THE MAGIC OF RIO . . .

A tall, gaunt black man wearing a pair of dirty white shorts and nothing else gave me the once-over. He whispered into Constanza's ear, turned, and left the room.

"I'm sorry, Senhor Hawthorn, but it will not be possible for you to accompany us to the sanctuary of the *exu*," she said.

I didn't particularly like the idea of Alberto going off without me. "Tell me something. Who, or what, is an *exu?*

"*Exu*, Senhor Hawthorn, is our word for the devil." She smiled, took Alberto by the hand, and led him toward the back of the house, where they disappeared into the darkness.

OVERSTEER

Ken Vose

AN AUTHORS GUILD BACKINPRINT.COM EDITION

Oversteer
All Rights Reserved © 1991, 2000 by Ken Vose

AN AUTHORS GUILD BACKINPRINT.COM EDITION

Published by iUniverse.com, Inc.

For information address:
iUniverse.com, Inc.
620 North 48th Street, Suite 201
Lincoln, NE 68504-3467
www.iuniverse.com

Originally published by Dell Publishing

Original cover art by Leslie Jean-Bart

ISBN: 0-595-08948-8

Printed in the United States of America

Jen and Ken.
This one's for you.

ACKNOWLEDGMENTS

This is a work of fiction set in the real world of Formula One racing. As I am not a member of the Grand Prix "circus," it was essential that I receive the cooperation of those who are. If I have, as I hope, succeeded in bringing the Vitale Team to life, I owe a great debt to those who contributed not only their valuable time but also their enthusiasm to the project. Thanks to all, particularly Jaime Manca Graziadei, Giancarlo Minardi, Barry Reynolds, Peter Collins, Willem Toet, Dr. Jonathan Palmer, and the following teams: Benetton, Minardi, Larousse, Ligier, Leyton House, McLaren and Ford Motorsports.

I also want to thank Lisa Wager, who thought F1 would make great background for a mystery. My editors, Brian DeFiore and E. J. McCarthy. John Cline, Bud Nealy, Chris Wallach, Kimberle Meredith, Steven Zwaryczok, and especially Ianto Roberts, the only person I know who's been reading *Autosport* for as many years as I have.

Last, but far from least, the one person without whom this never would have happened, my partner in life, literary and otherwise, Chris Tomasino.

THE FORMULA ONE SCHEDULE

BRAZIL	Rio de Janeiro	March 26
SAN MARINO	Imola	April 23
MONACO	Monte Carlo	May 7
MEXICO	Mexico City	May 28
UNITED STATES	Phoenix	June 4
CANADA	Montreal	June 18
FRANCE	Le Castellet	July 9
BRITAIN	Silverstone	July 16
GERMANY	Hockenheim	July 30
HUNGARY	Hungaroring	August 13
BELGIUM	Spa-Francorchamps	August 27
ITALY	Monza	September 10
PORTUGAL	Estoril	September 24
SPAIN	Jerez	October 1
JAPAN	Suzuka	October 22
AUSTRALIA	Adelaide	November 5

FORMULA ONE TEAMS AND DRIVERS

CAR#	DRIVER	CAR/ENGINE
1	Ayrton Senna	McLaren/Honda V10
2	Alain Prost	McLaren/Honda V10
3	Jonathan Palmer	Tyrrell/Ford V8
4	Michele Alboreto	Tyrrell/Ford V8
5	Thierry Boutsen	Williams/Renault V10
6	Riccardo Patrese	Williams/Renault V10
7	Martin Brundle	Brabham/Judd V8
8	Stefano Modena	Brabham/Judd V8
9	Derek Warwick	Arrows/Ford V8
10	Eddie Cheever	Arrows/Ford V8
11	Nelson Piquet	Lotus/Ford V8
12	Satoru Nakajima	Lotus/Ford V8
13	Peter Hawthorn	Vitale/Ford V8
14	Alberto Vaccarella	Vitale/Ford V8
15	Mauricio Gugelmin	March/Judd V8
16	Ivan Capelli	March/Judd V8
17	Piercarlo Ghinzani	Osella/Ford V8
18	Nicola Larini	Osella/Ford V8
19	Alesandro Nannini	Benetton/Ford V8
20	Johnny Herbert	Benetton/Ford V8
21	Andrea De Cesaris	BMS Dallara/Ford V8
22	Alex Caffi	BMS Dallara/Ford V8
23	Pierluigi Martini	Minardi/Ford V8
24	Luis Sala	Minardi/Ford V8
25	Rene Arnoux	Ligier/Ford V8
26	Olivier Grouillard	Ligier/Ford V8
27	Nigel Mansell	Ferrari/Ferrari V12

28	Gerhard Berger	Ferrari/Ferrari V12
29	Yannick Dalmas	Lola/Lamborghini V12
30	Philippe Alliot	Lola/Lamborghini V12
31	Roberto Moreno	Coloni/Ford V8
32	Pierre-Henri Raphanel	Coloni/Ford V8
33	Gregor Foitek	EuroBrun/Ford V8
34	Aguri Suzuki	EuroBrun/Ford V8
35	Bernd Schneider	Zackspeed/Yamaha V8
36	Stefan Johansson	Onyx/Ford V8
37	Bertrand Gachot	Onyx/Ford V8
38	Christian Danner	Rial/Ford V8
39	Volker Weidler	Rial/Ford V8
40	Philippe Streiff	AGS/Ford V8
41	Joachim Winkelhock	AGS/Ford V8

Only those who do not move do not die,
but then, are they not already dead?

Jean Behra
1921–1959

CIRCUIT NELSON PIQUET - JACAREPAGUA

CORNERS

1. MOLIKOTE
2. PACE
3. SUSPIRO
4. NONATO
5. NORTE
6. SUL
7. GIRAO
8. LAGOA
9. 90° GRAUS
10. VITORIA

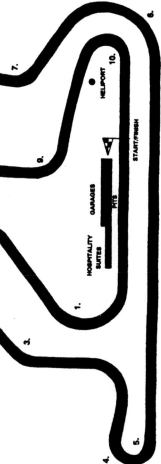

PROLOGUE

More than anything it's the smell that I miss: the mixture of hot oil, rubber, and gasoline. As soon as I walk into the pits it hits me and I feel alive. It smells like home.

Unfortunately, the only memorable smells reaching my nose for the past five weeks have been antiseptic in origin. First at the hospital in Oxford, England, and now here at home in Miami.

It's August 27. In less than an hour the lights will flash green three thousand miles away in the rain-soaked Ardennes forest at Spa to start the Belgian Grand Prix, and I won't be there.

For my teammate, Alberto Vaccarella, and the other twenty-five starters it will be the eleventh Grand Prix of the season. Only five more races to go before this season becomes yet another yearbook or highlight videocassette to put on the enthusiast's shelf.

For me, Peter Hawthorn, it means I have five more

weeks to get my ankles back into condition before the Spanish Grand Prix in Jerez. Five more weeks to think about things I'd pushed aside in the constant adrenaline rush of the racing season.

I have no memory of the crash that led to my newly contemplative state. In fact, I don't remember going to the track at Silverstone at all. Pierluigi Martini, whose Minardi was just behind me going into Stowe corner, thinks something broke in the left-rear suspension, but the car was so totally destroyed we'll never know for sure.

I've been told that it was pretty spectacular. The car got airborne after running over one of the curbs, then barrel-rolled five or six times. I still have the Bell helmet that undoubtedly saved my life. I pick it up from time to time as if touching it might somehow continue to bring me luck.

Shifting my body off the sofa, I move to the cockpit mock-up sitting on the floor in front of the television set. It looks like something you'd get if you mated a bobsled with a rowing machine, but for me it's just what the doctor ordered. At least that's what the doctor said after I told him what it was. The crew had constructed it with a pressure-adjustable clutch-brake-throttle assembly designed to help me regain the type of mobility I need before I can drive a race car again. It hurts like hell every time I use it, but the pain is nothing compared to what I'll feel if I can't rejoin the team for the last part of the season.

It's hard to believe that only eight months ago I was a thirty-five-year-old, ex–Grand Prix driver who had all but given up hope of ever getting back into the seat of a Formula One car. Then, at the Daytona twenty-four-hour-endurance race, a miracle happened. Or so it seemed at the time. . . .

CHAPTER

1

The team that hired me to drive at Daytona, Prather Racing, was a nice bunch of guys trying hard to make up with enthusiasm what they lacked in cash. Not one of the top outfits when you compared them with most of the Porsche teams or Nissan and Jaguar, but what the hell. It was the first race of the season and I had a decent ride. That was the good news. The bad news was that the team had to do really well in that race to attract a sponsor for the rest of the season, and from what I'd seen so far, its future looked a little dim.

The need for sponsor dollars was part of the reason they'd hired me. It looked good having an ex–Formula One driver on the team. There were six or seven in the field including Mario Andretti. Of course I was probably considered a bit more "ex" than Mario. Maybe that's why he was said to be getting $100,000 for the race. No one was saying that about me. I did have a handshake deal for the next two races at

Miami and Sebring, but I was already keeping my eyes open for something else.

"Pete. Pete Hawthorn."

The voice sounded familiar but I couldn't tell where it was coming from over the sound of the Cougar revving loudly beside me.

"Pete. Up here."

I looked up at the top of one of the many giant transporters parked in the paddock. I should have known from the Boston accent that it would be Paul White. Paul is an amateur racer whose job always seems to require his presence in a city where a race is scheduled. By the looks of the girl standing next to him he must have gotten a promotion.

"Peter Hawthorn, meet Stephanie Rand. Stephanie is doing some research on the psychological makeup of racing drivers. I told her you'd be glad to fill her in on your Oedipus complex and death wish."

The look she gave him said that this lady was definitely serious about her project. I'd met people like her before. Always running around with tape recorders, trying to find out what it's really like, "out there." She did have great legs, though.

"Seriously," she said, smiling earnestly. "We're having dinner with some of the drivers after the race tomorrow night. It would be really super if you could join us."

"Thanks, but I'll have to take a rain check. I already have a dinner thing scheduled."

"Is she anyone I know?" asked Paul.

"She's a he. Denis Windsor. Someone who knew my father back in the sixties."

6

OVERSTEER

The P.A. system crackled and popped into life to announce the mandatory drivers' meeting at the tech inspection building in five minutes.

I pointed to one of the loudspeakers, indicating my need to get over there.

"Good luck."

"Thanks, Paul. Bye, Stephanie. Nice meeting you. Good luck with your project."

"Thanks, you too. Listen, are you doing the Miami race?"

I knew what was coming as I nodded.

"Great. Maybe I'll collect on that rain check there."

I smiled my best noncommittal smile, waved, and set off toward the drivers' meeting. Miami, I thought. I already had a woman in Miami whose opinions on the psychological makeup of racing drivers I could do without.

The drivers' meeting, for all the usual talk of rules and regulations, could be boiled down to three words: Watch your mirrors. Not surprising when you consider the volatile mix that constitutes a twenty-four-hour endurance race: Take sixty-seven cars with vastly different performance capabilities, put in two hundred drivers of varying ability, have them drive enough miles to take them from the racetrack to Seattle, Washington, add darkness, a little rain, maybe some fog, and you've got the twenty-seventh annual SunBank 24 at Daytona, Florida.

The March-Buick I would be driving was one of the twenty-one faster GTP Prototype class cars. In fact it had won the race in 1984. That made me one of those who hoped the drivers in the slower classes would remember to look in their mirrors, at least occasionally. Nothing gets your attention quicker than a driver who's going 130 mph pulling out in front of you when you're pushing 200.

I walked back to the pits with my two co-drivers, Walt Addison and Les Bromley. Walt and Les were both good drivers but not as quick as yours truly. Normally in a situation like that I would have qualified the car and driven the first shift, but due to a series of mechanical glitches I'd only been able to do three hot laps in Thursday's practice session. Walt, who had been testing with the team since they bought the car, qualified at 1:54. Good enough for thirty-second starting spot. Not great, but the race was twenty-four hours long and if the mechanics could get the problems solved we had a chance of a good finish. For some reason the fuel pumps were not getting all the gas out of the tanks and into the engine where it could do us some good. It was okay on full tanks but as soon as about half of the fuel burned off the engine started cutting out intermittently, particularly in the two right-handers. It was enough of a problem on a clear track but with sixty-six other cars out there it could get a bit disconcerting to have the power disappear then slam back in when it felt like it.

Somebody called Les's name and he stopped to talk to a rotund polyester type with two young boys in tow.

I was about to ask Walt his opinion on the fuel pickup problem but I could tell from the look on his face that he really wasn't with me any longer; his mind had already shifted into race mode. Chances were he was thinking about the start, driving the opening laps in his mind. It's funny the way you can run laps inside your head, hitting every apex perfectly, every gearshift and breaking point. Once you learn a particular track it stays with you and you can replay it like a movie whenever you want. David Hobbs once said that he could remember every detail of a race he ran at Brands Hatch twenty-some years before. I wondered if David was driving this one or working up in the announcer's booth, since he usually did one or the other. Nice work if you can get it . . . and you can get it if you try. . . . Terrific, I thought, Walt is running the race in his brain and I'm singing Gershwin.

As soon as we got to our pit, Walt went into a huddle with team owner Henry Byers. I took it as a positive sign that chief mechanic Scotty McLean and the rest of his crew were busy polishing the car.

"Looking good, Scotty."

He looked up with a peculiar, crooked smile that was probably meant to be friendly. Scotty was wonderful with machines but not much when it came to interpersonal relations. I'd never driven a car he'd prepared before, but I knew he took a dim view of most drivers and the way they treated "his" cars.

"Does, doesn't she? Let's see how long you lot can keep her that way."

"Hey, Scotty. I'll treat her like she was my own."

"Good." He smiled again. "Just don't treat her like you treated that 962 last year. By the time the race was over that car had more nose jobs than Michael Jackson."

Scotty exploded into a wheezing laugh that was loud enough to turn heads two pits away.

He was right about the 962, though. We had somehow managed to destroy six nose sections, about one every four hours. While Scotty was repeating his witty remark to anyone within earshot, I buttonholed Dick Evans, the team's engine man.

"Think the pickup problem is licked?" I asked.

"I'm not sure. It stopped before I could find out what was causing it. I'd be ready for it if I was you."

"Right."

He grinned and went back to work setting up his tools and replacement parts in preparation for the start.

I don't care if you're behind the wheel, sitting in the stands, or standing on the pit wall as I was, the start of a motor race is something to see. All that raw energy suddenly unleashed by the waving of a green flag is enough to jump-start anyone's heart.

You'd think that when a race is twenty-four hours long it really wouldn't matter much who was leading at the end of the first lap, but you'd be wrong.

Every team manager up and down pit road had told their starting drivers the same thing: "Take it easy on the first lap and stay out of trouble." The drivers, of course, agreed. Most of them even meant it. But the moment the starter drops the green, the right foot takes control of your body, the infamous "red mist" descends over your eyes, and it's damn the team managers, full speed ahead.

As I watched the pace car pull down off the banking onto pit road I felt the hair on my arms begin to rise, anticipating the start. The field was accelerating now, the noise of 100,000 horsepower echoing off the walls and the giant concrete grandstand like a tidal wave threatening to engulf us all. From my perch atop the pit wall I saw the green drop as the front row came blasting by. Oscar Laurrauri in the Brun 962 dived into the lead as they came off the banking and headed into the flat, infield portion of the track but he was carrying too much speed and ran wide at the exit of the first turn. It seemed to take forever for the entire field to pass by. I caught a glimpse of Walt, surrounded by cars, in the middle of a high-speed traffic jam.

In no time the leaders were back up on the thirty-one-degree west banking with Brabham's Nissan in front, but as they disappeared down the back straight, Klaus Ludwig turned up the wick on the number-eighty-six Porsche and began to close in. By the time they burst into view again on the east banking, Ludwig had passed Lammer's Jag and before they passed the start/finish line he blew past Brabham and took the lead.

The opening lap was history. Two minutes down, 1,438 to go. The first pit stops were scheduled about an hour into the race, between laps twenty-eight and thirty-two. Most of the teams planned to change drivers during their first stops but Walt, who was an old hand at endurance racing, was doing a double shift. It

11

made sense, as he was the most familiar with the car and could probably diagnose any potential problem quicker than Les or myself. It also meant that I had two hours to kill before going to work.

"Scotty, I'm heading over to the motor home for some peace and quiet. Send one of the guys to get me about twenty minutes before my shift."

He nodded okay, but I knew he didn't approve of my leaving the pits this early on. Truth was, I had picked up some sort of bug and I wanted my stomach to be on its best behavior when I took over the car. I thought about explaining that to Scotty, but in this business that sort of thing is generally looked upon as an advance excuse for slow lap times. So I smiled my most ingratiating smile and went to find some Pepto-Bismol.

Unlike many of my racing brethren I happen to be a somewhat avid reader, books being second only to racing when it comes to escaping from other people's reality. Consequently, when Danny Teal came to get me he practically had to break down the motor-home door before I even heard him. Tom Clancy will do that to your brain. I put World War III aside, picked up my crash helmet, and headed for my chosen battlefield.

When I got back to the Prather pit I found everyone standing around Dick Evans, who was figuring out our fuel consumption on his laptop computer. I walked over to Les, who was peering over Scotty's shoulder at the dimly lit screen.

"What's up?"

"Hi, Pete. Fuel just started actin' up again and there's somethin' wrong with the dang radio."

"How many laps did he get in?" I asked.

"Thirty on the first shift. Twenty-five or so on this one."

"Where are we?"

"Twenty-first. Almost two laps down to Weaver."

"Weaver's got the lead?"

"Yup. Got about twelve seconds on the Nissan."

I looked out at the track then glanced at my watch. It was 5:35 and the sun was low over the west banking. Les smiled, reading my mind.

"Yup. You missed the worst of it. I remember driving into that sunset a couple of times and it's flat scary. You can't see diddly comin' off the banking into one."

"Quiet!" Scotty yelled. He clamped his hands over his earphones and jerked upright, like he'd just been plugged into an electrical outlet.

"He's coming in." His eyes darted around until they found, then locked on mine. "You ready?"

"As I'll ever be." My stomach tightened, my nerve endings sending their usual prerace signals. "What's our status?"

"Everything seems to be all right except for the pickup. Oh, and the goddamn radio only transmits one way, so you'll have to do without my expert advice when you're out there."

"Here he comes," hollered Danny as he stepped out onto pit road to mark the exact stopping point for Walt.

Walt was coming in, all right, and hot. For a mo-

13

ment I thought Danny would have to jump back over the wall to keep from getting run over but he stood his ground. Walt locked it up and slid to a stop right on the mark about an inch from Danny's knocking knees.

The second the car stopped moving, Bill Stack plugged in the pressure hose to activate the March's internal air jacks. The car responded by jumping up off the pavement as Jim Kirby and Chet Zwick got their powerful air wrenches whirring on the right-side wheels.

Walt had already opened the door and was crawling out, dragging his various wires and hose connections behind him. We touched helmets so he could shout in my ear. "Track's a little greasy in the infield. Brakes are okay. She's cutting out in the right-handers again, so don't get caught out. Be careful in traffic; there's a lot of crazies out there. And watch your mirrors, the leaders are really haulin' ass."

I clambered into the tiny sweltering cockpit, pulling the ends of the six-point seat belts into position.

Danny leaned in to attach the radio lead and water bottle hose coupling to my helmet, while Walt and I cinched up the seat belts to a point just this side of gangrene.

While all this was going on, Jack Woodland connected the two-inch gas hose from the overhead refueling rig to the quick disconnect filler coupling on the car and began feeding the volatile high-octane gasoline into the tanks.

By the time I was strapped in, the crew had changed all four tires and cleaned the windshield. As

OVERSTEER

I waited for the fuel tanks to top up, Scotty dived under the front of the car for a quick inspection while Danny rushed around checking the various air intake ducts for any debris that might cause the car to overheat.

Suddenly the air jack hose was disconnected and the car dropped down onto its new rubber. A spray of gas from the car's overflow vent indicated that the tanks were full, and as Jack yanked the fuel hose loose, Byers waved me out. I depressed the clutch, hit the starter, and put the gear lever into first as the guys gave me a big push on the rear wing.

I was calm now. The butterflies that had invaded my stomach took flight, moving down pit road in search of others hiding their anxiety beneath layers of fireproof Nomex.

I let the clutch out and checked the gauges as I moved past other crews trying to keep their cars alive while I headed for the pit exit. The entire exercise had taken about thirty seconds. The crew had done its job. Now it was up to me.

CHAPTER

2

The 3.56-mile Daytona course is unlike any other we run, in that it was designed for stock-car racing. The "good old boys" from NASCAR hold two major races there a year, pushing their three-thousand-pound sedans around the high-banked tri-oval at speeds in excess of two hundred mph. We sporty car types utilize most of the stock-car oval in addition to a flat, rather featureless bit of wiggly track laid out in one corner of the infield. This means that the March had to be set up to negotiate the flat, first-gear corners at thirty mph *and* be able to run balls out on the oval at two hundred.

The g-forces on the banking were so great that they more than doubled the weight of the car, pushing it down onto the shocks and tires. They would also double my weight, squashing me into my seat and pulling my head over as if there were an iron anvil hanging off the side of my helmet. Twenty-four hours at Daytona could be a pain in the ass if you didn't win.

The pit marshal gave me the all-clear and I accelerated onto the infield portion of the track, keeping well to the left, out of the way of any cars coming down off the banking through turn one. Moving quickly up through the gears, I was passed in rapid succession by a red turbo Toyota and one of the Fabcars. I decided to run behind them as they worked their way through the slower traffic. I figured that by the time they'd gotten through, any drivers they passed would still be checking their mirrors. Once my tires heated up to their optimum operating temperature I could worry about repassing them.

Must be nice, I thought, to drive for one of the top teams and not have to worry about going out on cold tires. The Jags had thermostatically controlled electric tire blankets to keep their rubber nice and toasty until needed. How fast do you want to go? How much do you want to spend? Amen!

Hard on the brakes for the first right-hander. Kept it smooth. The traffic ahead looked like the expressway on a Friday afternoon. The driver of a blue 911 saw me and moved to the right, giving me the fast line through the left kink. Downshifted. Four. Three. Two. Rear end got a little loose through the next right-hander. Corrected for it. A short burst of power into the sweeping left then back into third, headed for the banked oval. The Toyota and Fabcar had already climbed the tall three-story banking and moved off to my left.

The bump in the road where the infield joined the

oval was enough to shake the fillings out of your teeth. Then back on the power and up through the gears into fifth. Accelerating down the middle of the banking, the ribbon of concrete ahead curving upward into the top of the windshield like some giant amusement park ride. I began passing slower cars lower down on my left like they were standing still. Now, off the banking onto the long back straight, moving to the right near the retaining wall. The noise of the V-6 Buick roaring behind my head was already defeating my wax earplugs.

Down the back straight, right foot to the firewall. Maximum revs approaching the chicane. Two hundred mph. I was now moving the length of a football field every second. Flying on the ground. I loved it.

Past a yellow Argo, then on the binders, body pressed forward into the seat-belt harness. Left across the dirt at the apex of the corner. Two cars loomed up in front of me. I moved inside of the first, a Dodge Daytona, then a burst of speed, a quick turn to the right, then left and up onto the banking again. The red Firebird ahead was really moving. I followed it as it went past a group of four smaller prototype cars involved in their own race for position. Before I got by them the second car jinked to the right to make a pass, forcing me up into the "marbles" near the top of the banking. I kept my foot in it and went by them in a swirling cloud of grit. Some luck, I thought. Just as my tires were getting nice and hot I had to go up high and get a lot of junk stuck to them.

I approached the start/finish line. The huge timing-and-scoring tower grew large on my right; the sun shining directly into my eyes obliterated almost everything. I glanced at my mirrors and saw two blazing headlights coming up rapidly astern. I held my line as the Nissan blew by about two feet to my left. The air turbulence as he pulled in front of me to take his line for the corner made my steering go light for a moment, as if I were suddenly driving on glare ice. Then the front spoilers found enough clean air to glue the nose back to the track where it belonged. As I moved left into turn one, a couple of 962s flashed by on my right. Just like Walt had said: These guys were honkin'.

I spent the next few laps getting my mind, body, and the car into sync with the racetrack, establishing a rhythm that would allow me to run fast with the least amount of strain on man and machine. The sun had moved below the rim of the banking and lights were beginning to come on all around the track.

As I came to the start/finish line to complete another lap I saw the starter unfurl the yellow flag and wave it for all he was worth. I quickly eased off the power, hoping that the track ahead was at least partially clear. As I moved down into turn one the corner workers signaled me over to the right. By then I could see the problem. The Brun 962 had gone head-on into the guardrail and seemed to be wedged there. I caught a quick glimpse of tow trucks and an ambulance on their way to the incident and I knew that we probably were going to have a full-course yellow until they could get things untangled.

By the time I got around to the back straight I could

see the flashing yellow lights of the pace car moving through the chicane ahead of me. I slowed and joined the growing line of cars trundling along at fifty. I decided to let the team know what was going on and maybe begin to plan for our next pit stop, which was scheduled in about half an hour. I hit the mic button and spoke, hopefully, to my pit.

"Scotty. There's trouble down in one. It looks like it might take a while to clean up. Car is okay. No problem with the pickup. If you want me to come in before they go green, have Danny signal me. Over and out."

On the next lap, two of the cars ahead of me pulled out of line to enter the pits and I moved up behind the number-sixty Jag that Jan Lammers was driving with Raoul Boesel and Davy Jones. Twelve years ago Jan and I had both been rookie F1 drivers. Jan drove for Shadow and finished seven races while I drove for Klausen and never managed to qualify even once. My luck improved in 1980 when I partnered Eddie Cheever. I didn't actually finish any races that year but I did get to start in six of them. In 1981, Eddie moved to Tyrell and I went home to the States and an Indy car ride. Looking back, I'd say that Eddie had a better handle on things. As for me, the Indy car deal came to an abrupt halt when the sponsor pulled the plug halfway through the first season. I'd won a lot of races during the next nine years and was reasonably content with my lot in life but still, every once in a while, I would catch myself wondering: What if?

Arriving back at the accident site, I saw that the emergency crew had gotten the driver, Mauro Baldi, out of the car, which was about to be winched onto the back of a tow truck. In two, three laps at most, we'd be going green again. In the meantime, I was beginning to get hungry. Because I'd been feeling queasy I hadn't eaten anything for lunch and now I could practically hear my stomach growling over the sound of the engine. I had even begun to imagine the smell of the thick, juicy steaks they serve at Gene's Steakhouse. Then I realized that it wasn't my brain that was doing it to me, it was my nose. There were probably a thousand barbecue grills going full blast in the infield, and at the speed I was running I could smell them all, down to the last chicken wing.

The smell of food was also a reminder that I was having dinner after the race on Sunday with Denis Windsor.

I had done my best to keep him out of my mind since receiving his unexpected call early that morning. At two hundred mph you don't want your attention distracted, even for a second. But now, running under caution, I began to speculate about Windsor and his sudden reappearance in my life.

CHAPTER

3

I was fourteen when my father disappeared: vanished into the jungles of Brazil without a trace. If you've followed motor racing long enough, you probably remember the story. It even made the papers in New York, where my mother and I were living at the time. JUNGLE CLAIMS BRITISH RACER. RACE DRIVER LOST IN AMAZON. Items like those grabbed the public's attention for a day or so until they were pushed aside by a plane crash or quintuplets. He was nowhere near the Amazon, of course, but that didn't make it any the less real, or painful.

James Hawthorn, my father, was a moderately successful racing driver in the fifties and early sixties. He met my mother, Mary, in the Bahamas during Nassau Speed Weeks in 1954. She was beautiful, he was dashing, and something clicked. He took her back to England for the wedding and they settled down to live happily ever after.

OVERSTEER

As near as I can tell, things started going wrong early the next season. Mother, who had been swept up in the excitement of racing under sunny Caribbean skies, began to lose her enthusiasm in the chilly, rainswept pits of Silverstone and Spa.

Mary was two months pregnant with me when they left for France and the Le Mans 24-Hour Race, where James had a ride in a privately entered Gordini. They were in the Gordini pit together, waiting for James to go out, when the accident happened. Mercedes driver Pierre Levegh made contact with Lance Macklin's Austin Healey and was catapulted into the crowd just opposite them.

Levegh was killed instantly. Eighty-three spectators died with him.

Mary assumed that the race would be stopped or, at the very least, James would withdraw. With the screams of the victims still echoing across the track, the Gordini came in for its scheduled stop. Despite her pleas, James climbed into the car and joined the race. When he came back in to hand over to his co-driver, Mary was nowhere to be found. By the time the Gordini retired with gearbox trouble, she was on the boat train back to England. She never went to another race, not even one of mine.

I think he fully expected her to become her "old self" again after I was born, but Mary was through with racing. They still had strong feelings for one another but each of them must have known it was only a matter of time.

Before long, James began staying away from home. He'd find excuses for remaining at race venues after

each event, having a go at the women who hang
around the pits collecting drivers the way some en-
trepreneurial housewives collect Snow White com-
memorative plates. They kept up the pretense for six
years before Mary made her move. I was due to enter
school and she, having had her fill of Englishmen,
decided I was to be brought up in the States. The parting was difficult. James may not have been much of a
father but he was mine and I loved him. The fact that
I wanted to grow up to be "just like Daddy" probably
hastened our departure for Mary's hometown of
Miami, Florida, as much as anything else.

I was proud to be James's son and Mother never
discouraged my feelings for him. She even subscribed
to *Autosport* for me so I could keep up with his racing
exploits. I'd pore over each issue the moment it arrived from London, hoping he'd be mentioned in an
article or, if nothing else, listed in the race results.
The kids at school, who were quite snotty about my
British accent, were less inclined to bully me once
they'd seen James's photos in his racing gear.

I saw him last in 1965 when he made his annual
trip to Florida for the Sebring 12-Hour Race. I wasn't
allowed to go to the track, so he came to Miami for a
few days to see Mother and me. Our time together
was awkward. I was growing resentful that he wasn't
a real father to me like the kind my friends had, while
he was probably feeling guilty about the way things
had turned out.

If I'd known that I was never going to see him again
I might have acted differently but I was only nine and
couldn't imagine such a thing. He talked about my

coming over to England during the summer just as he had the year before and the year before that. I knew by then that I wouldn't be going to England, and to my regret I told him what I thought of his promises. After he left, mother comforted me with the reminder that they'd be racing at Sebring again next March. They did; but they raced without James. He'd driven his last Sebring. In fact James had driven his last major race anywhere.

James always had been partial to a dram of the sauce. But somewhere along the way, the drams kept multiplying until one day I opened the latest *Autosport* and wished I hadn't.

He had been involved in a rather nasty road accident while driving "under the influence." The "actress" in the car with him had been badly injured. James was unhurt but would probably be sentenced to a year in prison. In addition, the Royal Automobile Club had revoked his competition license until further notice.

He ended up serving three months but it would be three years before the RAC reinstated his license. We never heard a word from him during that entire period. Whatever I felt about it I kept to myself. At that time of life there are more things to think about than hours to think them in and no real way of expressing any of it. I hadn't yet discovered girls but I had baseball. I was actually beginning to think more about batting averages than I was about lap records.

Then, just after my fourteenth birthday, James's name appeared in *Autosport* again. Not in the racing news but in the section known as "Special Stage," which covered rallying. I remember reading the story with mounting excitement.

It seems that James was unable to get a competitive ride after the RAC reinstated his license, so he had begun co-driving in local rallies. Then, out of the blue, he was offered a drive in the biggest rally on the 1970 calendar: the World Cup. Given his circumstances, the drive was looked upon as yet another example of the eccentricity of the team's owner.

How else could you explain hiring a forty-four-year-old, ex-alcoholic with almost no rallying experience to race a Rolls-Royce Silver Cloud from London to Mexico City? The second Rolls-Royce in the two-car team would be driven by the team's owner and James's new benefactor, Denis Windsor.

Not long after the article appeared in *Autosport,* my mother and I each received a letter from James. She never told me what he'd written in hers but I remember thinking that it made her sad. Mine, on the other hand, was pure pleasure. He'd sent me a map of the rally route with all of the stages and checkpoints indicated as well as the dates each stage would begin and end. Using the map, I would be able to follow his progress day by day in my mind.

The teams were to set out from Wembley Stadium in London on April 19. Survivors lucky enough to complete the grueling sixteen-thousand-mile run would arrive in Mexico City on May 27.

Aside from a story that appeared in the *Times* when the rally began there was no real coverage of the event in the New York papers. So, although I knew when the cars were due in Stuttgart or Vienna, Budapest or Trieste, I had to wait until my weekly *Autosport* arrived to find out what actually had happened.

As you might imagine, the two Rolls-Royces received a good deal of prerace publicity and I devoured every word. My friends, who were caught up in the Mets' new baseball season, thought I'd gone off the deep end. While they were poring over news of the team's latest exploits, I was waiting for news from Europe, where the cars were due to arrive in the port city of Lisbon on April 26.

Of the ninety-six cars that set out from London, twenty-five had been eliminated during the 4,500-mile trip to Lisbon, leaving seventy-one to make the twelve-day ocean voyage to Rio de Janeiro.

For the drivers and crews there was time to relax in the sun for a day or two before catching the daily nonstop to Rio, where the rally would begin again on May 8.

By the time the mailman delivered the issue covering the start in Rio, James had already disappeared. According to the earliest reports, he and his co-driver, Trevor Alcott, simply failed to arrive at one of the checkpoints south of São Paulo. Long after the other competitors had passed through that checkpoint a search was begun, but the Rolls was nowhere to be found. Over the next few days the size and scope of the search increased but the results were the same. The Rolls driven by Windsor made it as far as Cali, Colombia, before breaking down for good. Windsor immediately chartered a plane and returned to Rio to help in the frustrating search.

On the fourth of June, the first, and as it turned out, only clue to the mystery appeared: Trevor Alcott. A group of surveyors found Alcott, dazed and incoherent, wandering along a road far from the rally route. After being treated locally for a broken arm and exposure, Windsor had him flown to Rio for further treatment.

Although Alcott made a full physical recovery, he had no memory of what had happened to James or of the whereabouts of the Rolls.

Upon his return to England, Alcott was admitted to St. Thomas's Hospital in London, the same hospital that treated Stirling Moss after his near-fatal crash at Goodwood in 1962.

Unfortunately, Alcott had no better luck in remembering what had befallen him than Moss did. Stirling, of course, has yet to remember anything that happened that day at Goodwood, so I supposed it was safe to assume that Alcott, if he was still alive, hadn't either.

Before long the world had moved on to other things and James's disappearance was forgotten. In time the memories dimmed and the scrapbook covering the rally and his disappearance got shoved farther and farther into the back of my closet. But I was my father's son, and no matter how hard she tried, Mother could no more keep me out of a race car than she could James on that terrible day at Le Mans.

When James was declared legally dead, Mary

agreed to marry her longtime suitor, Don Lambert. That was fifteen years ago, and unlike her first attempt at matrimony, they had managed to live happily ever after.

Now it seemed that Don and I were both going to lose her. She had been diagnosed with lymph cancer six months before, and despite radiation and chemotherapy, she was losing ground rapidly.

The part of my brain in charge of driving the car saw the starter holding up one finger to indicate that we'd be going green on the next lap. It was time to shut out the flood of memories brought on by Windsor's phone call and concentrate on the restart.

I knew the Jag up ahead would take off like a scalded cat when the flag waved and I intended to plant my nose under his rear wing and keep it there for as long as I could hang on. As we pulled up onto the banking everyone, including me, began weaving back and forth all over the track like some demented Chinese New Year's dragon, using the friction generated by turning the wheels left and right to put some of the heat we'd lost during the slow caution period back into our tires.

The cars at the front of the sixty-five-car train began to accelerate as soon as they came off the last corner. Everyone had their powerful driving lights turned all the way up, making it almost bright enough in the cockpit to read the fine print in the race regulations.

I put the hammer down and glued myself to the

back of the Jag as he went up high next to the wall. By the time we hit the start/finish line we had already passed ten or twelve cars. Down off the banking into one and I was still inches from the Jag. Along the short chute to the first right-hander. Cars all over the track, drivers scrabbling for real or imagined positions, paying scant attention to the faster cars trying to push their way through. Going into the right-hander, it happened; the engine coughed once then died. I hit the clutch, dropped it into first, then popped it. Just as the engine caught I got clipped from behind. Suddenly I was going backward. I locked up the brakes and backed into the guardrail with a neck-snapping jolt. I managed to keep the engine fired and as soon as the corner workers signaled that it was safe I pulled back onto the track.

I could see in my mirrors that the rear wing was tilted over to one side and the loud scraping noises coming from behind my head told me that at the very least, the rear bodywork was dragging along the pavement. I tried to get through to the crew to tell them what had happened but the one-way radio was now a no-way. I crept around as fast as I dared, trying to stay out of everyone's way. Before I could get back to the pit entrance the rear wing fell off, clattering away into the darkness.

As I moved down to our end of pit road I could see Scotty, waving his arms for me to hurry up and get there. When I finally ground to a halt, Scotty signaled me to get out, then disappeared to the back of the car. I tried to get the door open but the bodywork had flexed enough to jam it solidly shut. Danny, realizing what had happened, began pulling at the door from the outside. Then Bill joined in and with a loud screeching noise it popped open.

I climbed out, and before I could get my helmet unfastened, Scotty stuck his face up to mine and yelled, "Pickup?"

I nodded and he dived back into the engine bay. The rest of the guys had pried the deranged bodywork off and were checking the attachment points for damage before putting on the replacement section and wing. I pulled off my helmet and balaclava, took out my earplugs, and gave Les the bad news. "She quit totally going into the first right-hander, then somebody tapped me. I had to come around too slow to get any feedback, so take it easy for a couple of laps, in case the wheels fall off or something."

That tickled Les and brought on one of his goofy grins. "You dumb asshole," he said, then pulled on his helmet and climbed into the cockpit. Scotty straightened up to make room for the crew to put the new bodywork on. "Anything else?" he asked.

"Radio's gone."

He nodded, more to himself than to me, and started writing in the small, dog-eared spiral notebook he always carried.

"Go get a hot shower and some rest. I'll send Danny over for you later." With that, he bent over into the cockpit for some final words with Les. The hot shower sounded good, so I headed back to the motor home.

* * *

I don't know what felt better, the shower or just getting out of my sweaty Nomex long johns. The ventilation in the March was terrible. Les said it was like sitting inside a hot oven while guys beat on it with jackhammers. Close enough.

I poured myself some coffee and tried to get back into World War III. After reading the same page four times I decided it wasn't going to work. My mind was still on James. I lay down on one of the beds and drifted off into sleep without really intending to. I was jolted awake by Danny shaking my arm.

"Yo, Pete. Rise and shine."

"Danny. Thanks. Be ready in five minutes."

He shook his head and shrugged. "Take all the time you want. We're out of it."

"What happened?"

"Rear tire blew on the banking. Les kept it on the wall but it did a lot of damage to the right side. Anyway, Scotty says thanks and Mr. Byers asked you to call him tomorrow about Miami."

"Okay. Hey, thanks for all the help."

He started to go, then hesitated. "Pete. Can I ask you a question?"

"Sure."

"Is it true you raced against Gilles Villenuve?"

I nodded, smiling at the memory of Gilles and his Ferrari.

Danny got that faraway look some people get when they think of Villenuve. It's as if they can see him, at opposite lock, the tail of his car hung out at some impossible angle. "Neat," he said, then turned and left.

Now that it was over I could admit to myself that I wasn't all that sorry. The idea of crawling back into a damaged car that had no chance of winning and not much hope of even finishing was not all that appealing. I know because I've done it enough times. The challenge of forcing some recalcitrant lump of machinery to do things it doesn't want to can be a character-building experience. It can also put you in the hospital.

It took a few minutes to pack my gear before starting the long trek to the parking lot. The driving must have settled my stomach, because the greasy trackburgers at every stand I passed smelled delicious and I knew they were more dangerous than sprint cars.

As I drove away from the track I could still hear the cars buzzing around like angry wasps as they raced on through the foggy Florida night.

CHAPTER

4

That Sunday night, Gene's was packed with winners, losers, and assorted survivors of the twenty-four-hour grind. Exhausted but exhilarated, they were intent on consuming what looked to be whole sides of beef in a sharklike feeding frenzy. I could hardly wait to join in.

The maître d' indicated Windsor seated at the far end of the crowded dining room. On the way back there I noticed Paul, Stephanie Rand, and a couple of drivers being serious at a table on the opposite side of the room. I made a mental note not to look in that direction again.

As I neared Windsor's table a waiter who had been tossing a Caesar salad stepped aside and I saw that Windsor was not alone. His companion, who obviously recognized me, stood, smiling broadly. Windsor, on the other hand, just sat there staring at me.

Taking a quick gulp of his martini, he rose to make the introductions.

"Hello, Peter. I'm Denis Windsor and this is my partner, Ludovico Vitale."

Vitale, whoever he was, seemed genuinely glad to meet me.

"*Buona sera*, Signor Hawthorn."

While Vitale was enthusiastically pumping my hand, Windsor continued to examine me as if I were some sort of specimen. I was tempted to look down to make sure I had my pants on, but it was my face he seemed to be interested in.

"Is something wrong?" I asked.

He shook his head as we sat down, then drained his glass to the lone olive.

"I'm terribly sorry. It's just that . . . hasn't anyone ever remarked on your resemblance to your father? I mean, you do look like him in photographs but, well, in the flesh it's positively uncanny."

"Yes, sometimes. But I don't come across that many people who remember him. It's been a long time, you know."

"Yes . . . Yes, I guess it has."

At that point our waiter appeared with the menus and another martini for Windsor. I ordered my customary Campari and soda and looked at the menu. When I looked up, Vitale was staring at me. Did I remind him of someone too? He certainly reminded me of someone. It was the great Italian comic actor Alberto Sordi.

"Bad luck out there last night, Signor Hawthorn. Was the car badly damaged?"

"No. From what they told me I'd guess it can be fixed in time for Miami. Problem is, I'm not sure they have enough money to do it right."

"What will you do then?"

"If it runs, I'll drive it. If not, I guess I'll look for another ride."

"Is this possible on such short notice?"

"There are always a few seats open in the longer races, if you're quick enough."

We placed our dinner orders and Vitale selected a very expensive bottle of Burgundy. Although I still wasn't sure exactly why I was there, I knew my stomach would be thanking me before the night was over.

Windsor must have been reading my mind. He took a sip of his drink and said, "So, Peter, you must be wondering what brought us together tonight?"

"Well, obviously, I assumed it had something to do with my father. Maybe you just wanted to meet James's look-alike son. I don't know. I know I've always been curious about you. At least I used to be when I was younger. Your call started me thinking about things I hadn't thought of in years."

Before he could reply, the waiter returned with the wine and, somewhat nervously, removed the cork and presented it for inspection. Vitale sniffed it, swirled a bit of the wine around in his glass, held it up to the light, inhaled its aroma, and tasted it, all without seeming in the least bit affected. He smiled and pronounced it *"Magnifico!"*

As soon as the waiter had filled our glasses Windsor proposed a toast. "To the Vitale team."

"The Vitale team," I replied, raising my glass. The

Vitale team? Why did that seem to ring a bell? I began to detect the elusive aroma of a new ride, mingled with the heady bouquet of the wine.

Vitale obviously was enjoying this little cat-and-mouse game. He smiled conspiratorially at Windsor, then they both leaned in over the table. Not wanting to be left out, I leaned in as well.

"You see, Signor Hawthorn, we, Denis and I, have this dilemma. We have a new racing team. We have our first race approaching at the end of next month, for which we are constructing two new cars. But, as yet, and this is the problem, we have only one driver."

"What Ludovico is saying, dear boy, is that we would be most happy if you would consider joining our little venture for the rest of the season."

Now it was my turn to be nervous. I think it was the word *season* that did it. I didn't want to appear *too* eager but the offer of a full-time ride from a man who casually ordered a '55 Corton Clos de Rol like it was jug wine was downright appealing.

Now I knew what Cinderella must have felt like meeting her fairy godmother. It was hard, though, not to think about golden carriages turning into pumpkins.

"I'm flattered and I'm certainly interested. But I have to tell you that if Miami's your first race, I made a commitment to drive for Henry Byers there. That's if he goes, of course. If not, well, let's talk."

My answer seemed to confuse Vitale.

"Miami?" he said, looking quizzically at Windsor.

"Sorry, Ludovico. I thought he knew about the team. Peter, you must forgive me again. We're not planning to run at Miami. We're not talking about IMSA racing at all. Our first race is in Rio on March 26. The Brazilian Grand Prix."

"Jesus." With that brilliant reply I lost it as a rational adult male and turned into some sort of Gumby with a crash helmet.

Vitale refilled my glass. I pretended to be absorbed in the wine for a moment while I regrouped. As soon as Windsor mentioned Rio it hit me who Ludovico Vitale was. Like every other driver I'd read stories about all the new teams trying to break into Formula One now that the incredibly expensive turbocharged engines had been outlawed: Dallara, Rial, March, EuroBrun, First, Onyx, *and* a team called DV Racing. I couldn't remember what the *D* stood for but the *V* was sitting right there opposite me.

Windsor broke the silence. "Ludovico and I have known each other for a number of years. In fact, we always seemed to be bidding for the same paintings at one place or another."

Vitale broke in, laughing. "It was certainly an expensive way to discover that we have the same taste in art."

"Quite," Windsor agreed. "So when his partner, Paolo DeStefano, died so tragically last November, I offered to join the team and use whatever small expertise I might have to help make it a success."

Vitale interrupted again, waving his hands in the air. "Denis, as usual, is being overly modest. He has already made several valuable contributions both in the way things are run and in the team's personnel.

38

Including, I might add, suggesting that you become our second driver."

It was still too much for me to take in but at least I was able to start sounding intelligent again. "Vaccarella's your other driver, right? Formula 3000. Finished third in the championship last year?"

"*Sì*. Alberto is a very quick young man."

I could see that just talking about Vaccarella made him happy. He refilled our glasses and began looking around for the waiter. "Ludovico has been helping Alberto since his karting days."

"True. When he won the European Championship, I told myself that someday we would come to Formula One together. It's a good thing I did not know the cost or I might have suggested he study tennis."

With this he toasted Alberto then told the waiter, who had just arrived with our dinners, to bring another bottle of wine.

For the next few minutes our attention shifted from cars to steaks. But my appetite had suddenly gone south. The steak I'd been looking forward to now seemed totally unimportant. I guess it wasn't so strange when you consider that I'd been focused on the steak for twenty-four hours while I'd had a Formula One ride on my mind for nine years. I kept thinking there had to be a hitch somewhere. Yet everything they'd said seemed straightforward and reasonable. Everything, with one minor exception. "Why me?" It was only when Windsor began to answer me that I realized I'd said it out loud.

"As Ludovico said, Alberto is quick. He's certainly capable of winning any race he starts, given the right equipment. But, and it's a big but, he's young and he's got a typically Latin disposition."

Vitale gave a vigorous nod of approval and touched his chest. "He sometimes drives more with his heart than with his head."

"Right," Windsor continued. "Ludovico and I felt it was necessary to have an older, more experienced driver on the team. Not just for the calming effect on Alberto but also for the extensive testing program we have planned."

Now I really forgot about my food. An *extensive* testing program, the man said. That was what ultimately separated the teams at the front and rear of the grid.

Formula One races really were not won on Sunday in front of millions of spectators. They were decided during long days of testing in front of silent grandstands and empty camera positions.

"Signor Hawthorn. We do not have foolish expectations. We are not Ferrari, or Benetton, or even Minardi. That will come later. Our goal is to qualify for each Grand Prix and to improve our finishing position as the season progresses. If we can accomplish that much, I think we will be in a position next year to run in the points."

He looked at his watch and then straight at me. "I apologize, but I must leave now to make a connecting flight back to Milano. Do you wish more time to make up your mind or can I tell the team that we have found our second driver?"

"Signor Vitale. Mr. Windsor. You've got yourselves a race driver."

CHAPTER

5

After Vitale left for the airport, Windsor and I managed to finalize the deal over coffee and two of his Davidoff coronas. Great Burgundy. Cuban cigars. Be a pity if the car turned out to be a sled.

I had very little idea what the average journeyman G.P. driver was getting at that point. Those who didn't have a sponsor paying for their ride, anyway. I knew what Nelson Piquet was said to be getting. Six-point-one million. Of course, he had managed to win the World Championship three times. I decided to ask for about a third more than they offered and then compromise downward to somewhere just short of indentured servitude. The end result was actually better than I expected: equal number-one status with Vaccarella. No team orders as to finishing positions. A salary of $250,000 plus bonuses of $5,000 for qualifying ($7,500 if in the top half of the twenty-six-car field) and $10,000 for each World Championship point scored. These payments were to be made in addition to 10 percent of any prize money awarded the team in accordance with Formula One Constructors Association (FOCA) rules. I was also free to obtain personal sponsorship and to drive in any event that didn't conflict with the team's race or testing schedule.

I asked Windsor how the team got paid by FOCA so that I'd have some idea how much my share might amount to. He looked somewhat pained at the question, shrugged his shoulders, and said, "I haven't a clue, dear boy. Ludovico explained it to me twice before I realized that *he* was totally in the dark. Perhaps you can get one of the lads you know on the other teams to explain it, then you can tell me."

He smiled, then settled back in his chair and stared at me through the haze of cigar smoke. "I still can't get over how much you look like James. I was with him the day he disappeared, you know."

I nodded and waited for him to continue. He looked away from me and began the story I'd waited twenty-one years to hear.

"As you undoubtedly know, both of our cars had done respectably well in Europe but I was quite concerned as to how they'd stand up in South America. We had some special tropical bits made up in England but by the time they'd gotten through customs in Rio it was too late to do the work. . . . Sorry, I don't mean to get long-winded but being here with you tonight brings it all back so vividly. Almost like a film." He closed his eyes and returned to 1970.

"You should have seen the mob at the start in Rio. It

seemed as if the entire city was out in the streets. Everyone pounding on the cars for luck. We had dents from one end to the other. And hands. Thousands of hands. Ripping off all the sponsor's decals, numbers, everything . . . What a night. Anyway, the cars set off in the order they finished the European section, so James left about twenty minutes ahead of me. Once we got away from Rio and headed toward São Paulo we never saw another rally car unless we were passing them or they were passing us. And fog. A lot of fog. Thick too. Like London. Quite surprising, actually. Once it cleared we picked up the pace and made it without any incidents to our first refueling point just outside São Paulo. One of the local Castrol men said that the other Rolls had been through a good thirty minutes before. The organizers had canceled the first high-speed prime because of severe flooding, so all of us were going like the clappers to get to the second prime, called the Parana or Piranha or some such. It was only about 175 kilometers long but quite dodgy with washed-out bridges, mud slides, a god-awful mess."

He stopped talking to take another sip of cognac and another puff of the corona. I found myself suddenly impatient for him to get on with it. Even though I knew what the outcome would be, that James would still disappear into thin air, I needed to hear him say it.

"What happened then?" I prodded.

"Our next refueling point was in Curitiba. If anything, the roads were getting worse the farther south we went. It was pitch black of course and quite diffi-

cult to follow the recce notes, as some of the land-
marks had been washed away by the heavy rains.
Also we knew that there were two ways of getting to
Curitiba. The official route was the most direct but it
was supposed to be in dismal condition. The other
route was slightly longer but the first half of it was
over tarmac and seemed the better choice to me.

"Soon we were flying along what was practically a
motorway at well over the ton when we were passed
by one of the works Triumphs going in the opposite
direction. A minute or so later an Escort came by
flashing its lights, the navigator waving his arms signaling us to turn around, which we immediately did.
Good thing too. We found out later that a huge landslide had blocked the road about ten miles ahead.
When we finally arrived in Curitiba, we were told
that James hadn't been through. I didn't think too
much about it at the time. I mean cars were constantly breaking down, getting lost or what have you.
Anyway, we set off for the Rio Grande prime assuming they'd been held up by some minor mishap and
would turn up later. . . . Nothing of the sort as it
turned out."

"When did you find out that they were really missing?"

"Not until Buenos Aires. At that point there were
two cars missing and the organizers were actively
searching all possible routes on the theory that they'd
gone off somewhere in a big way. By the time we
arrived in Santiago the other car had been found but
there was still no trace of the Rolls. After our break-
down near Cali I chartered a plane and flew back to

Brazil to see what I could do, but it was hopeless. About a month later I was preparing to go back to England when Alcott turned up."

"I read that he was found wandering around miles away from the rally route."

"Quite so. And not one effing clue to what happened. I stayed with him in Rio for two weeks then had him taken back to London for more tests and such, but he was a blank. Didn't even remember bloody Brazil. Knew he'd started the rally but not a thing afterward . . . Can't tell you how sorry I am about the whole thing. Put me off motorsport for years. In fact, if it weren't for Ludovico, I doubt I'd ever have gotten involved again."

I could see that the alcohol was finally getting to him. Words starting to slur, eyes not quite focusing. He was even beginning to slip in and out of his strangely affected upper-class speech. It was time to say good night but I still had one question to ask.

"What about Alcott? Is he still alive? Could I get in touch with him?"

"He's alive, all right. Discovered he's been working for years as a lorry driver and mechanic down in Dorset. Seems perfectly fine, except for his memory of course."

"How'd you find him?"

"Didn't. He found me. Read about my joining forces with Ludovico and rang me up for a job."

"A job? You mean with the Vitale team?"

"Couldn't say no, could I? You'll meet him on Friday at the works in Italy." He stopped talking, gritted his teeth, and took a deep breath, which he held for about ten seconds before exhaling slowly. "Phew. Excuse me. Bit of heartburn, I'm afraid." He squinted at his watch then stood carefully.

"Must be off, I'm afraid. Car's waiting. Ring me at the hotel tomorrow about transport and the like. Glad we had a chance to chat about things. Safe home."

He turned and, with the deliberation of one used to heavy drinking, walked carefully to the restaurant door.

I picked up my cigar, which had gone out some time ago, committed the unpardonable sin of relighting it, then poured myself a final cup of coffee and tried to sort out all the information I'd just taken in. Unfortunately, the only thing my brain was suited for was sleep. As I passed the bar on the way out I saw Stephanie Rand trying to sit in Eddie Atkins's lap. The fact that he was standing up at the time didn't seem to matter to either of them. Ah, research. One more glass of wine and I'd probably have started looking through my pockets for that rain check.

The next morning I slept late, then made a leisurely trip down Route 95 to Miami. The weather was tourist bureau perfect. The fast lane was free of fifty-five-mph boneheads and an old Mulligan/Alan Eazer tape was trying to destroy all my stereo speakers.

The sunny day clouded over when I got to my apartment, listened to the messages on my answering machine, and heard my stepfather asking me to call when I got in.

I tried the house, got their machine, and had to listen to my mother's cheery voice telling me they weren't at home. I knew why he let the message stay on there, and he was right, but it killed me every time I heard it. Since Don wasn't home, I went straight to the hospital.

Until mother got cancer I'd never really minded going into hospitals. Now it was all I could do to walk down the corridor past the nurses' station to her room.

It was a semiprivate but, for the moment, the other bed was empty. A chair sat at the head of the bed with newspapers and magazines strewn on the floor around it. Don must have gone for a smoke or some coffee. I sat in his chair and looked down at her. She was sleeping fitfully, breathing through a tiny oxygen hose that disappeared into the wall above her head. Chemotherapy, even when it works, extracts a terrible toll. Her wig was askew, revealing the few wisps of her own hair that remained, and her nearly translucent skin was blotchy with black-and-blue marks. She couldn't have weighed more than sixty or seventy pounds. She reminded me of some tiny bird fallen from its nest. Too weak to fly. Waiting for the end.

I wiped away the tears and began to talk to her about the events of the past twenty-four hours. It didn't matter if she could hear me or not because I knew that soon even this one-way communication would be gone. I had just mentioned the incredible coincidence of my driving for Windsor and his rescuing me much the same way he'd rescued James's driving career when she awoke with a start, clutching my hand so hard I thought my fingers would break.

"Not Windsor," she said. "Not Denis Windsor. He

killed your father. Now he wants to kill you." She dropped my hand and started coughing violently.

"What the hell is going on . . . Peter, what did you do?"

It was Don and he was furious. He rang for the nurse then sat on the bed, cradling her in his arms. "Do you want to kill her?"

There was nothing I could say. As the nurse entered I stepped into the corridor and leaned against the wall. How could I have known she would react to Windsor's name that way? Or that she blamed him for James's death? True, if he hadn't given him the ride, he would never have gone to Brazil, but James would have gotten back into a race car anyway. If not Windsor's then someone else's. Don came out of the room glaring at me.

"You were talking to her about racing, weren't you?"

"Look, Don, I'm truly sorry. I don't know why she reacted like that. You know I wouldn't do anything to upset her on purpose."

He took a deep breath then exhaled most of the anger away.

"I know. Sorry. I'm just on edge. She hasn't got much time left and I just don't want her upset any. Okay?"

"Okay . . . Has the doctor said anything new? About, you know, time?"

"Nothing. Could be weeks. Could be months. I'm beginning to understand why some folks up and pull the plug. Not that I would, Pete. But I do understand."

I watched the tears well up in his eyes before he could turn his face away.

"If you're gonna be in town for a while, why don't you stop by the house. Can't really talk in this damn place. Can't even think straight."

"Thanks. I'd like that. I've got to go to Italy for a few days. We'll do it as soon as I get back. If you need me, leave a message and I'll take the next plane back. Okay?"

He nodded, trying to muster up a smile. The nurse came out and indicated it was all right to go back in. Mary was sleeping again as if nothing had happened. I kissed her on the cheek. Thank God for Don, I thought. We had our share of differences but I couldn't think of anyone I'd rather she be with now. Not even James.

I'd just left the room when Don came out behind me.

"Pete," he said softly. "I almost forgot why I called. Do you know someone called Windsor? Denis Windsor, I think it was."

"Yeah. He's the man I've just made a deal to drive for."

"I guess that explains it then."

"Explains what?"

"He called on Saturday and left a message for Mary. Said he'd be in touch. I guess he was looking for you."

"I guess."

He nodded absently and went back to his vigil.

CHAPTER

6

The Pan Am flight to Milan was uneventful, and as
the team had booked first class, I was able to stretch
out and get a few hours of airplane sleep.

As soon as I'd cleared customs and walked into the
terminal, a short, wiry man, wearing an expensive-
looking tweed shooting jacket, made a beeline toward
me.

"Welcome to Italy, Peter. I'm Barry Spikings. Team
manager. Car's just outside . . ."

He turned and walked briskly toward the automatic doors. I noticed that he had a slight limp, or as
Les Bromley would have said, "a hitch in his git-
along." It certainly didn't slow him down any. I hurried along in his wake, and by the time I got outside,
he already had the rear deck of a yellow Ford Escort
open. While I was stowing my suitcase and driving
gear he said something in Italian to the carabiniere
who seemed to be guarding the car. As the man burst

into laughter we climbed in and roared away, tires squealing.

"Being part of an Italian F1 team will get you practically anything over here. If we were with Ferrari, he'd probably have washed and polished it."

He aimed the car toward a rapidly closing hole between a bus and an ancient Fiat. Blowing the horn and shaking his fist, he snaked past them and out of the airport complex.

"I decided to pick you up myself rather than send one of the others so we'd have a little time to chat. Things at the works are pretty hectic, as you might imagine. We've been going around the clock trying to get one car ready for the open test session at Jerez that started yesterday, but we're not going to make it."

It began to rain as we pulled onto the A1 Autostrada and turned south toward Bologna.

"What's causing the delay?"

"Well, we were on target with the build program until DeStefano, he was Vitale's partner, went and got himself killed last November. Things just went into low gear for a while until Mr. Windsor joined the team and gave Vitale a bit of a goose."

"What actually happened to DeStefano?"

"Some sort of skiing accident near Gstaad. Too bad, really. He was the perfect team owner. Never any problems with money and he only came to races to party. Not like Windsor, who's actually run a team and wants to be involved in everything."

"What's Windsor really like?" I asked.

"What's he like?" Spikings was incredulous. "I was

hoping you'd tell me. I was given to understand that he was an old friend of the family. Quite frankly, I assumed that to be the reason we hired you. No offense, but your name wasn't exactly on everyone's lips when the subject of available F1 pilots came up."

He smiled when he said it, but it was clear that I'd better be able to deliver the goods. No matter whose friend I was.

By now the rain was coming down in buckets. I had just opened my mouth to answer Spikings when some jerk in a Mercedes came blasting past at about 150 kph, pulled over right in front of us, and promptly lost it. Spikings let out a stream of obscenities in various languages as he rapidly pumped the brakes and threw the car into a long slide. He corrected two or three times, got back on the throttle, and eased us past the still-gyrating Merc with inches to spare.

"Fucking idiot," he said. "Good thing this little bugger does what you tell it."

"Nice driving," I croaked as soon as I'd gotten my breath back.

"Thanks. More luck than anything else, as you bloody well know."

It dawned on me that this was the Spikings who had driven Formula Two and Formula 5000 back in the midseventies. He'd had a bad wreck at Zandvort my first year in Europe doing Formula Three.

"How long have you been with Vitale?"

"Three years. One in F3 and the last two in 3000. He's a good man, Vitale, and so was DeStefano. That's why I was hoping you could tell me something about

Windsor. Not that I think there's anything wrong with him. I just like to know as much as I can about the people I'm involved with."

Over the next hour I filled him in on Windsor's relationship with James, about the ill-fated Cup Rally and Windsor's unexpected reappearance in my life. I also told him, in no uncertain terms, that I intended to make a go of it in F1 this time around.

By the time we turned off the Autostrada at Modena the sun had broken through the clouds. Things were looking brighter outside *and* inside the car.

After the high-speed run from Milan, the old Via Emilia between Modena and Bologna was a monoxide-filled bumper-to-bumper nightmare. If you ignored the fact that the gas stations sold AGIP instead of AMOCO, we might as well have been in New Jersey. Didn't seem right for the old Mille Miglia route to have come to this.

"Well, here we are," Spikings said as he turned in to one of the small prefab industrial parks I'd just been damning in my mind.

"Not much on the outside but I think you'll like what we've put together. Those are our buildings over there." He pointed to one rather large and two smaller nondescript, boxlike constructions.

A bright yellow eighteen-wheel rig with SCUDERIA VITALE blazed in red across the side was the only indication that the buildings might house something other than a beer-can recycler or a widget manufacturer. The other thing I noticed was that the parking lot seemed full of turbo Escorts with a couple of Sierra Cosworths thrown in for good measure. Spikings answered my unasked question. "Vitale's brother-in-law's a big Ford dealer over in Bologna. The keys to the Escorts are in the office whenever you need a car. The Sierras are for Vitale and Windsor."

Spikings was certainly right about the reality of the place bearing no relation to its outside appearance. Just inside the small front door we entered a reception area that really got my attention. A marble floor, soft, glove-leather-upholstered furniture, paintings of racing scenes by top artists like Frank Gude and Nicholas Watts. And, as a centerpiece, Vaccarella's 1988 Formula 3000 car. The receptionist, a tiny doll-like girl named Gabriella who was speaking into two phones at the same time, handed Spikings his messages then buzzed us through the locked security door into the works itself.

We stepped into a large, brightly lit open area. My eyes went immediately to the center of the room, where, in perfect geometrical alignment, four race cars were being assembled. The one to the far right, which was nearing completion, already looked like a Formula One car. The other three were days or weeks behind it on the evolutionary scale.

About a dozen men wearing yellow jumpsuits were working away with quiet intensity on the embryonic racers. Spikings called out to one of them. "Rory, come over here. I want you to meet someone."

A large, bearded man turned away from the car on the right and walked over to us.

"Pete Hawthorn, Rory Hite. Rory's our chief mechanic and all-around miracle worker. I'm going to leave Pete in your hands for a bit while I get a FAX off to Ennio. Those radiator cores still haven't arrived from Rome."

Spikings turned, darted up an exposed metal staircase, and disappeared from sight.

"Outside suppliers will be the death of us yet," Rory said, sounding like a gruff Crocodile Dundee. "If we had everything we'd been promised, your bum would be strapped into a DV-1 at Jerez right now. Glad to have you with us, by the way. Alberto's a right rabbit but he has a tendency to bend things. So, what would you like to see?"

"Everything."

"Right. In any particular order?"

"From the beginning, I guess. It's been eight, nine years since I had to understand these cars and I'm sure nothing's the same anymore."

"Yes and no. Some of the computer stuff is pretty mysterious but we've got our fair share of whiz kids who think it's all a piece of cake. No matter what the computers say, it still comes down to more gas, less brakes. Right? Let's go up to the design department from whence cometh all good things."

The upper floor was set on a sort of balcony that ran completely around the room with a staircase at either end. The drafting department, which took up one end of it, consisted of a few large drafting tables containing drawings of various components, including front suspension geometry and a transmission casing. Hanging on a wall at the far end of the long narrow room were overlays of the car in full one-to-one scale. Save for Rory and myself the room was empty.

"Where is everyone?" I asked.

"Probably in the lounge having coffee or a cuppa tea. They've been at it since six this morning. But the man you really want to talk to is our design boffin, Todd Whitehead, and I know just where he is."

He pointed to a door next to the hanging full-scale drawings with a decal on it saying DANGER—RADIOAC-TIVE, and directly beneath it one of those little yellow BABY ON BOARD signs.

"Our CAD/CAM room. Todd's eminent domain."

He knocked and I followed him inside. The room was barely illuminated, the strongest light being the glow of the color computer monitor. If Whitehead heard us, he gave no indication of it. His attention was focused on a three-dimensional, revolving pro-jection of the transmission casing I'd seen the draw-ing of outside. I noticed he was wearing earphones connected to a small compact-disk player sitting next to the computer keyboard. Rory tapped him on the shoulder.

"Todd. Sorry to barge in but this is Pete Hawthorn. He wants to see some of the toys you're making for him to play with."

Whitehead turned away from the screen almost re-luctantly, switching off the CD player and removing his earphones. He was a lot younger than I'd ex-pected, not more than thirty. His hair was almost shoulder length and he wore a small gold earring in his left earlobe. He spoke with a soft, educated voice.

"Trying to find someplace new to stash the oil tank

56

that Byrne hasn't thought of over at Benetton. I've used his concept of putting the gear ratios ahead of the crownwheel and pinion but I don't like the way the tank is integrated. I'm sorry, who did you say you were?"

"Pete Hawthorn. I'll be driving one of your cars."

He looked me over as he stood, then nodded his head. I wasn't sure if it meant he liked what he saw or if he was merely acknowledging my necessary existence. "Welcome. I think you'll like what we've come up with. Nothing radical but she should run pretty respectably right out of the box. I think."

"Pete wants to get a feel for what we're doing. I thought you might run over some of the details of the car on the system here."

"My pleasure."

"Right. I'll leave you two alone then. Got to get back to work or we'll all be watching Rio on the telly." Rory left and Todd offered me a seat next to him in front of the screen.

"Good man, Rory. He's pretty much gotten us back on schedule. Barry and I thought the mechanics might resent Windsor bringing him in but it's worked out very nicely.

"So, before we start, I have to warn you that I tend to go on a bit about things that might not make sense to you. What I mean is, feel free to stop me. Ask questions. The more you know about the total design package, the better we'll be able to communicate about changes and updates. The DV-1 is a big opportunity for me and any help will be greatly appreciated. Okay?"

"Let her rip."

"To begin with, all of our design work is done using this CAD system. That's computer-aided design. We still do some preliminary drawings but this is the real workhorse. Frank Dernie over at Lotus calls these systems 'fast idiots' because they can only do exactly what you tell them to, but they do it incredibly quickly.

"Basically, it's a Prime 2755 thirty-two-bit computer incorporating their product design graphics system. That's the CAM part. Computer-aided manufacture. If it was up to the computer, you'd be testing at Jerez right now but, unfortunately, the only place the complete DV-1 exists is in here." He pointed at the blank nineteen-inch screen with a light pen and immediately the DeStefano-Vitale-1 began to come to life before my eyes. "We all agreed not to try anything too radical this time around, so the car is fairly conventional within the parameters of current F1 design." As he spoke the car was forming on the screen in a three-dimensional rendering. "The chassis is quite low and narrow with an overall height of 36 inches and a width of only 82.5. Like most of the new cars, we have low sidepods with a narrow cockpit area and needle nose. The wheelbase is rather long at 113 inches, mostly because you and Alberto are both about six feet tall and we had to have room for a reclining driving position in order to keep the airbox height down. Front track is 70.5 against 65.5 rear and we're right at 1,102 pounds. Transmission internals are standard Hewland DGB400 six-speed mounted longitudinally with the rear wing attached to the casing. We're using a single ATL fuel cell and we've managed to get the whole two hundred liters located aft of the cockpit. The monocoque is carbonfiber-Nomex honeycomb composite that we make right here in our own autoclave. Wings and sidepods are also composite. We may be right at minimum weight but the car is very strong. Shouldn't have any problems with flexing or anything like that. Suspension is also pretty conventional: double wishbone and push rods all around with Koni dampers. Outboard Brembo brakes with SEP carbonfiber disks.

"We're using the Cosworth DFR with Weber-Marelli injection. Signor Vitale wanted to go with the Lamborghini V-12 but Barry, Rory, and I convinced him that simpler is better. We've got Heni Mader doing the prep, so they should have a good power curve and not be prone to self-destruct. Also, we've been getting a lot of help from the Minardi team. They're about an hour away in Faenza. Vitale and Giancarlo Minardi are old friends and since they've been using the DFR it was easier to sell the V-8 concept to the boss. Any questions so far?"

"Ask it how many races I'm going to win this year."

He closed his eyes, touched the screen with the fingers of his left hand, waited a moment, then replied in a terrible Indian accent.

"I am having the utmost difficulty getting through. . . . Wait a moment. Yes . . . Yes . . . The all-knowing one asks, are you Senna? Are you Prost? Or are you the one who will make your humble designer look good by managing to get through pre-qualifying?"

"Okay," I said, laughing. "I surrender. From what I hear, pre-qualifying's going to be a son of a bitch, so I hope you're right about its being quick out of the box."

"That's the primary reason we've kept the car simple. It's also the reason we've invested so heavily in all the high-tech stuff: to save time. I mentioned our CAM capabilities? Right. Let's say I want to make the radiators larger for Rio. That's going to change the size and shape of the sidepods. Used to be that before we could check out the modification aerodynamics the model shop would have to spend hours making up new quarter-scale bits. Now, as soon as I do anything on the CAD system the info is digitalized and stored in the computer's memory.

"Then, by implementing the CAM numerical control system, a three-dimensional milling machine next door automatically cuts the wooden model to the exact specs. Saves days of fiddling because it's always constructed perfectly and any time we save here gives Maurice Heath, our aerodynamicist, that much more time in the wind tunnel and you a lot more practice time in the cars."

The door opened and Spikings stuck his head in.

"Everything under control here?" he asked, grinning.

"I think we've properly astonished him."

"Good. Can you come around to my office for a minute, Pete? You can spend some more time with Todd before you leave."

"Okay. Thanks, Todd. I'll be back."

"Anytime. I like generating feedback from the un-programmed modules in the system."

"Come again?"

"I think he means the drivers, Pete."

Todd flashed a quick smile and started to put his earphones back in.

"Who's on the CD?" I asked. "Philip Glass?"

"The Stones," he whispered. Inserting the other earphone, he cranked up the volume and went back into the world of recalcitrant oil tanks.

I followed Spikings around the balcony to the other side of the building.

"What do you think, so far?"

"I'm really impressed. I didn't realize Vitale was so well set. What the hell do all the poor teams do?"

"Hate to lay this on you, mate, but we *are* one of the poor teams. McLaren's got around 150 people and probably fifty million a year to spend, not counting all the engines and technicians supplied by Honda. We've only got forty people and even with our new sponsorship deal in place we'll be running on about 10 percent of their total budget."

"Who is the sponsor, anyway? When I asked Windsor about it he just changed the subject."

Spikings stopped in front of his office door. "The kind of money needed in F1 is getting harder to find every year. So, until all the *T*s are crossed and *X*s initialed we don't want word to leak out who we're negotiating with. There are at least two major teams that haven't got their money in place yet. We're hoping to make the announcement in about two weeks.

In any case you and Alberto will be the first to know so you can get your own personal deals finalized."

He opened the door and ushered me inside. It was small but, like the reception area downstairs, stylishly appointed with expensive furniture and artwork. On a large glass-top desk were phone, FAX, and copying machines along with a wooden model of the DV-1 painted in Vitale yellow.

A short, thin, balding man wearing a Vitale jumpsuit was standing with his back to us looking at a Frank Wooten litho of Moss and Jenkinson in the '55 Mille Miglia.

"Trev, look who's here."

The man stiffened when he heard Spikings's voice. He turned hesitantly, took one look at me, and nearly keeled over, grabbing a chair back for support. It was Trevor Alcott and he had just seen a ghost.

CHAPTER

7

Alcott was staring at me with the same mixture of fascination and dread I'd seen on Windsor's face back in Daytona. Luckily, the FAX machine chose that moment to come to life, breaking the silence and drawing his attention away from me. Regaining his composure, he attempted a smile, although the execution wasn't convincing.

"Excuse me. They said you look like James but, God, it's a bit of a jolt."

"I'm sorry. I didn't mean to upset you. . . ."

"No. No. Forget it." Now the smile was beginning to work.

"Trevor Alcott. Pleased to meet you. Mr. Windsor said you'd be wantin' to talk about what happened in Brazil and I'd be happy to, but I've got to go to Rome and pick up some bloody inventory. Would tomorrow be all right?"

I assured him that would be fine and offered to take

him to dinner at the Cavallino. He accepted readily, then ducked out the door quickly, as if being in the same room with me made him uneasy. It promised to be a fun dinner, if that was the case.

"Well, this is interesting," said Spikings, looking at the FAX that had just arrived. "It's from Signor Vitale in Jerez. Senna's quickest, which is hardly surprising, but Gugelmin and Capelli have got the March going quicker than Ferrari, Benetton, and Williams."

"Are they running interim chassis?"

"Ferrari's running the new 640 but it's the only one. Benetton's working on their active suspension system. Herbert had a right heart-stopper with it. Seems a battery lead fell off, knocked the whole system into full up, and put him off at the end of the straight."

"Is he okay?"

"Yeah. Probably a bit older, though." He chuckled.

I could well imagine he might be. Herbert still could barely walk after his big accident at Brands Hatch last summer. It made me glad that Todd and the rest of the team had opted for simplicity over innovation with the DV-1. Computer-controlled suspensions, electronic shift by wire transmissions and all might be the wave of the future, but that wave could too easily swamp a small outfit like this one.

"It's been a long day for you already and I'm sure you'd like a soak and a bit of kip. I've got your contract ready, so why don't you go on to the hotel, get some rest, then look it over. If you have any questions we can talk about it in the morning."

"I *am* starting to fade. And I'm starved."

"We've got you booked into the FINI in Modena.

Take one of the Escorts. Gabriella will tell you the way and ask her to direct you to the Trattoria da Felice. The food there is super."

"Do I need a reservation?"

"Did the pope come to Ferrari? It's just like what happened at the airport. Tell them you drive for Vitale."

Spikings was right about the food. I managed to get a table by playing tourist rather than racing driver, which allowed me to enjoy the meal undisturbed. One mention of my ride with Vitale and I would have spent the evening autographing everything from menus to individual squares of ravioli. When it comes to motor racing, there are no fans anywhere that compare to the Italians. They are known collectively as *tifosi*, an almost untranslatable word that, at least in medical circles, denotes uncontrollable spasms in people suffering from nervous disorders.

I went back to the hotel and just managed to finish getting undressed before falling into a jet-lagged dreamless sleep.

The next morning, over a caffe doppio strong enough to blast away any lingering cobwebs, I went over my contract. It was short, to the point, and accurate. Then, with the stroke of a borrowed pen, I officially returned to the world I had let slip through my fingers nine years before.

When I arrived at the works I found that the four tubs had changed in my brief absence. Like the mysterious pods in *Invasion of the Body Snatchers* they

65

had taken the next step in their transformation from caterpillar to butterfly.

There was an empty chair sitting about ten feet in front of the nearly completed DV-1. When I asked Rory about it he shook his head and grinned. "Alberto's due back from holiday today. When he's here he likes to sit there and watch the lads put 'his' car together. At first he sat there day and night but I had to put a stop to it before he sent us all 'round the bend."

"Put another one out next to it. My contract says we're equal number one, and if he sits, I sit."

The way he looked at me I knew he thought the loonies finally had taken control of the asylum.

"Are you serious?"

It took a long moment while I tried to keep a straight face before he started to laugh.

"Jesus Christ. If you didn't give me half a fright. Come on, let's go next door to composites and get your comical arse fitted to a seat . . . two chairs. Bloody hell."

The composite shop was in the larger of the two support buildings adjacent to the main works. Just inside the door, on a low platform, was a full-scale wood-and-aluminum mock-up of the DV-1 tub. But the thing that dominated the room was the autoclave against the opposite wall. Autoclaves are like giant pressure cookers that produce carbonfiber-molded race-car bits instead of corned beef and cabbage. Rory explained that they were just making up a batch of nose cones that were to be used in FISA-mandated head-on crash testing.

Go to any professional race meeting and see how easy it is to pick out the drivers when they're not wearing their driving suits. They limp. Not all of them, of course. Just enough to make the point. When you're running along at two hundred mph it's your feet that are out there in front of everything just waiting to get clobbered. Ask Rick Mears or Jacques Lafitte. Or Barry Spikings, for that matter. So in addition to crash testing, the Fédération Internationale du Sport Automobile rule makers recently moved the driver's feet back behind the center line of the front wheels. Let's hear it for composite nose cones and foot boxes.

The process by which carbonfiber composites are turned into safe, ultrastrong, ultralight components seemed closer in execution to Savile Row than Detroit. As I watched, a man took a large sheet of composite material, laid a pattern on it, and cut it with a fabric cutter like you would a pair of pants. Spikings explained that the composite already had been impregnated with a resin that would "cure" in the autoclave. Once tailored, the cut fabric is laid into a mold made from a full-scale mock-up of the nose cone, then cooked in the autoclave under a hundred pounds per square inch of pressure at five hundred degrees until the recipe says it's done.

The man who supervised this procedure joined us. "Ziggy, Pete Hawthorn. Pete's come to take a ride in the autoclave."

Ziggy only added to the Savile Row analogy. He

looked like an old-world tailor. He even talked like one. He had me put on a jumpsuit and climb into the mock-up, then he pulled out a tape measure. I expected him to ask me if I wanted the tub let out a little around the middle. Actually, what we were doing was one of the most important steps in the construction of the cars. During a Grand Prix, g-forces and other factors such as heat, humidity, altitude, and any mechanical problems with the car can wear down the best-conditioned driver. Anything that makes the task easier can mean the difference between winning, losing, or even finishing a race.

The next hour was spent literally tailoring the car to my body. The seat itself was formed around me with some viscous material that seemed like a cross between modeling clay and gelatin. When this hardened, it would be used as a mold from which contoured seats could be cast in composite whenever needed. The steering wheel size, thickness, height, and distance from my chest were set, as were the location, spacing, and alignment of the throttle, brake, clutch pedals, and gearshift lever. Final adjustments would be made at the first test session. All relevant data would then be logged, allowing the mechanics to set up any chassis for me in a matter of minutes. Add the custom contour seat and the car would be as comfortable as an old pair of slippers.

Spikings arrived just as we were wrapping things up. He and I headed back to his office to discuss my contract before going to lunch.

We were about to enter the main building when, with a blaring horn and screeching tires, a red Alfa

convertible slid to a stop a few feet away. Alberto Vaccarella, flashing an impossibly white smile, vaulted
out of the car, then leaned back in toward the girl
seated in the passenger seat and kissed her on the
forehead. It was the sort of kiss you'd give your sister,
only nobody you'd ever heard of had a sister that
looked like this girl. He whispered something then
helped her over into the driver's seat. I suppose she
was wearing a skirt but you couldn't prove it by me.
Spikings let out a rather plaintive sigh. "I'm too old
for this," he said, shaking his head in disbelief.

The girl gave a little wave, stepped on the gas, and
was gone.

Alberto looked at us and said, in a serious voice,
*"La vita e molto difficile per un corridore, molto diffi-
cile."*

Spikings smiled. "He says life is very hard for a
racing driver. Very hard . . . I'll bet it's hard, you little sod."

"You are Peter Hawthorn. I am Alberto Vaccarella
but you must call me Alberto."

If you were making a Hollywood movie about the
glamorous world of Formula One and you called central casting for the perfect driver, they'd send Alberto.
Tall, dark, and handsome. He fit the cliché like a
Nomex glove. The fact that he was also very fast, was
familiar with all the new European Grand Prix
tracks, and was the protégé of the team owner might
have prejudiced me against him.

But I was an adult, wasn't I? I decided I hated him
anyway. Blissfully unaware of my thoughts, Alberto
went inside to see how "his" car was coming along

while Spikings and I went up to the office. I exchanged my signed contract for the first of ten monthly $25,000 checks. My mood definitely was back on the upswing.

There was a message from Alcott, who was still in Rome waiting for some radiator cores, saying he'd meet me at the Cavallino at eight. According to Spikings, the problem with the radiator cores was typical of the supply hassles faced by all of the smaller outfits. Without the huge budgets available to teams like Ferrari or McLaren it was impossible to fabricate everything in-house. You've probably heard stories of million-dollar races being lost because a two-dollar part broke. Well, more often than not, the part that failed was purchased outside rather than made by the team.

Lunch turned out to be rather hurried as Spikings had to leave for Faenza and a meeting with his counterpart at Minardi, Jaime Graziadei. As incongruous as it might seem, given the temperature in Brazil, he was trying to borrow their old set of tire warmers to take to Rio. As Spikings told it, they were already secondhand, Minardi having gotten them from Ferrari. What was most interesting about the tire blankets was that we needed them now. Windsor, he said, had just left London on his way to Rio to make arrangements for a private two-day test session with the first completed car. By the end of next week I'd know pretty much what the rest of my year was going to be like. Not to mention the rest of my career.

The news about Rio had Alberto so excited he could

barely sit still long enough to finish his meal after Spikings left. I, of course, befitting my status as senior driver, tried to appear cool and unconcerned. I sipped my caffe doppio, cut and lit a petite corona, and wondered: Would the car be fast enough? Would I be fast enough? More importantly, would I be faster than Alberto? What, me worry? I was so busy with my interior monologue that I forgot all about my teammate, who probably thought conversation should be somehow interactive. "Sorry, Alberto. Must be jet lag. What did you say?"

"The knife you used to cut your cigar. May I see it?"

"Of course."

I took the knife out of its small, leather-belt sheath and handed it to him. I could tell he was impressed; people generally were. Other folding knives they'd seen or handled were usually of the Swiss army or small penknife type. The liner lock folder that Alberto was carefully scrutinizing was handmade by one of America's top knife makers, Howard Viele. Constructed from 440c stainless steel with anodized titanium bolsters and handle, it was as high-tech as the DV-1. I had begun collecting knives two years before after inadvertently going to a custom knife show to get in out of a rainstorm. The artistry and craftsmanship knocked me out and I was hooked. My collection was small, only ten knives, but each was a work of art.

"Have you ever been to Mugello?" asked Alberto.

"Nope. Never have. Heard it's a nice track, though."

"Fantastico. I have won there many times. It is very good for testing when we cannot have Imola. But in

the town, in Mugello, is a knife maker store. Nothing so fine as this, of course. I will take you myself, perhaps Saturday?"

"Sounds great. But not Saturday. I have to stop in Miami on my way to Rio, so I'll be leaving then."

"You have raced in Brazil, yes?"

"No, as a matter of fact I've never been to Brazil. In '79 the team wasn't ready for the South American races and in 1980 I didn't have a ride until Long Beach."

"So, we are going to have a good year, I think. I look forward to working with you and your great experience."

"I'm looking forward to it myself."

"Perhaps you will have dinner with me tonight. I will ask Angela to bring a friend. You remember Angela from the Alfa?" One look at my face and he knew I remembered Angela from the Alfa. I had to laugh. It was going to be hard not to like Alberto. "Thanks for the invitation. But I've already made plans to have dinner with Trevor Alcott at the Cavallino."

"The Cavallino? *Molto bene.* For me, always a place of dreams."

I arrived at the restaurant a few minutes early and managed to find a parking space on a side street close by. The Cavallino is a world-famous gustatory mecca for racing fans, particularly the Ferraristi.

Directly across from the main gate of the Ferrari works in Maranello, it has played host to the great, near great, and pretenders of every stripe for many years. Alberto was right when he called it a place of dreams. Its name alone, Cavallino, the prancing horse symbol of Ferrari, is enough to heat the blood of any aficionado.

Inside its yellow stucco walls is found the history of Ferrari: photographs, flags, helmets, trophies. Mementos of men who drove and died driving before I was born, as well as the heroes of my youth. As I was shown to a table I passed the tiny bar where my father probably stood with the likes of Musso and Behra, Collins and Schell. All of them gone now, yet somehow still among us in this place. I'm not sure if it's because I'm a second-generation driver or the circumstances of my father's disappearance, but I have this strong, almost overpowering sense of history. I probably felt about Spa or the Nurburgring the way others feel about Stonehenge. I remember in particular stopping at the Spa-Francorchamps circuit next to the small marker memorializing Dick Seaman's fatal crash and being overcome with emotion. When I first started racing back in the States, it was an enormous thrill to go to a track like Watkins Glen and drive where Graham Hill or Innes Ireland had won the Grand Prix. I've spoken about this feeling to other drivers, but for the most part they're not as sentimental, being concerned only with the job at hand.

I had just taken the first sip of my Campari when the maître d' approached with a well-dressed, very attractive young woman of about twenty-five. She was wearing a conservative business suit, and her close-cropped, reddish-brown hair gave her a boyish look. Not my type, I thought, as they drew closer. It was only when he was about to seat her opposite me that I stood up in confusion. She smiled and held out her hand. "Good evening, Mr. Hawthorn. Sorry to take you by surprise. I'm Anne Alcott Davies. Trevor Alcott is my father."

We remained standing for a moment. "Couldn't he find a parking spot?" I asked.

She smiled and shook her head. "He's not coming. Something he ate in Rome didn't agree with him, so I deputized myself to take his place. I hope you don't mind?"

"No, of course not. Please sit down. And the name is Pete." I did mind, actually. Was Alcott trying to avoid talking to me? It hardly made sense for him to think he could, what with our being on the same team. Maybe he just wanted to postpone it. Maybe I should stop being so analytical and talk to the person who did show up. "Is it anything serious?"

"What?"

"Your father, is it—"

"No. I don't think so. To tell you the truth, I think seeing you upset him somehow. He told me how much you look like your father and I know this dinner was an excuse to talk about Brazil. I just don't think he could handle it yet."

"I thought it might be a problem. He nearly passed out yesterday when Barry Spikings introduced us. Has he ever spoken to you about what happened?"

"No. But he didn't have much opportunity. Mother and he already were divorced by that time and I've only just gotten reacquainted with him in the last year and a half. It worries me, though."

"In what way?"

"Well, I knew of course that he'd had this accident in Brazil and that he couldn't remember anything about it. What Mother didn't tell me was that another man was involved who was never seen again. I know now that it was your father."

"How did you find out?"

"From Father. I was staying with him for a couple of weeks at his house in Dorset before going up to London on a job. I'm a free-lance writer. Nothing exciting, mostly travel stuff, but it has obvious advantages. Anyway, he got this phone call offering him a job on the Vitale team and it affected him somehow."

"Go on."

"He changed. Nothing major like Jekyll and Hyde but little things. He started drinking quite a lot and I knew he wasn't sleeping well because I could hear him walking around the house in the middle of the night. When I finally got him to admit something was wrong, he told me about the rally and your father, but not in any detail. He's always been a very private man, partly because of his background, I'm sure. He's got this sort of 'us and them' attitude about everything, whereas my mother wasn't like that at all. Probably explains why it didn't last. Well, I don't want to go on about this forever but, you see, I'm not like him. I've had a good education. I've been trained to ask questions. That's actually why I decided to come tonight. I'm worried about him and I was hoping you could tell me what's going on."

"I'll tell you everything I know, but let's order dinner first 'cause it's a long story. By the way, do you know who it was that called him about the Vitale job?"

"Yes. It was the team owner, Mr. Windsor."

For the next hour as we worked our way through pasta, fish, and salad I related yet again the story of James, Windsor, Alcott, and the World Cup Rally. As I talked I found the disappointment of dispensing rather than receiving information giving way to something else. I was enjoying the way Anne looked at me as I recounted the story and found myself embellishing things to make it sound more interesting. By the time our espressos arrived I was just about talked out. Anne hadn't said much, just one or two pointed questions that kept me on track. The only thing I found strange was her seeming lack of interest in racing. I mean, here she was having dinner at the Cavallino with a bona fide Formula One driver, yet every time the conversation drifted into racing lore, including my own checkered career, she'd shown nothing beyond ordinary politeness. Maybe she disliked racing because of what it had done to her father, much the same way Mary hated it because of James.

"I can't see why you have to go to Brazil now. I mean, I know you want to find out what happened to your father, but why now? I'm sure it's the pressure of going back there with you that's disturbed my father so badly. Frankly, I think Mr. Windsor was totally insensitive to have allowed such a thing to happen."

"Hold it. You think I'm going to Brazil to solve some sort of mystery? I'm going for the Grand Prix. It's the beginning of the season. You don't just not go to a Grand Prix. It's for the championship of the world. . . ." She looked at me as if I were mad as a hatter. And loud too, from the reaction of the other diners. "Sorry, didn't mean to act like a jerk, but to suggest not going to the Brazilian Grand Prix? Do you know what a Grand Prix is?"

"Well, let's see. There's Grand Prix tennis, Grand Prix bicycling, horse racing, running. . . . Which did you have in mind?"

"Gotcha. Have you ever been to a Formula One race?"

"I have never been to a motor race of any sort. And don't take that as some sort of personal affront. Other than father, I've never even met anyone involved with motor racing. I did watch part of the Indianapolis thing on television once with my ex-husband but it bored me silly. All that zooming around in circles. Like a dog chasing its tail. I'm sure it's terribly exciting but it's just not something I'm interested in."

Terrific, I thought. In the space of a week I meet two good-looking, intelligent ladies and what happens? The first one wants to know too much about racing and the second nothing at all.

"I hope I haven't hurt your feelings," she said. "I shouldn't be discussing a subject I know nothing about and if it weren't for my father I wouldn't. But don't you find it a bit odd that you, Windsor, and my father are all going to Brazil together, for any reason, given what happened there nineteen years ago?"

Fortunately, the waiter chose that moment to arrive with the check, giving me a moment to consider what she said before I replied.

"You're right. It does seem a little strange. But, believe me, it is a coincidence. There are sixteen races in sixteen countries. Brazil just happens to be the first one. Maybe your father shouldn't go. On the other hand, going back might help him remember what happened. Why don't you speak to Windsor about it?"

"I already have. He said pretty much the same things you did. He did say that if father didn't want to go, he could stay here and work at the factory. I don't know, maybe I'm just being silly." She took a quick look at her watch. "I'm afraid I have to get back to the hotel. Thank you for a lovely dinner. I do hope I'll run into you again. And good luck in the race. I'll watch for you on television."

"Thanks. Look, if your father does decide to go, I'll try and keep an eye on him, okay?"

"I was about to ask if you would."

If she kept smiling at me like that, I thought, she could ask me for about anything. It wasn't until I'd seen her off to Bologna that I allowed what she had said to sink in. I *was* going to Brazil to race in the Grand Prix, and nothing was going to get in the way of that. On the other hand, it certainly would be the perfect opportunity to find some answers if, after all these years, there were any to be found.

CHAPTER

8

I managed somehow to sleep during the entire flight from Milan to New York. Even the routine cabin announcements, which usually jolt me out of whatever level of doze I'm in, failed to interrupt my jumbled dreams. I say "jumbled" because I seldom remember anything more than fragments of intricate, exciting scenarios. Wide-screen movies filled with fast cars, beautiful women, intrigue, and danger. Considering what Anne had said the previous night, I could see where my dream movies might soon have to be reclassified as documentaries.

After changing planes at JFK, I spent the time heading south making lists of the things I had to do before the racing season began in earnest. I knew that from the middle of March in Rio until Adelaide in November most of my days would be spent strapped into the seat of an airplane or a Formula One car. Two incredibly fast conveyances, each of which relied on wings to make it function properly. The trick would be to get through the season with the wings on one keeping the thing up in the air while the wings on the other kept it down on the ground.

As soon as we landed I called Don to see how Mary was doing. Not unexpectedly, nothing had changed since I left and we made plans to meet that evening at the hospital. Then I screwed up my courage and called Gail Goodwin, the woman I'd been seeing on and off since my divorce. Gail had seemed to be everything my wife wasn't, which meant she was everything I was looking for at the time. Now we were both looking for a way out.

Well, I was definitely looking to break things off and I was fairly certain she felt the same way. My new ride presented the perfect opportunity to bring things to a head. After waiting for her answering machine to stop playing the refrain from "Home Sweet Home" (Gail was in real estate) I left a message inviting her to brunch at the Down Under in Fort Lauderdale. I knew I was in for a side order of recriminations along with my ceviche and stone crabs but I assumed that since we were both adults we could handle everything and still remain friends.

With that cheery thought I took a taxi home for a nap and a shower before meeting Don at the hospital.

I got to the Down Under early enough to assure us a waterside table. I was originally introduced to the restaurant by some friends who used to arrive aboard their Bertram, off-load everyone into the restaurant, then send the boat back out onto the water until it was time to leave. I assume the place is named for its location. If you don't come by boat, you have to drive down under one of the bridges that cross the Inter-coastal waterway to get to it.

As I waited for Gail I practiced various ways of say-ing what I wanted to say, trying to keep things as pleasant as possible. The more I thought about it the less sure I was that she felt the same way I did about things. I had just finished my second spicy Virgin Mary when I saw her coming toward me through the restaurant. As she passed a table of three tipsy-look-ing men who were dressed for the Henley Regatta, I watched their heads swivel around in unison until it seemed that the one with his back to me would wring his own neck. Gail had that effect on some people. Men people mostly. Tall, with jet-black hair and the milkiest skin I've ever seen. I'm sure she personally supports more than one sun-block manufacturer. I stood and she brushed her lips across mine as she slid into her chair. "Hello, Pete."

"Gail. You're looking incredible, as usual."

"I wish I could say the same about you," she re-plied. "Have you taken a good look in the mirror lately? You look terrible. Are you okay?"

"Yeah, just tired. I got in from Milan yesterday and ended up spending the night at the hospital."

"Is there anything new?"

"No. Still the same. It's just that Don caught some sort of bug and didn't want to take any chances, so I spent the night with her. I'll probably do it again to-night, then I've got to fly to Rio tomorrow."

"Rio?"

"I got a new ride. Happened while you were down in Aruba selling time shares. I'm back in Formula One. That's why I was in Italy, to meet the team. Anyway, we're testing the car in Rio next week."

"Formula One, wow. Congratulations. But isn't this a bad time to leave, you know, with your mom and all?"

"No choice. The Brazilian Grand Prix is in a couple of weeks and we don't even know if the car works."

"Pete, she's your mom, for Christ's sake. Can't somebody else test the car?"

The waiter arrived with our drinks, giving me some time to come up with an answer she'd understand, but there didn't seem to be one. "The doctor says she could go on like this for months. I'll just have to try and be here as much as I can." She stared at me for a moment before pulling a pack of cigarettes out of her bag. It was obvious she didn't particularly like my answer. Truth be known, neither did I, but it was the only one I had. She inhaled deeply, slowly blew the smoke out over the water, and let loose.

"Look, Pete, I'm not going to try and tell you how to run your life. We've been down that road too many times already. I know how much you love your mom and I'm sure you're doing the best you can. It's just that . . . I probably shouldn't be saying this, but . . . It's not like driving a car faster than anyone else is really meaningful, you know? Even a Formula One car. I mean with all the problems in the world today who cares what someone's lap time is? I'm sorry. You're a nice guy. I'm probably even in love with you. But it all seems so stupid. Arthur says it's because you didn't have a war to fight in. Maybe that's it. Maybe you need to be on the edge all the time, or be in danger. I don't know. It's certainly not the glamour. I've been in the pits enough the past two years to know there's not much of that around."

She had to stop for a breath, so I attempted to jump in. "Okay, wait a minute—"

"No. Let me finish. I've done everything I could to make this relationship work, but it's just no good. I know this is a terrible time to do this, what with your mom and all, but I can't help it. I really don't think we should see each other again. At least not for a while."

I couldn't believe my ears. It was as if she'd been practicing things to say just like I had. The only difference was, she'd gotten to say them.

"Pete. I know this is probably a big shock and I'm sorry. But what can I say?"

"You could answer one question."

"Like what?"

"Who's Arthur?"

Her skin flushed until she looked like she'd fallen asleep in a tanning parlor. "How did you find out about Arthur?"

"I didn't. You mentioned his name a minute ago. Some sort of veteran, I presume?"

"Don't be cute. Arthur happens to be the man I went to Aruba with and he is a veteran. He was a captain in Vietnam. Now he runs a very successful yacht brokerage company in Key Biscayne."

"Very meaningful occupation," I said, smiling.

"What with the way things are in the world and all . . ."

She flipped her cigarette butt into the water and stood abruptly. "Pete, sometimes you can be a real shit, you know?" With that she turned and marched out the way she'd come in, with the same head-turning results. Oh well, like the song says, breaking up is hard to do.

The Varig flight from Miami to Rio was one of those experiences that made you wish you'd stayed in bed. Particularly in my case, since I'd spent another night at the hospital and could have used some shuteye. Fortunately, Don had shaken off whatever it was he had and could be there with her again.

It should have been a comfortable flight. The team had booked me into first class, which I was beginning to get used to, but unfortunately, I seemed to be the only sane passenger in the cabin. Every other seat was occupied by a travel agent off on a free Brazilian holiday courtesy of God knew who. Before we were an hour out of Miami there was more champagne being sprayed around than I'd ever seen on a victory podium. Unable to beat them and having no desire to join in, I put on the headset, dialed in the jazz channel, and buried my nose in the Clancy book I'd started in Daytona.

By the time I arrived at Rio's International Airport and cleared customs I was totally wiped out and in no mood for the scurrying taxi drivers trying to outhustle each other for the pleasure of driving me to the hotel. I took a quick look at the team's Rio fact sheet, found what I needed to know, and marched over to the Transcoopass Taxi desk, where I bought a chit for the fare to the Inter-Continental. People who talk about how crazy the drivers are in Rome or Paris obviously have never been to Rio. The opening lap at Le Mans is safer. It's no wonder Senna's so quick.

Within minutes of checking into the hotel I was climbing into bed. I remember thinking before I fell asleep that if the team did anywhere near as well with the cars as they did with everything else, we were going to have a hell of a year.

CHAPTER

9

After a few hours of blissfully dreamless sleep, a room-service selection of fresh fruit and coffee followed by a soak in the tub, I was ready to face the day. The team was due in later that afternoon, with testing to commence the following morning. Having heard nothing to the contrary, I assumed that Rory and his gang actually had finished building the cars.

I debated going to the beach to check out the latest Brazilian bathing-suit fashions. I'd heard there was a new type of *tanga*, the famous Brazilian string bikini, called the dental floss. It was, in fact, at the top of my list of Brazilian cultural attractions, right up there with a trip to Sugar Loaf and a visit to the Carmen Miranda museum. I called the hotel gym about a massage and got an appointment for five P.M. Since it was already three, I decided to head for the hotel pool rather than taxi over to Ipanema or Copacabana beach.

OVERSTEER

The Inter-Continental has three pools, and it's a good thing, because the first one I checked out was full of hung-over travel agents who definitely were still in party mode. At the second I found an empty lounge chair just fifteen feet from two luscious Cariocas. Tall and tan and young and lovely and wearing what must have been the aforementioned dental aid.

I had just gotten settled and ordered a fruit punch without the punch when one of them stood, preparing to leave. Her back was toward me and if I hadn't already taken careful note of her front I would have sworn she was naked as a centerfold. As she slowly wrapped herself in what I later found out was called a *kanga*, I managed to study the construction of the alleged bathing suit. It had two nearly invisible straps that widened out slightly as they came down over her breasts, barely covering her nipples. The floss then continued southward where the straps converged at a tiny triangular cloth concealing what must have been some exceedingly well manicured pubic hair. The suit definitely gave new meaning to the term *bikini line*.

Noting my interest, she smiled at me and said something to her friend, which caused them both to laugh before she exited to great effect.

I decided to order some food and used the opportunity to ask the waiter, who spoke excellent English, if the girls were guests at the hotel. Bending over, so as not to embarrass me, he said he didn't know the one who had left but that the other was the daughter of a prominent Rio banker. Clearly off limits. So much for the things he knew I was thinking.

I settled for a club sandwich.

I was just dozing off when I felt a sharp pain on my stomach. I looked down to see a giant ice cube melting on my belly button.

"Peter. You cannot sleep in the sunshine like this or you will be sick."

Alberto stood above me, flashing his perfect smile. I was about to inform him of my encyclopedic knowledge of sun-blocking agents when I realized his attention had wandered. I turned and saw my dream Carioca looking at Alberto the way I'd been looking at her. "Hi, Alberto. Welcome to Rio. I already checked her out. She's the daughter of some big-shot local banker and I get the distinct impression that the hotel doesn't want her to be disturbed. So, is everyone else here?"

"No. Only one car was ready. Signor Windsor, Barry Spikings, and myself have come with some of the crew today. The rest will arrive with the other car tomorrow, I think . . . Her father is a banker? My uncle is also a banker. Perhaps she will know of him, you think?"

Now it was my turn to laugh. "I think it's entirely possible, Alberto."

He was on his way over to her before I finished talking. He squatted down next to her lounger and began speaking earnestly. Probably discussing the International Monetary Fund. I looked at my watch and realized it was time for my massage. As I left the pool, Alberto, who was now sitting next to her, began peeling off his shirt. I hoped the massage was going to hurt a lot.

OVERSTEER

* * *

When I got back to my room there was a message from Windsor lying on the floor just inside the door: eight o'clock dinner at Monseigneur, the hotel's French restaurant.

The massage had done its job and loosened up the tightness I'd accumulated from long airline flights and the tension over Mary's hopeless situation. I put in a call to my answering machine in Miami but thankfully there was no message from Don. I'd promised to check in every day at about this time and return home on the next available flight, if needed. From here on out it was a case of no news being the best news of all.

As I showered and dressed for dinner I wondered if Windsor and Vitale had concluded their sponsorship deal. I had already begun preliminary talks with a couple of marketing reps, and one agent had even contacted me. But without knowing who the team's primary sponsor was and what their requirements might be, it was hard to do anything concrete regarding a personal sponsorship deal. Signage space on a helmet or driver's suit can be worth a great deal of money if you're prepared to commit the necessary time and energy on behalf of the company laying out the bucks. I was definitely prepared.

Windsor and Spikings were already seated by the time I arrived at the restaurant. As Windsor stood to greet me I could tell he'd already had more than one of whatever he was drinking.

"Peter. Good to see you. Sit down, please. Alberto

will be along any minute. Now, if you gentlemen will excuse me, I must place a call to the works."

Watching him wheel away, I decided he'd had a lot more than just one. "Hello, Barry. Good flight I hope?"

"Perfect. I assume you know we only brought the one car?"

"Alberto filled me in. Is Rory finishing the second one?"

"No. He's here. In fact, he and the crew are already out at the track getting things set up. Nigel Dillard's putting the finishing touches on number two. They'll be bringing it in tomorrow afternoon, if it's ready. By the way, if you're thirsty I'd recommend that you stay away from the local stuff the boss has been sampling."

"What is it?"

"Caipirinha. Made with crushed limes, ice, and cachaca, which is some sort of fermented sugarcane. Probably make a hell of an octane booster."

"I think I'll stick to mineral water. What time do we get started in the morning?"

"Track opens at eight. We'll leave here at seven-thirty. By one o'clock you'll be able to fry an egg on top of your helmet out there. The plan is to run until about one, break until five, then pick up again for another hour or two when it cools down. That's assuming of course that the little darling will run for that long right out of the box."

"What do you think?"

"Ask me tomorrow night."

Spikings picked up his menu. "Food here's quite good, the fish in particular."

I had just begun to speculate on how the various appetizers might taste when Spikings began to chuckle. "Don't look now, but our young friend seems to have done it again."

I knew before I looked up exactly what I was going to see: Alberto and the pool maiden, arm in arm, walking toward the table. She was wearing a white strapless dress with a slit up the side, and though it covered a lot more territory than her poolside attire, it managed to be even sexier. Barry and I exchanged hangdog expressions and stood to greet them.

"Barry Spikings, Peter Hawthorn, may I present Signorina Esmandina Bracha, who has been gracious enough to join with us for dinner tonight." Alberto was beaming, as well he might be.

"Gentlemen. Please be seated. I know you are testing in the morning and must have many things to discuss, so, please, don't let me interrupt."

Her voice was soft and musical. I decided I was in love.

"Actually, Miss Bracha, we've done about all the talking we can about the cars until after these two put some miles on them." Alberto and I tried to look properly humble.

"Well, hello. What have we here?" Windsor said, squeezing himself in next to Esmandina. "Denis Windsor, at your service, Miss . . . ?"

"Bracha, Esmandina Bracha."

She put out her hand and much to everyone's surprise Windsor bent down and kissed it. Alberto looked embarrassed but she seemed amused by it. Windsor turned to the waiter. "In honor of the occasion, and our lovely guest, I think a bottle of Dom Perignon is in order."

Champagne and cachaca. What a combination. Maybe Windsor was confused and thought we were in Rio for carnival.

"I just spoke to Ludovico. The other car will be arriving on schedule tomorrow afternoon. Miss Bracha, would you like to come to the track tomorrow and watch the test?"

"No, thank you very much, but as I told Alberto, I must fly to Brasilia tomorrow on business. Perhaps there will be time during the open tests next month. If not, I will surely see you in the pits during race weekend."

"Ah, well, that may be a bit sticky. FOCA pit passes are quite hard to come by for the Grand Prix itself, but I'm sure I can work something out."

"Thank you again, but it won't be necessary. I attend the Grand Prix every year and credentials have never been a problem. Alberto tells me you have recently become involved with the Vitale team. Have you a long interest in motorsport or is this just a pastime . . . a hobby?"

"Hobby? Not in the least, dear girl. Not in the least. As for how long I've been involved in the sport, let's just say long enough for Peter here's father to have driven for me. Right, Peter?"

"That's right." This was getting better by the minute.

"Actually my hobby, as you put it, is fine art. Paintings, particularly by the old masters. I've managed to put together a modest collection, which I would be most happy to show you any time you're in London."

My God, first he kisses her hand and now he wants to show her his etchings. What next? The waiter had opened the champagne and poured some for everyone but Alberto and myself. Windsor lifted his glass.

"To the beautiful city of Rio and its most beautiful inhabitant, Esmeranda Bracha."

"Esmandina."

"Come again?"

"Signorina Bracha's name is Esmandina."

Alberto was getting a little hot under the collar, and while it was true that Windsor was acting like a jerk, it didn't make sense to let things get out of hand. When in doubt, change the subject.

"You mentioned that you have to go to Brasilia on business. Do you work with the government?"

"No, although my father does on occasion. I myself am a designer of sportswear for women."

"How fascinating." It was Windsor again, looking for another opportunity to put his foot in his mouth. "Perhaps you might like to meet some of the top people at Benetton. My partner, Ludovico Vitale, knows the family quite well."

"I appreciate your kindness but I am already acquainted with them through my family. In fact, I'm sure Father must know Signor Vitale, as he used to know poor Signor DeStefano."

Just a flicker of something changed in Windsor's eyes. He poured himself another glass of champagne and signaled for the waiter. "I think it's time we ordered some supper. I don't know about the rest of you but I'm starving."

While everyone was placing their orders, I decided to probe a bit around Windsor's reaction to DeStefano's name. "You were there when it happened, weren't you? In Gstaad when DeStefano had his accident?"

He answered me quickly enough but I could see that he was becoming wary as he fought the effects of the alcohol. "Yes. Terrible tragedy. Terrible."

"What happened, anyway?"

He took a deep breath before continuing. "Don't know exactly. We had breakfast together, then I drove over to Lausanne to look at a painting I was interested in. Paolo went skiing, as he did every morning, but somehow he got off the regular ski trail and went through one of the areas that were closed because of possible avalanches. There was a giant slide and he was gone. It took two days to find his body.

"Weren't there reports of shots being fired in the area?" asked Esmandina.

"It was mentioned at the inquest, yes. From what I understand, the local police investigated but found no proof that it had happened. How is it that you're so well acquainted with the event?"

"I was there."

"In Gstaad?"

"In Saanen, which is quite nearby. One of my father's friends has a chalet there and we go often on holiday. Father and Senhor DeStefano knew each other through business only but I know he thought quite highly of him."

"Everyone did, I gather. I only wish I'd had the opportunity to know him better. Terrible business." He poured himself another drink, but this time it was agua minerale that went into his champagne glass.

"Please, enough of this talk. I do not wish to be sad tonight. Tomorrow is a great day for the Vitale team; the beginning of a new life for all of us. I'm sure Signor DeStefano would not wish for us to be sad. We must dedicate ourselves to his memory and make the team a great success."

Alberto said this with such conviction and passion that he embarrassed himself, blushing through his deep tan. It was the sort of thing that made him so likable and, if Esmandina's reaction was any example, so irresistible to women.

I guess we all secretly shared Alberto's sentiments because the rest of the meal was spent concentrating on the food, which was excellent, and listening to Alberto and Spikings tell war stories about their time in Formula 3000. Windsor, in a complete reversal, stopped drinking entirely and seemed content to listen to others tell their tales. At ten-thirty I excused myself, returned to my room, set the alarm for six, and crawled into bed. There were many things that had been said and, more importantly, left unsaid that evening that were vying for my attention, but I forced myself to push them aside in favor of sleep. As Alberto so aptly put it, tomorrow was a new beginning. Just the same, I wondered what Alberto was doing. . . .

Say good night, Peter.

CHAPTER

10

The twenty-minute ride to the circuit was accomplished in almost complete silence. I didn't know about Alberto but I was focused on flattening out my emotions. This was a day for cool, analytical thinking. Spikings tried to make small talk for a minute or so, realized it wasn't working, and concentrated instead on driving us there as quickly and smoothly as possible.

The Jacarepagua track, which was renamed in 1988 in honor of Brazil's three-time world champion, Nelson Piquet, is not one of the most beautiful on the Grand Prix tour. Although it's surrounded on three sides by mountains, the circuit itself is flat and almost featureless. It was constructed on a giant landfill when the area had little economic value. Now rumor had it that this could be its last race. The city of Rio recently had declared bankruptcy and was considering tearing up the track to sell the land, which was now worth a fortune.

In a way I was glad I had never driven here before. The fact that the entire team, men and machines, was starting fresh made our goals seem more clearly defined and somehow more attainable.

Spikings parked the car behind a row of dilapidated old brick garages. It was not yet eight in the morning, but it was already quite hot. I looked over at Alberto, who was pulling his gear out of the trunk, caught his eye, and gave him the thumbs-up sign. His uncharacteristically tight-lipped smile said that he was as nervous as I was. Just as I was about to ask Spikings where the car was, it exploded into life not more than fifty feet away, roaring loudly for a moment as the revs climbed, then coughing to a halt. The sound was followed almost immediately by the pungent aroma of hot exhaust gases. We followed Spikings through a passageway to the front of the garages and there it was: the bright yellow DV-1 gleaming in the blazing Brazilian sun. I was in love again. Rory and Carlo Dacco, Vitale's engine man, were huddled together watching the mechanics securing the engine cover over the rear of the car. Aside from Vitale's distinctive yellow livery there was no indication of any sponsor visible on the car. In fact, the only names painted on the bodywork were mine and Alberto's, one above the other on the side of the low airbox cowling just behind the cockpit. I was pleased to see that mine was on top, although, as I would later discover, it was only because my name had fewer letters in it.

"Everything ready?" Spikings asked loudly. Everyone stopped what they were doing to welcome us.

"Ready as she'll ever be. Engine runs, wheels turn, we'll break the lap record then stop for lunch. That all right with you two?" Rory was certainly in good spirits. He bear-hugged each of us as he kept chattering away. "We just finished running through the final assembly checklist. All we have to do now is set up the cockpit. Who's doing the honors, Barry?"

"Pete'll take her out first."

I looked at Alberto and shrugged. He smiled and nodded his approval but I could see the disappointment in his eyes. It reminded me of a beauty pageant I once judged. When the final runner-up was announced, she squealed and applauded along with everyone else, hugged and kissed the winner, but there was no joy in her eyes. Spikings knew what the score was and he got things moving immediately.

"Pete, you can change in the garage. Alberto, you stick with me in the pits. I want you in on the debriefings whenever he brings the car in."

As Spikings continued to get things organized I went into the garage, found a folding canvas chair, and began to change into my business suit. After stripping down to my underwear, I pulled on fireproof Nomex calf-length socks, long johns, and a turtleneck pullover. Over this came the driver's suit, which was made of Pyrotect and Nomex and was triple-layered for extra protection against fire. It was the same suit I'd worn at Daytona, and although it had been cleaned, it still had a familiar, lived-in odor. Finally I laced up the high-top Simpson Nomex boots and headed back outside. The whole procedure had taken less than ten minutes yet I was already sweating profusely. Add a Nomex balaclava, gauntlet gloves, and helmet to the equation and I would soon become a perfectly self-contained steam room. I had never been in an accident involving a serious fire but I'd seen a few, and no amount of discomfort would dissuade me from wearing whatever it took to buy me sixty seconds to get myself out of a burning racer.

When I walked back onto the pit apron, I was surprised to see Signor Vitale standing by the car waiting to greet me. Windsor also had arrived and was off to the side talking to Rory.

"Signor Vitale. This is a nice surprise. I didn't think the rest of the team was due until tonight."

He shook my hand and clapped me on the back. "That is true, but I could not miss this moment, so I chartered an earlier flight. What do you think of the car?"

"Bello. Molto bello."

"Sì. Sì." He embraced me and for a moment I thought he was going to cry. It was definitely time to get the car out onto the track. I disengaged myself, went over to the car, and climbed in. I eased my legs down into the long tunnel leading to the pedals up inside the foot box, then wriggled my body around in the seat to make sure everything felt okay. As I placed my feet on the pedals, checking for positioning, travel, and feel, Rory leaned in, snapped the steering wheel into place, and began cinching up the belts. The car seemed to fit me like the proverbial glove. Next, Spikings plugged the intercom connector into my helmet receptacle and gave me my first instructions. "Vitale wants to make sure you can get out of the car quickly in case there's any trouble. Wait for my signal, then get your bum out of there as fast as you can. Rules say you've got to be able to get out in five seconds or FISA won't let you attempt to prequalify. You ready?"

"Sure." The fact that I was all psyched up to drive the car rather than bail out of it didn't enter the conversation. Actually, it did make sense to test it out first, and this was yet another comforting example of how the team had its act together. Once Spikings had his stopwatch ready he gave me the signal to haul ass. With one hand I grabbed the central locking handle positioned over my stomach and released the belts while the other hand was operating the quick-release lever to disconnect the steering wheel. I threw the wheel aside, gripped the sides of the cockpit, and raised myself up enough to pull my feet free. Scrambling up a little higher, I got my feet under me then pushed myself up and out of the car. The only thing I'd neglected to do was disconnect the emergency air hose that was plugged into the front of my helmet. It did manage to disengage itself but not before yanking the helmet down so far over my eyes that I couldn't see a thing as I stepped out of the car. I must have looked like someone playing pin-the-tail-on-the-donkey because everyone seemed to be having a good laugh as they watched me fumble around. When I got it straightened out I asked Spikings, "How fast?"

He shook his head. "Almost seven seconds.

Shouldn't be a problem, though, once you've done it a few times. Want to give it another go?"

"Later, Barry. For now, let's see what happens if I stay in the car, okay?"

He nodded, still smiling, and set about getting me strapped in and hooked up again. Almost seven seconds, I thought. Christ, I was going to have to chop two seconds off my time in order to qualify to pre-qualify. Rory squatted down and spoke to me through the intercom. "Engine's warmed up but that's about it. Track's green, tires are cold, and the brake pads haven't been bedded in, so take it easy. Once things warm up a bit check the basic stuff then bring her in so we can see what's what. Okay? Good luck."

As he moved away I turned on the master switch and fuel pumps, then waited a moment for the starter to engage. The engine caught almost instantly and I rolled my foot on and off the accelerator to bring the fluid temperatures up to their proper settings. I looked up from the instruments and saw the entire team staring intently at the car, waiting for something to happen. I took a couple of deep breaths, tuned out the hopeful faces, selected first gear, hit the gas, let out the clutch, and smoked the tires as I headed down pit lane with the rear end cocked sideways. I hadn't done it on purpose but if I'd known the effect it would have on the team I certainly would have. Spikings, who was not at all impressed by what he took to be hot-dogging, told me that the mechanics decided at that point that I was all right or, even better, that I might actually be Italian. Vitale thought that was a great notion and in fact it became one of his favorite stories until he ran out of people to tell it to.

The first lap I motored around slowly, watching the instruments and taking note of things about the track that I'd never see once the car was up to speed.

A lot of drivers like to walk around a new track or drive it in a rental car before taking out their race car but I've never found that to do me much good. Afterward, when I have the track embedded in my consciousness, I'll go to certain troublesome spots for a closer view or watch other cars in action there. What I had done in preparation was to run a videotape of the last Brazilian Grand Prix, playing the shots taken from the in-car camera over and over again. It was something I'd never tried before and, surprisingly enough, the track actually seemed familiar.

As soon as everything was warmed up I started checking out what Rory had called the "basics." First, I began to nail the throttle, running up through the gears, making sure the car went where it was pointed without darting to either side, getting a feel for the clutch and shift linkage. Once I was going at a fair clip (about 125 mph) I backed off the throttle abruptly, again checking for a pull to either side. When I was satisfied with these tests I began using the brakes harder as I approached each corner, but I still wasn't ready to push it too far as I moved through them. If something was going to brake or fall off, I preferred it to happen while I was going in a straight line.

After three laps I pulled back into the pits. The moment I stopped, Rory and the crew got the car up on jacks and began checking everything for signs of breakage or things starting to come loose.

"How is it so far?" Spikings wanted to know.

"She tracks fine under acceleration and braking. Everything feels tight but I haven't gotten up to any real speed yet. Linkage seems a bit notchy from fourth to fifth and back. Could be that it's just stiff, though."

"All right. As soon as Rory's satisfied, give it some more of the same but this time you can take the revs up to ten thousand." He disconnected the intercom and went to fill in Alberto, Windsor, and Vitale.

So far, so good. I was already beginning to feel comfortable with the car but I knew that things could change in a hurry once I started getting up to racing speed. Now it was time to start earning my salary, extending the car and myself.

CHAPTER

11

It's a heady, exhilarating feeling, knowing you're the first person in the world to get into a new race car and put it through its paces. I don't want to sound mystical (or loony, depending on your point of view) but when I moved the gear lever into first I felt the car shudder, then begin to vibrate as if it were alive and straining to unleash its power. I managed to get out of the pits without any histrionics and did a couple of slow laps, warming up the tires again and checking to make sure the brakes were ready for some hard use. When most people think of F1 cars it's usually in terms of speed or cornering ability, but what is most astonishing to me is their stopping power. At speeds close to two hundred mph when you hit the brakes it's as if a giant fist punched you in the chest, and in less than two seconds you find yourself crawling along at fifty-five mph. I knew it would take me more time to acclimate myself to the shortened braking distances employed today than to any other aspect of Formula One.

As I passed the start/finish line for the third time I began to pick up the pace, shifting into fifth, then sixth, and bringing the revs up to 9,800. As I approached turn one I went down to third, then swept through the right-hander at about 125 mph. The car felt stable enough as I went down the short straight to Carlos Pace Corner, a long, double-apex left-hander. I was getting some understeer as I turned into the corner, so I lifted slightly then got back on the gas and up through the gears to fifth on the next straight. The notchy feeling in the shifter was already smoothing out. Into Suspiro Corner, really moving quickly at about 140 mph. More understeer. Corrected for it with another lift off the throttle then back on the power where the camber of the corner changed on the exit. That one is going to be a bit hairy at full power, I thought.

Back into third for another right-hander, Nonato, then a quick spurt and down into second for the Norte Hairpin. Very bumpy. In fact, the whole track was very bumpy. Two hours out here in hundred-degree heat was going to be like climbing into the ring with Mike Tyson.

Onto the long back straight: third, fourth, fifth, sixth. The huge grandstands flashing past on my right seemed endless. They were empty now but on Grand Prix weekend they'd be filled with 100,000 Brazilians, yelling their heads off for Piquet, Senna, and Gugelmin. Running at ten thousand rpm, only eight hundred short of maximum, and the front end was beginning to feel light. Not enough to break loose but hardly confidence inspiring. Sul Corner was coming up very quickly. Touched the brakes, went down into fifth, and turned in, going about 145 mph. Once again the front end refused to cooperate but at this speed it was worse, pushing me rapidly toward the outside of the track. A quick dab on the brakes and a slight lift got me through all right, but I knew we'd have to do something about the understeer before trying another quick lap. I motored through the final series of corners and pulled onto pit road.

It was ten A.M. and for the next three hours the routine would be the same. Two or three laps on the track followed by adjustments in the pits to correct the various problems as they emerged. Every change, no matter how small, was logged into the team's computer along with any relevant comments. By the end of the season all the correct settings for each of the sixteen Grand Prix circuits would be on file, ready to be called up for test sessions, computer simulations, wind tunnel work, or for our return to those tracks next season. I'm one of those drivers who really enjoy this sort of work. Testing, to me, is probably the most important thing a team can do to stay competitive. For a driver it takes a different sort of skill and, in many ways, is more difficult than being able to drive quickly during a race. At least that's what I keep telling people.

As one o'clock approached there were already some facts that were becoming quite clear: The DV-1 was fast in a straight line but had a tendency to go light at the front. This could become a significant problem in traffic when turbulent air coming off the wings of other cars upset the airflow over its own front wings. As soon as the second car arrived we could begin to check that out. The car worked reasonably well in all of the slow-speed corners but the high-speed understeer defied any simple solution. So far, the only thing that helped was adding downforce to the front wing, which meant adding downforce to the rear wing to keep the car balanced. The end result was a car that couldn't get out of its own way on the straights.

The other thing I discovered was that my neck muscles were giving out. The Brazilian circuit is unusual in that it's run in a counterclockwise direction. That means that whatever muscles you've built up on all the other clockwise tracks have a hard time coping with Rio's long left-handers and their high g-loads. So, when Spikings suggested I give it a rest and let Alberto do some of the work, I was only too happy to oblige. I could understand now why it was not uncommon to see drivers being lifted from their cars at the conclusion of the race there.

While the mechanics were setting up the car for Alberto, he and I had a quick talk. "I don't know what more I can tell you other than what I've reported so far. The track is really bumpy and there's not enough rubber down to do any good at all. I haven't taken her over ten thousand yet except on the back straight. There's so much front wing cranked in it's like driving a snowplow, but at least it'll turn in. Rory's making some adjustments to the camber before you go out. I don't know but I don't think that's the problem.

Maybe you can figure something out. Anyway, have fun."

"Alberto, you set?" Spikings called out.

"*Sì. Momento.*" He turned his back on Spikings and the others. "Peter. I may ask a favor?"

"Of course."

He reached into his pocket, pulled out a small digital stopwatch, and handed it to me. "I know Barry said no times yet but I would like it for my own keeping. Okay?"

"Sure, why not? You can do some for me later."

"*Grazie.*" He smiled that smile and ran over to the car. I walked into the garage, opened a cold bottle of water, and drank it down in one long pull. I couldn't believe how tired I felt. Hearing the engine fire, I went back outside to watch Alberto do his stuff. Vitale was saying something to him over the intercom and Alberto's helmet was bobbing up and down in agreement. As soon as Vitale finished, Alberto blipped the throttle a couple of times then popped the clutch and smoked the tires as he charged down the pit lane. You could probably see him grinning right through his helmet. Spikings came over and elbowed me in the ribs. "It's your fault, you know, him doing that, so be careful. This isn't some bloody kid's game."

I kept my mouth shut and nodded as Windsor and Vitale joined us.

"Peter, you look absolutely knackered. Well done, though. We're already ahead of schedule on today's checklist. Aside from the understeer, I mean, it's just a matter of time till it comes right. What do you think of the car?"

OVERSTEER

"Yes, Peter, tell us about the car," Vitale said. They were both looking at me like expectant fathers. I did my best to reassure them that the baby was all right. "I think the car's going to work. It's predictable. It feels solid and with the wings trimmed back it'll really move. Once we lick the understeer I think we'll have ourselves a qualifier."

Alberto came blasting by to complete his first lap and I could tell from the sound of the engine that he was already standing on it. The three of us joined Spikings out by the guardrail. He was down on the ground chalking up a big EZ sign on the pit board.

"Going a bit too quick, is he?" Windsor chuckled. Vitale immediately came to the aid of his young protégé. "No. No. I'm sure he is only getting a feel for the car. He has waited a long time for this, you know."

"Right. But if it's all the same to you gentlemen, he can wait just a bit longer." Spikings stood and looked at his handiwork. "Remember what happened at Mugello the first time he went out in the new 3000?"

"Show him the sign," Vitale said. The memory must have been a vivid one.

We stood and listened to the scream of the engine rising and falling in pitch as Alberto brought the car through the 90 Graus Corner and along the short straight to the Victoria Hairpin. As soon as he exited the turn we could see as well as hear him rocketing toward us, the sound of the engine getting louder with each upshift. I was thankful I'd left my earplugs in. Spikings held out the sign as Alberto flashed past in a 160-mph yellow blur, already downshifting to fifth for the first right-hander. As quickly as he had appeared he was gone from sight.

"I'm going to bring him in after this lap, then we can sit down with Rory and—" He stopped and spun around toward turn one. The track was totally quiet.

"Rory! What happened? What's he saying on the radio?"

Windsor and Vitale both looked stunned when Rory answered, "Radio's dead."

"Shit," Spikings said as he sprinted for one of the rental cars. The ambulance parked at the pit exit was already out on the track by the time Rory, Spikings, and I had gotten the rental car moving. Windsor and Vitale were just getting into their car as we exited the pit lane. No one spoke as Rory pitched the car through turn one and onto the short straight leading to Pace Corner. We could see the ambulance, lights flashing, stopped near the exit of the corner. Then the DV-1 itself came into view. It was upright and the cockpit was empty; two very good signs. As Rory skidded to a stop near the ambulance I could see Alberto standing next to one of the paramedics. He waved to us to show he was okay and started walking back toward the wrecked car to meet us. It was apparent that he was hurting, and considering the way the car looked, it wasn't surprising. Vitale ran past us, looking relieved but scared. We all converged on the DV-1 at about the same time. It was hissing and burbling as steam and water escaped from one of the smashed radiators.

Alberto was quite plainly shaken. "Was my fault. I was trying different swaybar settings and come in too hot. First the understeer, then bang, oversteer. I go onto the curbing and into the air backward. Then I was spinning around for one or two times until I hit the wall and everything stop." He looked so sad I couldn't help but feel sorry for him. Rory and Spikings were already poking around the car trying to assess the extent of the damage.

"What do you think?" I asked Rory. He looked up and managed a smile. "I think the tub is okay. If it is, we should be able to get her back in action by tomorrow. Foot box took a helluva jolt, but it held up. We'll check this one off as part of the mandatory front-end crash testing, eh Barry?" Spikings grunted something, obviously unamused. Rory shrugged. "I'd better get back and tell the lads they won't be chasing any bird tonight."

As he walked back to the rental car Spikings shook his head disgustedly. "One more little incident like this and we can probably kiss any chance of qualifying here good-bye."

"Come on, Barry. It's not that bad. At least we've got something to work with. I've driven a lot worse cars than this, believe me."

"That was then, this is now. Last year, Patrese's Williams was the fastest nonturbo. He managed a minute thirty and something. It took a minute thirty-five-seven just to make the show. We're ten seconds plus off that and I doubt if anything less than a minute thirty will get us through pre-qualifying. Come on, let's collect Alberto and try and figure out what we're doing."

"You said we were ten seconds off last year's qualifying time. How'd you know that if we weren't doing any times this session?"

He smiled and held up a Heuer digital stopwatch. "I said I didn't want you two playing beat the clock today. I didn't say anything about my not keeping track of things. Come on, let's go."

I had to ask myself if agreeing to take Alberto's lap times had been partly to blame for the accident and the answer I came up with didn't make me feel very good.

As it turned out, there would be no debriefing with Alberto because he'd been taken to the hospital for the usual X rays and "observation." I hung around the garage for a while as Rory and the crew worked on the car. Fortunately the tub was all right, most of the damage being confined to the suspension, nose cone, and bodywork. Rory decided to concentrate on getting it repaired immediately, just in case the second car was delayed in transit. I didn't envy the mechanics the task they had ahead of them. But, as I said to Rory, "At least it'll be cooler working here at night."

He looked at me like I was nuts. "Give me the bloody heat anytime," he said. "I know what it's like here at night. We're the brightest thing for miles. Every type of flying creature you can imagine, and some you wouldn't want to, will come down out of the hills to visit like some medieval plague of locusts. First they'll overpower the bug zapper, then they'll bathe in the bug spray, and then they'll proceed to crawl all over our insect-repellent-soaked flesh. Right, lads?"

Rory certainly had a way with words. A couple of the mechanics who understood English looked about as green as the oil in the drip pan. Since nothing in my contract mentioned going one-on-one with giant flying cockroaches, I opted to return to the hotel for a massage, an early dinner, and sleep. If anyone could sleep after that speech.

I was walking through the hotel lobby when I heard someone call out my name. I turned and spotted a woman waving to me from the registration desk. It took me a moment to figure out who she was. Not that Anne Alcott wasn't memorable, I thought as I walked over to her.

"Hello, Pete. Remember me now?"

"Hello yourself. Sorry for the blank stare. I won't say you're the last person I expected to see here, but it is a nice surprise. Did you come in with the rest of the team?"

"Yes. Father's still not acting himself as far as I'm concerned, so I thought I'd better come along and keep an eye on him."

"Have they gone straight to the track?"

"No. They're having some sort of trouble in customs with the paperwork on the car. He said it might take hours, so I came on ahead. I've been fighting off a cold or the flu or something and I'm about to drop."

"I'm pretty tired myself. You coming out to the track tomorrow?"

"Quite honestly, it all depends how I'm feeling. Tell me, have you made any progress solving your mystery?"

"You mean the understeer?" As soon as I'd said it I

knew what she was talking about. Christ, I thought. I must sound like a real asshole. "You mean my father. No, I haven't made any progress. In fact, I haven't even had time to think about it. We've been having teething trouble with the car. In fact, Alberto crashed it today. It's okay. He's fine. Wasn't too bad. They'll have it repaired by morning."

"Thank God he wasn't hurt. Do forgive me but I really must get up to my room before I fall asleep here in the lobby."

"I'm sorry. Look, uh, how about dinner tomorrow night? If you're feeling better, of course."

"That would be lovely. Thank you."

"If you're not out at the track, I'll buzz you when I get back to the hotel."

"Good. I'll look forward to it. Good night." She smiled as if she knew something I didn't, then turned and followed the bellhop who was carrying her luggage to the elevators.

I made a massage appointment and was headed to my room when Windsor intercepted me. "Peter. May I have a moment, please?"

"Sure. How's Alberto?"

"Nothing broken, thankfully. Ludovico insisted that he stay in hospital overnight, just as a precaution. Had Todd and the others arrived by the time you left the track?"

"No, but they're at the airport. I just ran into Anne and she says there's some sort of screwup with the paperwork at customs."

"Christ. I'd better get out there then." He paused, looking puzzled. "Anne, you said. Anne Alcott?"

"Yeah. She came out to keep an eye on her father."

"Good, that's just what we need, some bloody nursemaid underfoot." He seemed angry for a moment, then abruptly changed moods. "Oh, well, can't be helped, I suppose. Dinner tonight?"

"No. Thank you. I'm for bed as soon as possible. What's tomorrow's schedule? Same as today?"

"Later, I should think. Let's say we'll leave here at eight-thirty. All right?"

"Whatever you say."

"Fine. I'd better be off. See if I can't expedite things at the airport. Show those people how it's done, eh?"

He blustered off to do battle with the Brazilian customs officials. Probably challenge them to dueling carnets or something.

As I rode up in the elevator, I thought back to what Anne had said. I had a couple of free days after the test session. Maybe I'd spend them here instead of returning to Miami. Considering her father's involvement, maybe Anne could be persuaded to stick around as well. Two heads are better than one. Holmes and Watson. Last Tango in Rio. Even then it didn't occur to me that I might actually discover anything.

CHAPTER

12

The next morning was nothing like the previous two, with overcast skies and an 80-percent chance of rain predicted. Out at the circuit, the humidity was already oppressive. Rory and the mechanics were seated at a long wooden folding table having breakfast when Barry and I arrived. The effect of the all-nighter was visible on their faces, giving them the look of extras in a George Romero film. None of this showed in the car, though. Sitting a few feet away, the DV-1 looked exactly as it had before Alberto's shunt. I noticed that the tires were encased in electric warmers that must have arrived with the second car. Rory peered at us over the rim of his coffee cup and tried, without success, to sound cheery. "G'day, Barry. Pete. You ready for a bit of a thrash before the sky pisses on us?"

"Mornin', Rory. Guys. I'm ready. Car looks great. You all did a helluva job. Thanks."

"All in a night's work. How's Alberto doing?"

"He's fine but the docs want him to sit today out," Barry replied. "Vitale and Windsor went to check him out of the hospital and take him back to the hotel. They should be here in about an hour. By the looks of that sky, I'd say we should get moving. If the weather holds, we can try and get the second car out for a few laps at the end of the day, if it's ready. Where is it anyway?"

"Number one's all warmed up and set to go whenever you say. The rest of the lads are getting number two ready inside that garage three doors down. They're using yesterday's settings, like you said."

"Fine," said Barry. "I think I'll go have a word with Nigel while Pete gets changed."

I had put my Nomex underwear on back at the hotel, so it was only a matter of minutes before I was climbing into the cockpit. As Rory helped fasten the belts, I asked about his predicted insect invasion of the night before. He pointed to two huge garbage bags just outside the door of our garage. "They're in those," he said. "All the ones we could find anyway. Don't worry, though, we got 'em all out of the car, I think." He winked and stood up, laughing.

"Very funny, you bastard," I muttered into my balaclava. Actually, I guess it was. After all, that's why we'd come to Brazil, to get the bugs out of the car. For some reason that lousy pun put me in an incredibly good mood, and as I moved out onto the track I felt certain that the solution to our handling problems was at hand.

When you drive a car that's been damaged in a

crash, you're particularly sensitive to any changes in the way it handles that might signify something undetected by the mechanics during the rebuild. With that in mind I spent the first few laps going through the same routine I'd used when I first took the car out the day before. Once I was satisfied that all was well, I came in for a quick inspection to confirm the diagnosis. The sky was growing darker by the minute and the wind had begun to pick up as I went back out. I knew it would only be a short time until the rains came, so I decided to concentrate on the two fast left-handers, Suspiro and Sul. I was going about 150 mph when I turned into Suspiro. The understeer was there but not as pronounced as I'd remembered, although it still required a slight lift to restore front-end traction. I got the next two corners right and was able to pull a few extra revs on the back straight. The front end wanted to wander, but again the problem seemed less severe than it had the day before. I got on the brakes and went down into fifth then turned into Sul. The understeer was more pronounced now and the pressure of four and a half g's really took its toll on my aching neck muscles. I touched the brakes and *whap,* the rear end came around so fast I was caught completely off guard. The car shot to the outside of the track just at the exit of the corner, hit the curbing backward, letting air get underneath, and flipped. I remember seeing the ground flash by underneath me as the car went over, the sound of the engine screaming out of control, and not much else until I was scrambling out of the cockpit. Someone should have had a clock on me then. The ambulance arrived just as I was turning off the master electrical switch and I was quite happy to allow the paramedics to lead me over and sit me down inside it. As they asked questions and checked my vital signs, Barry stuck his head in. I could see the concern in his eyes and did my best to reassure him. "I'm okay. Really. But the car's a mess. Much worse than yesterday. I don't know what happened. . . ."

He held up his hand. "Don't try and talk until the medics are finished. I know what happened and it had nothing to do with you. The rear wing came off. We spotted it in the sand trap about halfway through the corner. Rory's collecting it now. They're going to run you over to the hospital for some X rays and things. I'll be along as soon as I phone the boss. You're sure you're all right?"

"Yeah, I'm fine, really." He patted my arm then ducked out the ambulance door. It was finally starting to rain and by the time we left the track it was coming down in buckets.

Two major crashes in two days. Not quite the way we'd pictured things. Thankfully, the second car was okay and we could get back to work as soon as the weather cooperated.

The hospital routine took most of the day to complete but in the end I got a clean bill of health. Windsor and Vitale, who had just taken one of their drivers out of the hospital, had to turn right around and come back for the second. Probably not their idea of a perfect day either. By the time we left, the sun was shining again and rapidly evaporating the last traces of the rainstorm. Sun or no sun, there would be no more testing that day. In fact, from the way Windsor was talking on the drive to the hotel, there might not be any more that week. "It's possible that the wing mount was damaged when Alberto went off, although Rory says it checked out all right. That means it could have been some sort of structural failure. We can't take a chance on having another incident. Isn't that right, Ludovico?"

"Denis is entirely correct. I have spoken to Todd and he recommends that we suspend the test and return to Italy immediately. What do you think, Peter?"

What did I think? My instincts told me that the wing mount had been overstressed during Alberto's shunt. On the other hand, my brain told me it would be stupid to take a chance when the designer of the car said to stop the test. "Look, we all know there's still a lot of work to do before the car'll be ready to race. So if you want to keep going, I'm ready." So much for logic.

"Denis told me this is what you will say but I cannot agree. We will return the cars to the factory and then resume testing at Ricard on the first of March."

"I'm afraid I must second Ludovico, and if you wake up tomorrow feeling anything like Alberto does today, you'll be glad as well."

Windsor pulled up in front of the hotel to let me out. I was already starting to stiffen up. "That part I don't doubt a bit. Whatever decision you make is fine with me. If you need me for anything, I'll be soaking in the tub."

While the tub was filling I tried to reach Anne but

she wasn't in the hotel. Then I tried Alberto, who wasn't taking any calls. Finally, I called my machine in Miami, which played back a string of unimportant messages, including one from Gail asking me to call when I got back. We'd see. I pulled the new Jonathan Valin book out of my suitcase then eased myself into the steaming water, determined not to emerge until I was wrinkled like a prune.

The bath did its job and within minutes of slithering out I was in bed asleep.

The phone jolted me awake, and after assuring Anne that I felt a lot better than I actually did, we agreed to meet in the lobby in half an hour. I wanted to go for a walk before dinner to help ward off the stiffness that, in spite of my lengthy soak, was taking hold of every part of my body. Anne suggested we go to nearby São Conrado beach to watch the sunset. Sounded perfect to me.

The warm evening air felt almost velvety as it blew in off the ocean to the accompaniment of a guitar somewhere down the beach. A lone hang glider circled lazily as it descended from the cliffs of Pedra Bonita high above us. This was why people who didn't drive race cars came to Brazil.

I could sense that Anne, who had hardly spoken since we left the hotel, was disturbed about something. "You seem worried. Is everything okay with your father? I never even got to see him at the track today."

"He's fine, thanks. As a matter of fact, he called about an hour ago to see how you were. He also told me about **the wing** falling off. He said you were lucky not to have been killed."

"Well, I don't know about that. Years ago maybe, but these cars will take an incredible amount of punishment. Other than a few aches and pains I feel fine, honestly."

"I suppose if Signor Vitale hadn't canceled the test session, you'd be back in the car tomorrow?"

"I suppose. Hey, come on. It's my job. The wing came off because of Alberto's crash. It doesn't mean the car's unsafe, and it had nothing to do with the understeer problem. Just one of those things, like falling off a horse. The best thing to do is get right back on before you start thinking too much about it."

"Have you ever fallen off a horse?"

"No. Actually, I can't stand horses. But that doesn't mean the principle's not valid." She fought it but finally had to smile.

"As long as you're in such an expository mood, perhaps you could explain just what it is that's the matter with the steering under your race car?"

"I'll try. I assume you want to know what understeer is? Right. Well, understeer and oversteer aren't really involved so much with the steering as with the way the car behaves when it's cornering. Understeer means the front end of the car wants to keep going straight ahead when you want it to turn. Oversteer's just the opposite. You turn into a corner and the back end of the car gets loose and wants to spin the car around. In the States, we say 'push' or 'loose' to describe what's happening, but not in F1. Make any sense?"

"I think so. It sounds like what's happened to me if I've come off the motorway a bit too quickly."

"You've got it. When the car's trying to push you off the outside of the exit ramp, that's understeer, and at 150 or so you want the car to go where you point it, not where it wants to go. That's very good."

"Don't look so self-satisfied. It's not that difficult a concept to master. It's *why* you'd choose to go around a corner at 150 'or so' that's hard to conceptualize."

"Let me try one more example. There was this famous racing driver back in the thirties named Tazio Nuvolari. He was being interviewed and the guy asked him how he could climb into a race car day after day when he knew he had a good chance of getting killed. This was back when drivers got killed fairly regularly. Anyway, Nuvolari asked him if he expected to die in bed, and when the guy said yes, Nuvolari asked him where he got the courage to climb into bed every night. . . . See what I mean?"

She shook her head and changed the subject. "Father says they're packing everything up to go back to Italy. Are you going to continue to test the cars there?"

"Not in Italy. There's a big test session coming up at the Paul Ricard circuit in France. A lot of teams will be there, so that's what we're aiming for. Actually, I'm thinking of staying here for a few days. Figure I'll poke around, see what I can turn up about what went on during the Cup Rally. I was hoping to finally have that talk with your father too."

"I know. He's mentioned it as well. Maybe tonight

after dinner. He said he'd be back at the hotel around nine."

"Good. And speaking of dinner, I heard Alfredo's is pretty good, so I made a reservation, if that's okay?"

"Of course."

I was trying to think of some clever way of suggesting that she stick around Rio as well when two small boys, about seven or eight years old, started dancing around us, laughing and holding out their hands for money. One of them beat on a beer can with a stick while the other sang. I'd just put my hand into my pocket to look for change when Anne yelled, "Look out behind you." I started to turn when something hard smashed into my back, driving me onto my hands and knees in the sand. I caught a glimpse of Anne, who was screaming her head off while trying to keep the kid who had been hitting the beer can from stealing her purse. I lunged toward him and got clobbered again. This time they caught me over the left ear. It was a glancing blow but the pain was intense. Much worse, in fact, than what I'd experienced when the car flipped. I rolled quickly to one side just in time to dodge another blow from the long wooden board being wielded by a third, larger boy. He lost his balance for a moment when he failed to connect with my head and that gave me the opening I needed. I kicked out and caught the end of the board, causing it to fly up and land squarely on his nose. From the shriek he let out it must have hurt like hell. I certainly hoped so, at any rate. I tried to get my footing but kept slipping and churning up sand. The kid I'd just hit was holding one hand over his bloodied nose and yelling something in Portuguese to his friends. The three of them took off like jackrabbits, spindly legs and bare feet flying. I could still hear their laughter after they disappeared from sight. I knew it was senseless to chase them. By the time I got off the beach they'd have melted back into their *favela* shantytown on the hillside. I plopped down next to Anne, who was sitting quietly, staring at the strap she was holding. It was all that remained of her purse. "Anne. Are you all right? Anne?" She looked up slowly, focused her eyes on my face, and gagged. "Anne. What is it?"

She pointed at me, her hand trembling. "You. You're covered with blood." Without a mirror I couldn't tell what my face looked like, but from the amount of blood, mine and the boy's, splattered on my shirt and pants I must have been a sight.

"Believe me when I tell you it looks a lot worse than it is. Come on," I said as I stood and helped her up. "We'd better get back to the hotel. Did they get anything besides your purse?"

"My shoes are gone."

"Your shoes? Are you sure they're not in the sand here somewhere?"

"No. The little boy, the one that was singing? He had them in his hand when they ran off. Don't you think you should get to a hospital rather than the hotel?"

"No. I'm pretty sure I'm okay. I'll have the hotel call a doctor to take a look at the cut over my ear in case I need a couple of stitches or anything." I put my arm around her and we made our way across the beach

and back to the hotel. The few people we passed
shook their heads and made sympathetic clucking
noises, giving me the distinct impression they'd seen
that sort of thing before.

Anne finally stopped trembling when we got inside
the hotel lobby. There, our appearance did cause a
commotion and we were soon surrounded by managers, assistant managers, security men, and assorted
guests, each of them putting in their two cents' worth.

We were soon ushered into the manager's office to
await the arrival of a doctor and someone from the
local police. Anne was pretty calm now and when the
manager suggested something to drink we both
agreed that a cognac would go a long way toward
making things right in the universe. He had no
sooner sent out for the drinks than the phone rang.
He picked it up, nodded, then handed it to me.
"Senhor Hawthorn. It is the hotel operator, for you."

When I got up off the sofa to take the phone, I felt a
stab of pain in my side that nearly took my breath
away. My bruises must have bruises, I thought, as I
placed the receiver to my undamaged ear. "Senhor
Hawthorn, you had a call from the United States
about thirty minutes ago from a Senhor Lambert. He
requests that you call him immediately. . . . Hello?
Did you hear me? I said you—"

"Yes. I heard you, sorry. Did he leave a number?"

"Yes. Do you wish me to put the call through for
you?"

"Yes, please." She told me to hang up and she'd ring
me when she got through. As I put down the receiver
I had a terrible sick feeling in my stomach. There was

only one reason he'd call me here. I was aware that someone, probably the doctor, had come into the office behind me but I couldn't seem to get away from the telephone. It held me rooted there, waiting.

"Peter . . . Peter. What is it, for God's sake?"

It was Anne and she sounded frightened. I tore my eyes away from the phone and turned to explain what was going on. She was standing next to her father, clutching his arm tightly. Before I could say anything, Alcott let out a strangled cry, whispered the name *James,* and crumpled to the floor between us.

CHAPTER

13

It was only on the flight to Miami that I could begin
to sort out the chaotic events of the preceding night.
In a way, the beach attack and its confusing after-
math at the hotel helped soften the news of my mother's death. Or at least it prevented me from dwelling
on it at the time. Fortunately, the doctor had arrived
within moments of Alcott's collapse. He checked him
over and immediately called an ambulance to transport him to the hospital. Then he administered a sed-
ative to Anne, who had taken about all the emotional
abuse she could handle for one day.

I took the call from Don on a house phone out in
the lobby, managing to escape the Marx Brothers–
like arrival of Alberto, Windsor, Vitale, Spikings, and
the police. Don was pretty broken up and in need of a
friend. I reassured him that I would be on the first
flight out. After asking Spikings to take care of my
travel arrangements, I went with Windsor, Vitale,

Anne, and her father to the hospital. While Alcott was being worked up in the emergency room, I had myself checked out. Nothing broken but my ribs were severely bruised and it took ten stitches to close the cut behind my ear. I decided not to tell Anne about Mary. I could see she was close to the breaking point and figured it was better not to burden her with my own disturbing news.

When I got back to the hotel, my ticket to Miami was waiting at the desk along with a note from Alberto and Spikings expressing their sympathy and offering to do anything they could. Vitale had already told me to take as much time in Miami as I needed. There would only be one car available to go to Ricard, he said, and Alberto could handle the test alone, if necessary.

The next morning I left a letter for Anne, who was still asleep, spoke briefly to Windsor and Vitale, then checked out and headed home.

By the time I arrived at my place there were already a number of comforting messages on the machine from various friends, as well as one from Don with directions to the funeral parlor.

I've never liked going to funerals, skipping them altogether whenever possible, but there would be no avoiding this one. I hadn't discussed the arrangements with Don because I'd felt instinctively that he would do the right thing. But as I entered the large brick building and was directed to "viewing chapel number two," I began to feel queasy, wondering if the casket would be open. I honestly didn't think I could stand around and chat with people if it was.

As I stepped into the dimly lit room, Don, who had been sitting in the front row near the open casket, stood and gave me a little wave. I could tell he'd been there for some time by the haze of bluish smoke hanging over that end of the room. When Don walked back to greet me, I put out my hand only to have him step beyond it to embrace me. He stepped back, took a long drag on his cigarette, and tried to conjure up a smile. "Pete . . . I know how you must be feeling. But she's at peace now. It's better if you keep reminding yourself of that. . . . No more suffering. I know you'll want some time alone with her. I'm going to walk around the block, get some air . . ."

I could see tears starting to glisten in his eyes and felt my own beginning to well up. He embraced me again but this time it wasn't surprising, just natural. After he left and closed the door behind him, I walked down the aisle toward the casket. There were a lot of flowers. Mary would have liked that, I thought. She always loved fresh flowers. Seeing her like that was not as difficult as I'd feared. It looked something like her but not enough to fool anyone who'd loved her the way she really was. I sat down in one of the chairs across from her and allowed the memories to come flooding in. Childhood things, mostly. And James . . . I remembered my father with her as if it were yesterday. It was my birthday, I don't know which one, but I was opening presents. They were watching me and they were holding hands. I remember how good that made me feel then, and how sad today. It was then that I realized that this wasn't just Mary's funeral, it was James's as well. He'd been gone for nineteen years. Dead, almost certainly, but the doubt remained. Maybe that was why I'd been secretly, even unknowingly, reluctant to search out the truth. As long as there was a mystery there was doubt. A possibility, however remote, that he wasn't dead. There, in that room, the doubt vanished. James was dead and had been all these years. In accepting that for the first time, I left childhood behind me. Daddy wouldn't be coming home. Even if his body could be found, it would no more be James than the cosmetician's version of Mary across from me was my mother.

I don't know how long I sat there, probably a lot less than it seemed, but at some point I realized that Don had returned and was sitting a couple of chairs away.

"Sorry. I didn't hear you come in."

"No need. Folks are going to be coming in a few minutes and if it's all right with you I'd like to close the casket."

"Go ahead. I was going to ask you if we could anyway."

He crossed and gently closed the lid, placing a large wreath of roses on top. "This one's from us. . . . The viewing is over at nine. Why don't you come back to the house then. There are some things Mary wanted you to have, and maybe we could just talk for a while. Okay?"

"Thanks. I'd like that."

I found a pay phone next to the men's room and

placed a call to Rio. Anne was at the hospital but she had left word for me to call her the next day.

I spent the next hour or so talking to a lot of sympathetic people, most of whom I didn't know. A few of my local friends stopped by, as did one or two of the drivers who had arrived in town for the upcoming IMSA GTP race, including my Daytona co-driver, Les Bromley. He and I stepped outside for a smoke and some shoptalk. "So," I asked, "you driving Henry's March next weekend?"

"Yeah, me an' Walt figgered ol' Henry'd get hisself into trouble out there if we wasn't around."

"Henry's driving again?"

"Yup. Couldn't have you, so he went for the next best thing, I guess."

"I guess. What else is new? I hear Gurney's got the new Toyota ready."

"That and the group-C car from Japan. Should be fun. Nothin' that would interest no Formula One big shot, though. How's the new car?"

"Got some minor problems, like terminal understeer, but I think it'll work out. Thing that's impressed me so far about the team, and Formula One, is the technology. It's gotten to be like NASA or something."

"Ah, I knew there was somethin' I was fixin' to tell you. You know I used to do all that high-speed motorcycle stuff, right? Well, this old boy I know offered me a shot at the Land Speed Record in this top-secret car he's building. Guess they figured anyone who'd strap hisself to a jet-engined cycle would do about anything. Probably right too."

"You gonna do it?"

OVERSTEER

"Dunno. Meeting with the man right after the race on Sunday. Might be fun if the money's right. Easy too. No downshiftin' or apexes or none of that shit. Just run on down the road in a straight line. What time's it gettin' to be? I got me a lady to impress out at Joe's Stone Crab at seven-thirty."

I looked at my wrist before I remembered that my Rolex was now being worn by some skinny kid with no shoes. "Sorry. Don't have my watch, but it must be after seven."

"Better be goin' then. Listen. Like I said, I'm real sorry about your ma. If there's anything at all I can do or if you just want to go out and get shit-faced, gimme a holler. Okay?"

"I might just do that, thanks."

Les headed for the parking lot and I took a final puff on my cigar before going back inside to see how Don was doing.

We arrived back at Don's house about ten-thirty, after stopping to pick up a couple of six-packs and a pizza. Don went into the kitchen to get things ready while I fell back into the familiar old overstuffed living-room sofa. The beer was icy cold and I could tell from the first swallow that it was going to be tough sticking to my self-imposed one-beer limit.

With the exception of my ribs, which still hurt like hell, the other scrapes and bruises had joined together into one large dull ache that seemed to encompass my entire body.

"The stuff I was telling you about, that Mary left for you? It's in that shopping bag next to the TV. You'll have to excuse the mess. I haven't had much inclination to straighten up lately."

Mess? The only sign of a mess I could detect was in front of me, where the ash from my cigar had fallen off. I brought the shopping bag over to the sofa and was about to look inside when Don came in with dinner and my second beer. We wolfed down the pizza without much conversation. The moment we finished, Don whisked the dirty dishes into the kitchen, returning a minute later with more beer, the bottle of Laphroaig single-malt scotch I'd given him last Christmas, and two glasses. "Don. If I have any more to drink I'm going to end up spending the night on your sofa."

"No, you won't. You're staying in the guest room." He poured two shots of the whisky, handed one to me, and began speaking purposefully. "Pete. You know I'm not one for beating around the bush. When I think something needs to be said, I say it." He threw down his shot and poured another. "I never really gave you a fair shake and I'm ashamed of myself for it." He hung his head and I thought he was going to start crying again, but the moment passed. He downed his second whisky and poured a third. I took a sip of mine and felt its warmth moving down toward my stomach.

"Come on, Don. Don't be so hard on yourself."

"No, Pete. It's true and now I'm gonna tell you why. First off, it had nothing to do with racing. I know Mary hated it, and she had her own reasons, but I never did. Hell, before we got married I used to go up to Daytona every year for the 500. Didn't know that, did ya?" He poured yet another drink, overfilling the glass and letting the liquid form a little pool on the coffee table. I knew he was drunk when he didn't try to clean it up. "It wasn't even you at all," he declared. "It was James. She still loves him, loved him, I mean. Shit. I'm not sayin' she didn't love me. She did. She really did. But she never stopped loving him. A man knows those things, y'know?"

I didn't know what to say, so I just nodded and took another sip.

"An' you look just like him, you know? That's stupid. Of course you know. Every time she'd see you it'd remind her of him. Got so I couldn't stand the sight of you. I'm sorry, Pete, I really am. Can you forgive me?"

"Don, there's nothing to forgive. You made Mary happy. You loved each other and she was happy and I'll always love you for that."

Now he was crying. He drank the last of his whisky and stood, slowly. "Thank you for saying that. I have to go to bed now. G'night." He swayed out of the room and in a minute I heard his bedroom door close.

I finished the last of my drink then cleaned up the coffee table before taking myself off to bed. I'd always known that Don didn't approve of me, but it never entered my head that his feelings were that strong, or the reason behind them. I set the alarm for seven, figuring that would give me plenty of time to get back to my place to get ready for the eleven o'clock funeral service.

After tossing around for what seemed hours, I faced the fact that I was too keyed up and too tired to sleep. I thought about watching TV but I didn't want to take a chance on waking Don. Then I remembered the shopping bag.

I found a lot of my childhood in that bag: report cards, finger paintings, school book reports, and a program from a school Christmas pageant in which I played the lead shepherd. There was also a small diary and two scrapbooks.

I organized the pillows behind me and opened the larger of the two. To say that I was surprised by what I saw would hardly convey my astonishment. The book contained what seemed to be a complete record of James's racing career. I recognized a lot of the clippings because I'd saved them as a child. I'd thrown them away when he had let me down once too often. Mary undoubtedly had rescued them from the garbage and then continued to add to the collection. Don must have known about it. No wonder he was so jealous of James. The second book was even more startling, covering my own racing career from my first amateur successes right up to the end of the previous season.

If the scrapbooks were a surprise, the diary was a revelation. From the time of their breakup until his disappearance, James and Mary had stayed in touch. Not just phone calls and cards on holidays and special occasions, but on a regular basis.

The time I was most interested in was the period leading up to the World Cup Rally, and I wasn't disappointed, for there, between the pages, was a thin, onionskin airmail letter from James dated March 15, 1970. As I read the words I could hear his voice as if he were in the room with me.

My dearest Mary,

I know that I've failed in many ways to live up to your expectations, and to my own as well. I offer nothing in my defense. I am what I am and we both know it. But, and this is important, I'm also what I can be. Does that make any sense? I'd hate to think that I've gone through all that I have and brought pain and shame on my loved ones (and you and Peter are my only loved ones), without learning a thing or two.

I've just landed a plum ride in the upcoming World Cup Rally which runs from London to Mexico City, but that is only part of the reason I'm writing to you. There are opportunities connected with this event that far exceed the excitement or challenge of the actual race. Opportunities that offer great financial reward. If things work out as I've planned, for once, then I shall definitely retire from motorsports competition. I know that I've promised this more than once already, but you must believe me when I tell you that this time I will do as I say. I have spoken again to Ornaro about that land in the Chianti country and it is still available. The price has gone up but if things go according to plan that will be of little consequence. Sorry for being so cryptic but I'll explain everything to you when I arrive in New York, probably on the thirteenth or fourteenth of May.

All my love to you and to Peter. Pray for me (us).

Yours eternally,
James

I had just refolded the letter and put it back in the diary when the return address caught my eye: *James Hawthorn, c/o David Livesey, 23 Leinster Gardens, Bayswater W2 London, England.* I didn't know who David Livesey was or if he still lived at that address or even if he were still alive, but considering the other recent coincidences, it seemed worth checking out. All at once everything that had happened over the past few days caught up with me and I fell asleep with the letter in my hands.

Don and I both got through the next day on some sort of automatic pilot. The church service was brief and the interment took place under a blazing spring sun. It was the sort of day Mary would have enjoyed. Maybe she did, somehow.

When I returned to my apartment that afternoon there were messages from both Spikings and Anne. I called Spikings first. He told me that Todd had been unable to pinpoint the cause of the understeer using computer data from the Rio test but that he had some aerodynamic modifications he wanted to explore in the wind tunnel. Todd and I were to meet in Oxford, England, in two days to conduct the wind tunnel tests. Then, if they proved successful, we'd try them out on the third chassis, which would be shipped to Silverstone as soon as it was completed. In the meantime, Alberto would take chassis number two to Ricard to attack the problem via changes in the suspension geometry.

As soon as I finished with Spikings I reached Anne in Rio. She told me that her father had had a mild stroke. Nothing really serious, but the doctors said it would be safer for him to remain in Brazil until the team returned for the race rather than risk all the air travel necessitated by the team's schedule. Anne was staying with him, at the team's expense, and seemed really pleased when I said I was returning to Rio as soon as I finished testing in England.

Other than a brief visit with Don and a trip to the cemetery, I spent the day before my flight soaking my aching body in the tub and wondering what changes Todd had in mind.

CHAPTER

14

Another night spent crossing the Atlantic, headed for London's Heathrow Airport.

I had brought Mary's diary as well as the clippings pertaining to James's disappearance with me to re-read during the flight. I always took at least one good mystery book along on any trip, but this was different. This time I was playing detective. Unfortunately, neither the clippings nor diary revealed any secrets at thirty thousand feet that hadn't been apparent at sea level, so I reverted to my real profession and became a sleeping race driver.

The weather was atypically sunny and gorgeous the next morning as I made my way out of the airport and west on the M4. The wind tunnel was part of the Royal Military College of Science in Shrivenham, which was somewhere between Oxford and Swindon. According to Spikings, Todd and Maurice Heath would wait for me at the hotel, then take me there with them. Benetton was letting Vitale use the wind tunnel that afternoon and all of the following day, as they had already packed up and left for the open test at Ricard.

Once I was off the motorway, the roads to Bibury, where my hotel was situated, kept getting more and more narrow, making me uncomfortably aware of driving on the "wrong" side of the road. It usually took me a day or two before I could relax and drive instinctively while sitting in the passenger seat.

I found Bibury to be a picture-perfect Cotswold village, with beautiful old stone houses and a stream meandering through the middle of town, which I later discovered was chock full of trout.

The Bibury Court Hotel managed to be large and cozy at the same time. A converted Jacobean manor house, it had sheep grazing on one side, the trout stream on another, and a centuries-old cemetery between itself and an equally old adjoining church. It was a long way from the HoJo's in Daytona Beach, and I'm not just talking about mileage.

The trout stream was the reason we were staying in such elegant surroundings. Hotel guests had fishing privileges, and Maurice Heath was an avid fisherman. In fact, when I checked in I was asked to meet him at the stream, "as soon as it was convenient."

Heath, like Todd Whitehead, seemed young to be chief aerodynamicist for a Formula One team. Except for his curly blond beard he barely looked old enough to be served a drink in a pub. As I approached, he was standing knee deep in water, flicking his fly rod back and forth in a graceful fluid motion. "Excuse me. Are you Maurice Heath?" He made one more perfect-looking cast before coming out of the water.

"Yes. And you must be Peter Hawthorn. Have any trouble finding the place?"

"No, not at all. It's really something."

"The food's quite good, the bar convivial, and the trout highly selective. So far they've managed to ignore all of my best flies. Do you fish?"

"Nope. Love to eat them but never could get worked up over the catching part. Is Todd here?"

"He's over at the Benetton works in Whitney, finalizing the arrangements. The tunnel is on a military base and we've got to have proper documentation to get in. Still, until Mr. Windsor comes up with the million pounds we need to build our own, this is a godsend."

"A million pounds. Well. And Windsor's paying for it?"

"That's my understanding. He had me draw up a complete plan for the facility along with my cost estimates. One million one hundred and forty-seven thousand pounds, to be exact. We're supposed to begin construction in May and be operational in time to use it on the DV-2 in the fall. Here comes Todd."

"Well, I see you found our little hideaway. Welcome. I'm really sorry about what happened in Rio, but I'm sure you'll be glad to know that it *was* caused by Alberto's shunt. The wing actually held up very nicely. It was the securing bolts that were overstressed. They looked all right but should have been changed on general principles. Won't happen again, I can assure you. We have time for a bite of lunch before heading over to Shrivenham, if you're hungry."

"Sounds good to me."

"I'll join you in a few minutes as soon as I get my gear stowed," Maurice said as he dismantled his rod. "Any news from Ricard?"

"Yes, and it's not all that encouraging. I'll tell you both about it over lunch."

As he said, the news from Ricard was not so hot. In addition to our team, Arrows, Dallara, Osella, Rial, and Zakspeed were all there with their new spec cars. Alberto was reporting a lot of instability whenever he ran close to other cars, and had already spun a couple of times without hitting anything. De Cesaris's Dallara, which had the same type of engine we did, was second quickest behind Patrese's interim spec Williams-Renault. De Cesaris's 1:09.7 lap time was totally beyond the reach of the DV-1, which had barely broken 1:17. Todd and Maurice, to their credit, refused to be panicked by the reports and their confidence went a long way toward reassuring me that I hadn't somehow gone and stepped in shit again.

After lunch, Todd drove us over to the military base, where we were checked out thoroughly by the MPs before being allowed on the grounds. If you took away the various howitzers, tanks, and missile launchers that were sitting, sculpturelike, on the lawns, the place would have been indistinguishable from most small universities. The building housing the wind tunnel was an industrial-park-type structure located at the far end of the base near the riding stables.

Immediately on walking inside, we were in the midst of what, to a child, might pass for Santa's workshop. There were scale-model boats, jet fighters, helicopters and missiles, as well as odd bits and pieces of things waiting to be put to the aerodynamic test. I watched as Maurice and Todd set the one-quarter-scale DV-1 into place and began hooking up what seemed to be hundreds of spaghettilike plastic tubes to various parts of the model car. The actual wind tunnel wasn't very impressive. It reminded me of a couple of large sections of industrial-air-conditioner ducting with a gap of about five feet in the middle where the things to be tested were placed.

Todd must have noticed the way I was looking things over. "Have you ever been to a wind tunnel test before, Pete?"

"Nope. This is a first."

"Maurice. You're the expert. Why don't you explain what we're doing?"

"It's nothing much, really. Sort of like a fan in a box that can simulate the behavior of a car, or what have you, moving through the air while it's actually standing still. We're fortunate because this particular tunnel has a rolling road, like a treadmill. This way we can study airflow under the car and over the rotating wheels as well. Air moving through these bits of tubing allows us to measure air pressure at specific points. The computer will take a reading every twenty seconds, measuring drag, downforce, transversal force, lateral forces, and so on, at speeds up to two hundred mph. At this point in the car's development, we can actually do more to increase top speed here than Carlo can by squeezing more horsepower out of the engines on the dyno."

"Which is why we wanted you here, Peter," Todd interjected. "This model is set up exactly the way the car was in Rio when you brought it in to hand it over to Alberto. What Maurice and I want you to do is talk us around the circuit. Tell us everything you can remember about the way the car felt. We've got all the basic technical data from the engine computer black box, but until we get our on-board telemetry set up you're our most important databank."

"But don't think you have to explain everything in technical terms. Be as subjective as you want. Be poetic if it suits. Look at this as a new approach to going faster. A 'new age' approach, if you will."

"All right, Maurice. Don't let's get started on that. What he means is that we don't want to discount any knowledge about the car's behavior. Rory will be bringing in chassis number three tonight. He and the crew will set up at Silverstone and begin implementing the changes tomorrow. You should be able to test them on the circuit the next day."

Todd flipped some switches and air began to rush through the tunnel, blowing across the model sitting in the open space. As the fan blades picked up speed the noise level rose, but not so as to drown out conversation. The car was still stationary but the rolling road zipping by underneath it had the wheels spinning at high rpm. He hit another switch and the machine slowly came to a halt. "Works," he said, grinning. "All right, Peter. Tell us about Rio."

For the next four hours I did lap after lap in my

mind, trying to make Todd and Maurice feel what they would never experience for themselves: driving a Formula One car at speed. By the time we were finished, I wouldn't have been surprised to walk outside and find myself in Brazil.

When we got back to the hotel, I decided to try to reach David Livesey. I was in luck. Not only did he live at the same address but he insisted I come to see him before I left England. I knew I'd have most of the next day free, so I agreed to drive down to London for afternoon tea at his place.

When I told the boys about my plans during dinner, they assured me that I wouldn't be needed again until we went to Silverstone. Then I made the mistake of asking what they'd found out in the wind tunnel, and they told me. They weren't speaking any language I was familiar with, but they told me anyway.

CHAPTER

15

The next day dawned drizzly and gloomy. As soon as I finished breakfast, I put on my rain gear and set out for London. The Cup Rally had been sponsored by the *London Daily Mirror* and I wanted to go there and see what material, if any, they might have about the event.

Traffic in London was worse than I'd ever seen it. Luckily I stumbled upon a parking garage within walking distance of the newspaper offices. The rain was coming down harder now, the streets a sea of black "brollies," the chill March air cutting through my unlined raincoat and sweater. I wondered what it was like up at Silverstone. I decided to call Rory at the end of the day to make sure the test was still on for the morning.

Because I hadn't made an appointment, there was no one at the paper that I could talk to about the rally. There was, however, a newspaper morgue, and after paying for the privilege, I found myself in a small brightly lit room waiting for someone to deliver me some clues. I had requested all the issues for the months of April and May 1970, and when the clerk wheeled in the first batch I could see I'd be sitting there for some time.

When you read old newspapers, it's hard not to get caught up in a nostalgia trip, trying to remember where you were when such and such a thing took place. APOLLO 13 MOONSHOT LAUNCHED. IAN SMITH WINS MAJORITY IN RHODESIA. MILLION-POUND ART THEFT AT LYDDON HALL. NIXON PLEDGES WITHDRAWAL OF 150,000 U.S. TROOPS FROM VIETNAM. JACKIE STEWART FAVORED TO REPEAT AS FORMULA ONE WORLD CHAMPION.

There were also, of course, stories about the upcoming World Cup Rally, and as the April 19 starting date drew closer they increased in size. There were feature stories on many of the teams and in the April 12 issue I struck pay dirt.

GOING FIRST CLASS ALL THE WAY
Reported by Sam Roberts

One of the most unusual teams set to depart Wembley Stadium Sunday next is that of Denis Windsor and James Hawthorn in a matched pair of Rolls-Royce Silver Clouds. Windsor, who only began rallying professionally last year, is confident that he and co-driver Billy Gibbons are up to the task. "I am well aware that this is the most difficult rally our team has yet attempted, but I have every confidence in our equipment and in every man involved in this great undertaking."

OVERSTEER

Windsor went on to single out for praise the driver of his second car, James Hawthorn. Hawthorn, a well-regarded sports-car driver in the late 1950s and early sixties, was the focus of a rather sensational legal case. His imprisonment for causing an auto accident while under the influence of alcohol led to his suspension by racing authorities. Having paid his debt to society, he has recently returned to competition as a rally driver. Mechanic Billy Gibbons, who will be co-driving with Windsor, informed us that there have been a number of special modifications made to the team's Silver Clouds in preparation for this gruelling grind. The famous Rolls-Royce self-levelling suspension has been replaced by springs and heavy-duty Koni shock absorbers. The large-diameter steering wheels have given way to ten-inch-diameter units from the Austin Mini. The air conditioners have been removed to avoid overheating in the extreme climate of South America. Special heavy-gage steel bumpers have been fitted fore and aft and large-diameter, tubular steel rollbars will surround the occupants.

There was a major relocation of the exhaust system with the pipes now running up and over the roof in order to avoid being dislodged by the rough terrain. Extra driving lights are necessary, as are metal skid pads to protect the underbody. Sixty-gallon fuel tanks have been placed in the boots, giving the cars a range of nearly six hundred miles.

Pictured below, from left to right, are the two team cars and their crews: Denis Windsor. Billy Gibbons. James Hawthorn. Trevor Alcott. Now it's on to Mexico City.

I copied that item and continued reading. The biggest stories were in the issue that reported on the start the following weekend and the coverage that followed as the cars moved through Europe. For once, the rally drivers got more coverage than their Formula One counterparts at the Spanish Grand Prix, where Jackie Stewart's Matra defeated Bruce McLaren and Mario Andretti.

While rally reports from Europe were published every day, and in more detail than anything I'd read before, they offered nothing that would shed any light on James's disappearance. Reports from South America were sketchier, and said little that had not been covered in *Autosport.* James's Rolls had last been seen on May 9. Mention was made of his having turned up missing in the Monday, May 11 edition. It was right under the report from the Monaco Grand Prix, where Jochen Rindt had taken his Lotus to victory on his way to what would become his posthumous World Championship.

It wasn't until I read the May 20 issue that something finally jumped off the page demanding attention.

TEAM OWNER JOINS SEARCH FOR MISSING COMRADES

British businessman Denis Windsor's World Cup Rally aspirations ended south of Cali, Columbia, yesterday when his Rolls-Royce Silver Cloud suffered an irreparable rear-suspension failure. Leaving the stricken vehicle in the care of his Canadian co-driver, Richard Harrison, Windsor immediately chartered an aircraft to return him to Brazil to aid in the search for his missing teammates, James Hawthorn and Trevor Alcott. Hawthorn and Alcott were reported missing ten

150

days earlier somewhere south of São Paulo. A massive search effort by rally organizers, aided by units of the Brazilian police and armed forces, has yet to uncover any trace of the missing men or their Rolls-Royce Silver Cloud.

Windsor, who is the proprietor of Cars of Distinction in Surrey, has vowed to do "everything humanly possible" to find his teammates with "no regard for the cost or time involved."

I went back and reread the section that had caught my eye: "Leaving the stricken vehicle in the care of his Canadian co-driver, Richard Harrison . . ." Who the hell was Richard Harrison? And where was Billy Gibbons? I went back over all of the issues that had mentioned the team but found no mention of Harrison and none of Gibbons once the rally had begun. Then I remembered the photograph of all the rally crews posed together in Wembley Stadium the day before the start. I read the tiny print that listed everyone present. Windsor was there, as were James and Alcott, but neither Gibbons nor Harrison was present. I made copies of the relevant stories and packed it in. It was time for tea with David Livesey. He'd been James's co-driver at one time, so perhaps he'd know something about Gibbons/Harrison.

The drive to Livesey's took me past Marble Arch, then out along Hyde Park by Lancaster Gate. The part of Bayswater opposite Kensington Gardens was a mixture of old English gentility and Asian immigrants. I parked in front of the grandiose—in name

151

only—Henry VIII Hotel, which was almost directly across from number 23 Leinster Gardens. Like the rest of the neighborhood, the building looked as if it had seen better days, but the street and sidewalks were clean and there wasn't a dirty window in sight.

I'd no sooner rung the bell than the door opened to reveal a short, stocky, late-sixtyish man with a few wisps of curly white hair and a drinker's ruddy complexion. He stared at me with his mouth open, but by now I was used to this reaction.

"Afternoon, Mr. Livesey. As you can see, I'm Peter Hawthorn."

"Sorry, lad. I din't mean to stare, but—"

"You look exactly like James," I said, finishing his sentence for him. "I know. People keep looking at me as if they'd seen a ghost."

"I should think they would. Come in. Come in. No sense standin' here when there's a warm fire and good whisky inside."

So much for tea, I thought, as I followed him in. The flat was small, dark, smelled of pipe tobacco, and felt like home should feel. There was an antique gas fireplace trying its best to imitate a roaring fire and there were pictures. Hundreds of them. Framed photographs in all shapes and sizes sitting on shelves, tabletops, and every other available surface.

Having hung up my raincoat, Livesey picked up the pipe he'd been smoking and began poking the tobacco around the way all pipe smokers do. "After you called, I did some digging around in the spare room. That's where I keep everything I don't need but can't throw away, and I found some things for you to look through. Would you like a dram to take the chill off? No? All right then. Have a seat by the fire while I put the kettle on."

My eyes had grown accustomed to the dim light, and while he was in the kitchen, I began looking at his extraordinary photo collection. With the exception of what were probably some family pictures, the entire collection was composed of race cars, drivers, and crews. The time period covered seemed to be from the midforties to midseventies.

"Noticed my little collection, have you? There's lots more but I ran out of room long ago. Will you take milk, lemon, or Glenmorangie?"

"Lemon, please."

He had cleared off a small table beside the fireplace to make room for a china tea service and a half-full bottle of whisky. "Would you prefer a brandy, perhaps?"

"No. Believe me, if I was going to have a drink, that would be it."

"Your father liked single-malt, you know. Liked it a bit too much, he did, poor James." He handed me my tea then poured himself a cup of scotch with a bit of tea for flavoring. "Well, cheers then. It's been a long time since I've had a chat with a Grand Prix driver, let alone a friendly drink. It's all so bloody serious now, isn't it? More money too." He laughed. "Well, bugger the money. The fun's gone out of it if you ask me. I stopped going to the races after Hunt retired. Just watch on the telly now. Listen to me go on. If you want to say somethin', you'd better jump in and say it." He poured himself another cup but thought better of adding any tea. "It was the World Cup Rally you wanted to know about, wasn't it? Well, ask away."

"I know you were my father's regular co-driver, so why did Trevor Alcott get the World Cup ride? From what I understand, he was nowhere near as experienced as you."

"True. True. Quite bitter I was about it, I can tell you. But it was no fault of James's. No. It was the team owner. Mr. High and Mighty Windsor. He wanted Alcott on the team. Money talks, doesn't it? 'Course, the way things turned out, maybe he done me a favor. Poor James. He deserved better. Excuse me. Must go to the loo. Tea runs right through me. That envelope next to your chair there? Take a look inside."

It was crammed full of old snapshots of Livesey when he was about my age, and with him in many of them was James. Except for the difference in driving gear, I could have been looking at pictures of myself. Livesey returned and poured us each some more tea. Well, one of us anyway. "You must have known James pretty well?" I asked.

"As well as anyone, I guess. But he wasn't all that easy to get close to, your father. Not after the trouble anyway."

"I know he wasn't drinking anymore but what about other problems, like gambling, betting on the horses, that sort of thing? Something he'd need to get his hands on a lot of money to take care of?"

"He may have wagered on the nags now and again but I don't think he was much of a gambler. What makes you think he needed a lot of money?"

154

OVERSTEER

"As I said on the phone, my mother died recently, and when I went through her things I discovered that James had been writing to her about his plans to strike it rich so they could get back together again. Mostly, it was in a letter with your name and return address on it. He talks about making a big score, intimating that he's about to come into a lot of money."

"I don't know. James was always sort of mad at the world, wanting to get even for things he'd brought upon himself. I don't mean to speak ill of the dead, particularly James, but I think he wasted a lot of time and energy plotting and scheming, always going on about how he was going to 'show the bastards.' "

"Would you mind reading his letter? Maybe something will ring a bell, I don't know."

"Of course. Got to get my glass out, though." He reached down between the cushion and arm of his chair and pulled out a large magnifying glass. "Eyes are no better than my damn kidneys." He took the letter and slowly moved the glass back and forth until he'd finished, then went back over it again. "No, don't see much here that means anything. Except that he got the dates wrong."

"What dates?"

"Says here he'll be in New York on the thirteenth or fourteenth of May. Rally didn't end until the twenty-seventh."

"Maybe he just made a mistake about the dates."

"Could be, but he'd have known just where the car was going to be every day from the pace notes and route map. By then he should have had it memorized. Want to see it?"

"What?"

"The route map. I got it out after you called."

"Absolutely. In fact, I'd like to see anything you've got on the rally."

"Thought you might. Whatever I've got is in here." He picked up another manila envelope from the floor and handed it to me. "Take your time, and if you got any questions, just ask. Shall I put on another pot?"

"Not for me, thanks. But if you—"

"Got all the tea I need right here." He grinned, pouring another helping of scotch into his teacup. He stood and stepped over to look at the envelope's contents with me. *Autosport, Motor Sport,* and a few other magazines, the "official" rally route map, some snapshots taken at Wembley Stadium, and a copy of the group photo I'd seen at the *Mirror.* "Were all of these pictures taken on the day before the start?"

"They were. The newspaper got all the crews together for a big picture of the lot. I went down to wish James, and some of the other lads I knew, luck."

"Was Billy Gibbons there? I couldn't find him in the official photograph anywhere."

"Billy Gibbons, no. Funny you should mention Billy, God rest his soul . . ."

"He's dead, then?"

"Must be close on ten years now. Hit-and-run. He was comin' out of a pub. Knowing Billy, he'd had a few. That's why he wasn't at Wembley. He'd been out celebratin' the night before and he had a run-in with some right villains. Bashed him pretty good they did too. It's why he missed havin' his picture took. He was in hospital. Thought to myself, and I'm not proud of it, I thought, well, maybe I could take his place, you know? I really wanted to go on the big one. I asked James to put in a good word for me with Windsor, but he said it was too late. Windsor'd already gotten some other bloke. Canadian, I think he said he was. I was pretty angry about the whole thing, so I just went home. Didn't even go back for the start." He took another sip of "tea." I could see I was beginning to lose him to memories and alcohol.

"Harrison . . . Richard Harrison."

"Who's he?"

"The man who replaced Billy Gibbons."

"Never heard of him. Bloody Canadians."

"I'd like to stay and talk a bit longer but we're testing at Silverstone in the morning and I want to get up there for an early dinner and a good night's sleep."

"Stayin' at the Green Man?"

"How did you know?"

"Where else would a race driver stay at Silverstone?"

He had me. "Look, why don't you come out to the track? Be my guest. Might be fun. Then we could talk some more. Yes?"

The invitation brought him partway out of the fog. "You're a good sort. What time would I be wanted?"

"Well, we're starting at eight. If the car's okay and I can keep it on the concrete, we'll be going till about three. Let's say eleven. Then we can talk over lunch."

"I'll put it on my appointment calendar," he said, and winked.

"Right. Would it be okay if I borrowed this stuff? I'd like to look at it some more tonight."

"Keep it, son. No need for it to go on gatherin' dust here. Are you trying to find out, then? About what happened to James?"

"I guess I am."

"Good. You know, I always wondered what would've happened if I'd been in the car with him. Things might have been different, I don't know. . . . Who did you say that fellow was that took Billy's place?"

"Richard Harrison."

"Now that I'm thinkin' about it all again, I do seem to recall the name. Is he important?"

"I don't know what's important. I'd just like to talk to him if he's still around."

"I'll poke around in the spare room. See what I can come up with. All right. Off with you now. Till tomorrow."

"Till tomorrow."

CHAPTER

16

I arrived at the Green Man Inn, which was only a mile and a half from the track, to find Rory, Todd, and Maurice in the bar discussing the new aerodynamic mods. My ribs were really hurting, so I decided to join them there for a snack, then go up to my room for a soak and lots of sleep. During our discussion, I told them I'd invited Livesey to the session and described his incredible collection of racing photos and memorabilia.

"Speaking of old racing photographs," Todd said, indicating the large collection hung throughout the room. "Is your father in any of those?"

"I'm not sure. There used to be one over there, just inside the doorway to the dining room. Actually it was a photo of Moss and Ireland, with James leaning against a car in the background, but it was a pretty good shot."

"We shall have to have a look when we go in to dinner," Maurice said, before polishing off his lager.

"Do me one favor, all right, Maurice?"

"Of course."

"No matter how tempting it is, don't tell me how much I look like him, okay?"

"Not superstitious about it, are you?" asked Todd.

"Superstitious? No. I'm not superstitious about anything as far as I know."

"Good thing," said Rory, grinning at the others, foam hanging off his beard.

"All right. What's going on that I don't know about?"

"It's your car number for the season," Rory replied. "Number thirteen."

"If it does bother you, it can probably be changed to something in the forties," Todd said. "It's just that the team was assigned thirteen and fourteen, and Alberto didn't want anything to do with thirteen."

"No problem. I don't believe numbers are lucky *or* unlucky. In fact, the only number I'm interested in at all is thirty-one."

As I got up to leave, the three of them looked at each other to see if anyone knew what I was talking about. "My room number, gentlemen. Good night."

Entering the paddock at Silverstone was a much different experience than at Rio. For one thing, I'd driven there on a number of occasions. More important, Silverstone was a track with a real sense of history. During World War II, it was one of the hundreds of airfields from which British and American bombers took off for raids over Germany. In 1948, the RAC staged the first postwar British Grand Prix there, which was won by Villoresi's Maserati. It was also the fastest circuit on the current Grand Prix calendar, with a 153.054 lap record set by Nigel Mansell in '87, driving a Williams-Honda. Three of the corners, Copse, Stowe, and Club, are of the 150-mph variety, while Abbey curve is in the 175-mph range. It was the ideal place to work on high-speed understeer.

If you've ever read anything about Silverstone, or watched races televised from the circuit, you will generally find it described as flat, but in reality it isn't. The entire track, which follows the perimeter road of the old airfield, is constructed on land that slopes gently downward from a central point in the middle. This has the effect of giving all of the right-hand corners a slight negative camber, which can catch you out. Unlike Daytona, where the positive camber of the banking combines with gravity and centrifugal force to stick the car to the track surface, these same forces at Silverstone are doing their damnedest to hurl you off it.

At least the rain had stopped, but there was some standing water in the paddock, which meant that portions of the track might still be wet as well.

Once again, the mechanics had the car warmed up and ready to roll when I arrived. The tire warmers were doing their thing for the rubber while a large space heater in the garage did the same for the crew. It was cold. At least I was dressed for it. For once, the long johns and heavy driver's suit proved good for something other than fire protection or displaying sponsor logos. I assumed that Vitale had not put his sponsorship deal together yet, since the only change to the car's paint job was the addition of the dreaded thirteen and the deletion of Alberto's name.

"Ready to take a crack at it?" It was Maurice's voice, coming out of a giant fur parka that all but obscured his face.

"I'm set. Where's Todd, in there with you?"

"Very droll. He's off checking to make sure the fire and ambulance chaps are in place. We're shorthanded because Rory's come down with some sort of bug and can't get away from the loo. That's Todd's car coming now, so we might as well get you buckled in."

I wriggled down into the cockpit and we began hooking up the usual belts and hoses. Todd joined in, and after reminding me to take it easy until the brakes were bedded in, we started the engine and moved slowly down the pit lane.

As soon as everything was properly warmed up, or as near as it could be under the conditions, I brought the car in for a final inspection. Everything checked out, so I set off to do a few hot laps while the car was still in its Rio configuration. This was done to establish a baseline against which the various modifications could be compared. Although I'd never sat in this particular chassis before, the car felt totally familiar and predictable. Unfortunately, one of the predictable things was the understeer, which was just as nasty as I'd recalled. My best time with the Rio setup was 1:17.340. Not fast enough to have qualified for last year's British G.P. Then it was back to the pits, where Maurice and Todd began to weave their magic spell. I remained in the car while the mechanics unfastened and lifted the main section of bodywork up and off the chassis, replacing it with another that didn't really look much different. Out again. The understeer was still present, but the time had come down to 1:16.530. In again for a new nose cone: 1:15.211. A new airbox: 1:15.005. Finally, a smaller, three-tier rear wing: 1:14.930. That would have been good enough for twenty-second place on last year's starting grid.

When I climbed out of the cockpit after that lap, it was as if everyone on the team had gotten ten years younger in just 1:14.930. I felt pretty good about it myself. I would have felt even better if my ribs hadn't been trying to poke holes in my side. The high g-loads in the right-hand corners were putting an incredible strain on them and I was relieved to find that it was already time to break for lunch. The crew took the car back to the garage for a thorough inspection before the afternoon session.

Maurice, Todd, and I drove back to the Green Man for a quick bite and a lengthy discussion. The most interesting thing was that the understeer problem hadn't changed. The aerodynamic modifications had improved the car's straightline speed to such an extent that it overcame the handicap of the wing settings needed to make the car turn into the corners properly. Now, if we could begin to dial out the understeer, we would be in really good shape.

We had just finished eating when Rory joined us and, declaring himself cured, ordered a pint. "I've been out to the track. Everything checks out. I told the lads to be ready to go again at one-thirty."

"Rory," Maurice said, pointing at him. "What have you done to your face?"

Todd and I must have looked pretty surprised because Rory laughed as he massaged his now clean-shaven chin. "Glad t'see you lot are so observant. Decided to take it off before we go back to Rio. Itches too much in the heat. Not to mention all the bugs gettin' stuck in it," he said, winking broadly.

Suddenly I remembered Livesey. "What time is it now?"

The three of them looked at their watches like commandos getting ready for a raid. Todd replied first. "It's six past one. Plenty of time."

"Rory. The guy I mentioned last night, David Livesey? Did he show up after we left?"

He shook his head. "Not as of ten minutes ago."

"Strange. He said he'd be here at eleven."

"Maybe he got held up or something," Todd said.

"Maybe. I wonder if he tried to call me. I'm going to check the desk and see. Be back in a minute."

Livesey hadn't called, so I called him, or attempted to, only to be told by the phone company that the line was temporarily out of service.

Back at the circuit, the whole routine began again. Two or three laps at speed, then back in for minor adjustments: change the antirollbar and camber settings front and rear, reset springs and shocks, more toe-in, less toe-in. If it was adjustable we adjusted it. After two hours of this, the pain in my ribs was beginning to affect my concentration. I knew Rory had brought one set of qualifiers from Ricard and I decided it was time to make one final banzai lap before quitting. I pulled back into the pits again. As the crew put on the qualifying tires, Todd and Maurice walked purposefully around the car, peering at things and trying not to look nervous.

Qualifying tires are· made from a softer, stickier rubber compound than normal racing tires and it takes less than a lap to heat them up to optimum working temperature. Then you have one lap where you'd swear they were made out of crazy glue before they start to fade. You may get a second hot lap out of them, but that's it. Once the tire has done its job, it begins to self-destruct and it's time to bring the car back in.

This run would require every ounce of concentration I could muster. All the experience I'd accumulated over the years, plus the willingness to hang my balls out on the nose cone. Ten-tenths time.

I brought the car up to speed pretty quickly. Not flat out, but moving right along. I had the lap I was going for burned into my brain and I knew I'd be ready for it when I hit the start/finish line. I wasn't sure about the tires, but I didn't think I'd be good for more than one lap. I came out of the right-hander at Woodcote and nailed it, hitting the start/finish line in fifth at 140 mph. Into sixth, still accelerating. Under the Shell Bridge: 160. Everything felt perfect. Pits went flashing past on the right. Copse Corner was dead ahead. I didn't touch the brakes till the hundred-meter marker on the left. Then down to fourth and into the corner. Negative camber made the car go light for a moment and I started getting some understeer. I lifted slightly, then nailed the throttle, hitting the apex on the right and drifting out toward the exit. The left-side tires went up on the curbing, jarring the car as they rode up onto it, then caroming off and propelling it toward Maggotts Corner like it was shot from a cannon. Left through Maggotts at 170 and on to Becketts Corner. Becketts led onto the long straight, so the better exit speed I had, the more top end I'd see. I hit 175 then moved over to the left to set up before getting hard on the brakes. The track was slippery there but the qualifiers had it covered. Down to third and it was understeering again. I lifted for a split second then went flat out down to the apex and hit it on full power. Into fourth, I drifted out toward the rumble strips at 120. Again the tires gathered it in and in a instant I was sweeping through Chapel curve. Into fifth, sixth. Hanger straight, which is slightly downhill, helps the car accelerate even quicker. The airflow was buffeting my helmet enough to make my vision blur and the noise was incredible. I bent my head forward into a "tuck" and it stopped. I'd have to tell Maurice. Up to top speed. Rory was out there somewhere with a radar gun checking it out. If it wasn't 190 we were in trouble. The front end felt a little light but not too scary. I lifted off the throttle slightly to get the car settled for Stowe Corner and before I even touched the brakes the deceleration from the aerodynamic drag of the wings exceeded one g. I'd heard that you can get through Stowe flat in sixth. Not today, José, I thought. It's a very quick, double-apex corner, so the entry was critical, but again the understeer got in the way. Corrected for it, then got back on the gas. The track dips downward into the first apex then immediately runs back up toward the second, making the car really stick. I hit fifth and was through it. Snatched sixth: 170. Then a quick run to Club Corner: 175. My heart rate was going for the Guinness record. On the brakes, down to fifth. Fighting understeer again. I went through it at 155 and headed for Abbey curve, a fast, bumpy, left sweeper. Flat out through Abbey. Just a flick of the wrists and I was accelerating toward the Woodcote chicane. Up into sixth: 175; 180; 185. Got hard on the binders again at the Foster's Bridge. Gravity was trying to suck my body out through the nose of the car as it came down to seventy for the chicane. Second gear, then turned into a tight left-hander, stabbed the throttle, and swung right. Full power again. Finally got some oversteer as the rear wheels spun, fighting for grip, then grabbed hold and sent the car rocketing back to the start/finish line.

The moment I crossed the line I felt like an eighteen-year-old kid in a hundred-year-old body. What an idea for a movie, I told myself, beginning to laugh. I actually felt giddy as I made my way back around the circuit. A boy and his qualifiers. Thank God everyone else was smiling when I pulled back into the pits.

"Well, don't all speak at once," I said as I pulled off my balaclava. "What was it?"

Todd looked at his clipboard as if he didn't know the time by heart. "1:13.248. Good enough for fifteenth starting spot last year."

"Well, all right." It looked as if we were going to have a season. I started to push myself up out of the cockpit and was jolted by a stab of pain. I didn't yell but the look on my face must have said something to Todd because he yelled. "Rory. Maurice. Quick, give me a hand getting Pete out of there. Is it your ribs?" he asked.

I just nodded and let them slowly raise me out of the car. "Do you think anything's broken?" Maurice really sounded concerned. "I think we should call in the ambulance crew and have them run you over to the hospital for a checkup and X rays."

Todd looked up. "Rory, would you call—"

"Already done. They're on their way."

"I'll go in the ambulance on one condition," I told them.

"What do you mean?" Todd asked.

"You two ride with me so we can run through that lap while it's still fresh. When are we getting that on-board telemetry system you were talking about anyway? Last I heard, you said it was in the pipeline?"

"As a matter of fact," Todd replied, "we should start testing one right after Rio. That's the reason Barry stayed at Ricard with Signor Vitale. They're going to take a look at the MRG system that Ligier uses. It's made in the States but they have a facility at Ricard."

By then the ambulance had arrived and the three of us climbed in for the ride to the hospital. I went over the lap in detail, breaking down every corner, curve, and straight into their component parts, then answered question after question as they both took notes. They seemed really interested in the fact that the car had bottomed out in a couple of spots. There was almost no fuel on board and it should have been too light for the skid plates on the undertray actually to touch the track surface, particularly as it hadn't done it in Brazil, which was a much bumpier circuit.

The X rays showed a hairline fracture in one rib and the doctor who taped me up said I shouldn't get into a race car for at least two weeks. He was young and very earnest, so I agreed, knowing full well that the open tests in Rio would begin in half that time. Then I got the pole position for mendacity by lying to the others, telling them the doctor had recommended a one-week layoff.

The team was returning to Italy the next morning, but I decided to head for Heathrow and catch the overnight Varig flight to Rio. The painkillers the doc had given me would guarantee a flight-long sleep and when I woke up in the morning it would be summer again.

By the time I arrived at the airport and got things squared away, it was nearly time to board. I put in a call to the hotel in Rio and left a message for Anne about my arrival. Then I tried to call Livesey again, to say good-bye and make plans to see him in July when I was back for the British Grand Prix, but the line was still out of order.

Once I was settled into my seat, I took two of whatever it was the doctor had prescribed and began to look through the newspapers the flight attendant had given me. I wasn't really concentrating when I remembered that the Miami race had been run the day before. With all that had been going on, I'd completely forgotten about it. As the plane moved into position for takeoff I found the brief race report in the paper. The Nissan had won, which was no surprise, with Jag second, a Spice Firebird third, and one of Gurney's Toyotas fourth. No mention of Les or the Prather team. I'd have to call from Rio and see how they did. I was just about to fold the paper up and stuff it in the seatback pocket when something caught my eye. It was a small piece, down at the bottom of the page, surrounded by soccer news.

EX–RALLY DRIVER DIES IN FIRE

David Livesey succumbed today to injuries sustained in an explosion and fire that swept through his Bayswater flat. According to police, the explosion was caused by a gas leak in the victim's fireplace.

Livesey, who was sixty-eight, is best remembered for his near win of the 1959 RAC Rally in a privately entered Ford Zodiac. He retired from active competition in 1975.

Funeral arrangements have yet to be announced.

Livesey, dead. That stupid fireplace. Another link to the past, to the Cup Rally, to James, was gone. I tried to remember everything he'd told me, but the pills were already taking hold, and before the no-smoking lights were extinguished, I was asleep.

CHAPTER

17

There was a message from Anne waiting for me when I arrived at the Inter-Continental saying that she was visiting her father at the clinic and would return about one P.M. Not surprisingly my ribs were giving me a lot of grief, so I decided to use the time to bake them in the sun.

Neither Esmandina nor anyone nearly as distracting was poolside. After making myself comfortable on one of the lounge chairs, I began to compare the rally map Livesey had given me with the road maps I had bought at the airport. My plan was to retrace James's path from the time the Rolls left Rio until it disappeared somewhere between São Paulo and Curitiba. I don't know if it was the heat, the humidity, or just plain weariness, but the next thing I knew I woke up to find a lovely, bikini-clad body lying about a foot from me. For some reason the head attached to the shapely lower extremities was looking at my maps.

Sensing my stare, she turned and gave me a big smile. In the time it took me to register that it was Anne, she'd already picked up on the fact that once again, I'd failed to recognize her.

"Remember me?" she said, with a wry smile. "Dinner at the Cavallino? Muggings on the beach?"

"Hey. No fair. I just didn't recognize your . . . uh, I mean I knew it was you as soon as I saw your face. . . . You know what I mean." God, I thought, I sound like a total doofus. At least she was laughing. "Never mind. How's your father?"

"He seems to be much better, thank you. The doctor says he'll be discharged in two days. I told him you were coming back and he asked me to bring you out tomorrow."

"I'm glad he's feeling better. You know that I really have to talk to him about some things?"

"I know. But you must promise me that you'll stop if he seems in the least bit upset by your questions. Yes?"

"Promise."

"Now, tell me about these maps. Where did you get the old one? Are you planning to follow the route again, now? Of course you are. May I come along? I'm sure I could help. I speak Spanish and a little Portuguese. Very little, actually . . . Why are you looking at me that way? Am I being silly? Never mind, don't answer that." As she laughed again I caught a glimpse of what she must have been like when she was a little girl, and it gave me a warm feeling.

"Yes, I am planning to retrace the route and, of course, you can come along. How I got the route map is a long story, but one you should know about." Now she was looking at me the way I'd always imagined young coeds looked at dissolute visiting poets. I filled her in on all of the happenings in England and why I needed to question her father about Livesey, Billy Gibbons, and Richard Harrison. As I spoke, the laughing little girl gave way to the businesslike young woman I was more familiar with.

"Aren't you worried that something might happen to you because of all this?"

"Why?"

"The accidents of course. First the one on the rally, then Billy what's-his-name gets hit by a car. Now your Mr. Livesey's flat blows up. Three men dead, plus my father, who's missing a piece of his life."

"Four men dead," I said, then explained. "Vitale's original partner, Paolo DeStefano, was killed in a skiing accident a few months ago."

"Don't you find it all a bit odd, then?"

"Yes and no. Remember, the rally incident happened nineteen years ago and Billy Gibbons didn't die until almost ten years after that. As for Livesey and DeStefano, the police said they were both accidents. I'll grant you that it's an unusual set of coincidences but I doubt it's some dark conspiracy. On the other hand, if there is some sort of weirdness going on, maybe it would be best to keep you out of it."

"Not on your life, Peter Hawthorn. Your father never came back from Brazil, and while mine did, part of him is still out there somewhere. If we can find out what happened, maybe I'll be able to give him back what he's lost. Besides," she said, brightening up again, "haven't you ever heard that two heads are better than one?"

"Okay. We'll get started first thing in the morning." Sometimes, I thought happily, the best-laid plans do manage to work out. "I've made arrangements to rent a jeep for a few days. First we'll go and talk to your father, then head south. I don't know if it'll be possible to follow the rally route after all these years, but we'll just have to do the best we can. You free for dinner tonight?"

"No. I wish I was but I picked up an assignment while you were away. I'm doing a piece on Rio for a new travel guide. I've got a meeting this afternoon, then dinner tonight with one of the editors of Brazilturis. In fact, I'd better get changed now or I'm going to be late. Sorry."

"That's okay. I'm going to do some more work on the maps then go pick up the jeep. How early can we see your father tomorrow?"

"Anytime after nine. It's only about half an hour away."

"Eight-fifteen out front?"

"Super." She stood, wrapping herself in a short, terry-cloth robe, gave me a quick smile, and trotted off to work. I watched until she disappeared inside then opened up the maps again.

At eight-fifteen the next morning I pulled the red Toyota jeep up in front of the hotel, and while I was backing into a parking space, Anne came out, looking great in T-shirt, shorts, and sneakers. "Good morning," she said, tossing the small canvas duffel she was carrying behind the seats next to my gear. "You didn't say if we'd be returning tonight, so I thought I'd better be prepared."

"Good. We won't get to São Paulo until sometime this afternoon, so it'll probably be easier to stay somewhere down there tonight." I smiled, trying not to look too happy at the prospect.

"Did you have any luck with the maps?"

"I found all of the main checkpoints from São Paulo down to the Uruguayan border but I didn't have much luck with the primes."

"What's a prime?"

"Primes are special sections of a rally where the roads are closed to regular traffic and the drivers go flat out to set the fastest elapsed time. They can be pretty dangerous, particularly when conditions are bad, which they were back then. It's already eight-thirty, so we'd better get started. Where exactly is the clinic?" I spread out the map of Rio and the surrounding area.

"It's here, near Seropedica," Anne replied, pointing to a small town northwest of the hotel.

"Great. It's close to the main highway south. We know that the Rolls made it past São Paulo, so I figure we might as well head straight down there before we start nosing around."

"You're the boss. May I have another look at those maps?"

"Sure. Look for a place called Piedade, southwest of São Paulo. It was the first checkpoint after the cars left Rio, so it seems like a logical place to begin."

* * *

We arrived at the clinic a few minutes past nine. A small, two-story brick building set on a gentle hillside, it looked clean, well cared for, and expensive. The nurse at the reception desk said that Alcott was waiting in the lounge.

One look at the man who stood to greet us and I knew that Alcott wouldn't be returning to the team for some time, if at all. He seemed to have aged at least ten years and, although he was still the same size, appeared almost frail. He and Anne embraced akwardly before he limply shook my hand. "Pete. Thank you for coming. I feel terrible about what happened at the hotel the other night. I don't know what got into me. I saw all that blood and then I guess I just blacked out."

"Come on, it was hardly your fault. I'm just glad you're doing okay. I understand you're getting out of here pretty soon."

"Day after tomorrow, thank God. Not a bad place, this, but I've had about enough of it. So tell me, how's the new car coming along? Will she be quick enough to qualify?"

"It'll be close but I think we'll make the show."

"Well, that's good news, isn't it?" He eased himself back into his chair, pulled out a pack of cigarettes, and lit one while I moved chairs for Anne and myself over next to him.

"Now, what's all this about your taking Anne off on some wild-goose chase to look for the Roller? It's been nineteen years, man."

"I know how long it's been. I know I probably won't

be able to find anything either. But aren't you curious about what happened? Don't you ever want to fill in the blank space in your life?"

That got to him. I could see it in his eyes. But what was he thinking? There was another possibility I hadn't taken into account. What if he didn't want to remember? He'd only met me twice. The first time he nearly passed out and the second he ended up in the hospital. Maybe Anne was right and I shouldn't push him to do something he might not want to do.

I could see that she was getting tense but I had to take things a little further now that I was there. "Did Anne tell you I saw David Livesey when I was in London?"

His surprised look answered that. "He gave me a copy of the original route map and some photos of you and James and the rest of the crew at Wembley the day before the start. Would you like to see them?"

"Not right now. I'm feeling a bit tired. I think I could do with a lie-down."

Anne, who had been very patient to this point, now got very protective. "That's all right, Daddy. No more questions today. Time enough for that when you're out of here. Right, Peter?"

I wanted to be nice and agree with her but I wasn't quite ready to let go of it. "Yes, definitely. There is one thing, though. Before he died, Livesey told me that Billy Gibbons couldn't do the rally because he'd gotten banged up in a fight and that he was replaced at the last minute by a Canadian named Harrison or something. Do you remember him?"

"Harriman, I think it was. Richard Harriman. Did

you say Livesey was dead?" The mention of Livesey's death had struck a nerve and Alcott looked frightened.

"Sorry, I thought Anne had told you. An explosion. Police said it was the gas fireplace. So, you knew this Harriman guy?"

"Not really. I seem to remember meeting him at Wembley but that's about all, I'm afraid."

"Any idea what happened to him?"

"Haven't a clue. What's he got to do with all this anyway?"

"I'm not sure. But with Livesey and Billy Gibbons dead and your memory gone, I'm running out of people to talk to."

"Peter. That's enough for now." The edge in Anne's voice was as sharp as a samurai sword. I made a point of looking at my watch. "You're right. We should be on our way. Trevor, good to see you again. I wish you were feeling a little better so you could come along with us. Never know, it might even jog your memory." He got that frightened look again, and Anne bent down and kissed him on the cheek. "You get some rest now. Pete and I will be back in time to pick you up."

As we were leaving the room I turned back to see Alcott trying to light another cigarette with trembling hands. I knew Anne was angry, so I kept my mouth shut as we got back into the jeep and headed for the highway. It would take about four hours to get to São Paulo and I was sure I could smooth things over before we arrived.

CHAPTER

18

During the first hour of the trip south the atmosphere was frosty, even though the jeep had no air conditioner. Traffic was moderately heavy and moving along at a good clip, so I concentrated on driving while I waited for Anne to start the conversational ball rolling.

"Was it really necessary to frighten Father by talking about Livesey's death?"

So, she thought he looked scared too. "I'm sorry, but I had no idea he'd react that way. Do you think it's possible he remembers more than he's letting on?"

"I suppose he might be, but I honestly don't think so. Not on a conscious level anyway."

"What do you mean?"

"I'm not sure exactly. I told you that he'd changed somehow, almost from the minute he got the call about joining the team. At first, he seemed excited about everything, including meeting you, but the closer it came to happening, the moodier he got. Then, when he saw you in Italy, I think it unleashed something bad in his subconscious. That's why he avoided seeing you again. And for good reason, considering what happened in Rio. I think he needs psychiatric help. Peter, I don't want him to get his memory back if it's going to have some terrible effect on him. Does any of this make any sense?"

"Sort of. But, on the other hand, if the memories are there, bubbling around just below the surface, we might be able to discover what really happened if we could help him break them loose."

"That's just what I'm afraid of. I don't mean to sound cruel, but I don't want the price of finding out what happened to your father to be the loss of mine."

With that, we lapsed back into silence for another fifty or sixty miles.

"Do you ever think that your father might still be alive?"

"Not in any rational way, no. But the idea is certainly still there in my brain. I don't want him to be dead, and I've never seen him dead, so maybe he isn't. That sort of thing. As long as my mother was alive it was different somehow. Now I need to try and resolve things so I can accept the fact that they're both gone. I guess that's really why I'm doing this now, after all these years, so I can close the books on my childhood once and for all."

"Even if it means destroying someone else?"

"I don't know. . . . No. Not intentionally, anyway."

OVERSTEER

"You know, we're very much alike, you and I. I just hope we don't hurt one another because of it."

She got quiet again and when I looked over a few minutes later she was sound asleep. Then I started to think about what she'd said and the old fantasies returned. What if James actually were alive? Maybe he had amnesia like Alcott, only worse? Maybe he didn't want to be found and the accident was a convenient excuse to disappear? Maybe it wasn't even an accident? Once I got started on these scenarios they ran through my head for the rest of the trip.

As we neared São Paulo, I reached over and patted her on the arm. "Rise and shine, Sleeping Beauty."

"Where are we?"

"Place called Guarulhos. That's São Paulo dead ahead with all the tall buildings and smog. Take a look at the map and see if you can figure out how we can get to the other side of the city without getting stuck in the middle of it. The place looks gigantic."

"It is," she said, opening the São Paulo map. "It's the fourth-largest city in the world after Shanghai, Mexico City, and Tokyo. Population, ten million. There, aren't you glad you brought along your own travel writer? What's our destination?"

"São Roque. It's about forty miles the other side of the city."

She studied the map for a moment or two. "Got it. See if you can get onto the Via Presidente Dutra. That should take us to Avenue Otavio Alves de Lima, which looks like it runs across the northern end of the city and out the other side."

I will never complain about traffic anywhere again

as long as I live. São Paulo must be what New York taxi drivers envision in their cabbie nightmares. Millions of cars. One-way streets that never go the right way. Traffic endlessly diverted one way, then another, due to construction or sheer capriciousness. Before long we were totally lost. I spotted a parking space and pulled in to take a break and, I hoped, get directions from one of the locals. For some reason, the locals all seemed to be Japanese. Then we noticed that the street signs were in Japanese. There were Japanese characters on the movie marquees and store window signs. In fact, we seemed to have been diverted all the way to Tokyo. Anne stopped a well-dressed young man and, in her best halting Portuguese, pointed to the map and asked where we were. He replied in perfect English that we were in the Liberdade section of the city, then proceeded not only to furnish us with a workable escape route but gave us the names of the two best sushi bars in town. We do indeed live in remarkable times.

It was nearly five o'clock before we finally departed São Paulo and headed up into the hills. São Roque was only about forty-five minutes away by the clock, but it was like time travel to another world. For one thing, we left the overwhelming air pollution behind. You can say what you like about America's tough automobile emission controls, but one drive through most any major foreign city will make a believer of you.

The Hotel Alpino, which had been highly recommended by the man at the car-rental place, lived up to its billing. Set in a eucalyptus and pine forest, it had a

European feel to it that went with the clean mountain air. We had adjoining rooms with balconies overlooking a swimming pool, and after a day bouncing around inside a hot jeep, nothing could have looked more inviting. Well, almost nothing. Anne knocked on the connecting door and when I opened it to let her in I nearly lost it. She was wearing a *kanga,* which by Brazilian standards was probably considered modest. By that I mean it was more angel-hair pasta than dental floss.

"Is something wrong?" she asked, enjoying my reaction.

I made a point of looking her over, then told the truth. "Not that I can see," I replied, going into my famous, leering, Groucho Marx imitation. "And from where I stand, there's not a lot I can't see."

She surprised me again. This time by blushing and acting flustered. "You go ahead. I'll be out in a few minutes." With that, she managed a rather weak smile, then backed through the door into her own room. Women.

I was toweling myself off when she arrived at the pool about fifteen minutes later wearing the terry-cloth robe and green bikini she'd had on in Rio.

"No amusing remarks, please," she implored with a smile.

"No, ma'am. Nothing even remotely amusing will find its way past these lips."

She dropped the robe on the chair next to mine, walked to the deep end of the pool, and dived in. I went over and sat down with my legs in the water to watch her swim. By now I could tell, the way you usually can tell, that we probably were going to end up in bed together. After all, she had insisted on coming along *and* made a point of bringing an overnight bag, not to mention the *kanga.* I'd done my part by booking adjoining rooms, but I knew this couldn't be played out in standard, "two lonely people find each other attractive and make happy, uncomplicated, no-strings-attached love" fashion. There was a lot more baggage with us than our two overnighters. I wondered if I should let her make the first move. I was brought out of my reverie as Anne stood up in the water and smiled at me. "Penny for your thoughts?"

"I was just thinking how nice it would be to go to bed with you. You can give me the penny later."

"I guess I asked for that." She climbed out of the pool and sat down beside me. "How long were you married?" she asked.

"Five years."

"That's all?"

"Seemed longer. How about you?"

"Seven. I was twenty-one. He was thirty-four. He made television commercials. Very glamorous, very successful. Then he started going bald and suddenly he was obsessed with growing old: changed his diet, started running, joined a gym, *and* started sneaking out with his actresses. I guess I knew what was going on but I thought it was just a phase, something that men go through when they turn forty. Then I came home two days early from an assignment and found him in *our* bed with two girls whose combined ages probably didn't total mine, and I was only twenty-eight. In any event, to make a long story short, that was a year ago and I haven't been to bed with a man since."

What the hell do you say after hearing a story like that—"I'm sorry your husband was such a turd, but all men are not alike, you know"? Yuck. At that point, she leaned against me, put her head on my shoulder, and whispered into my ear. "I hope you won't think me terribly wicked but I'd like to go to bed with you as well and I think we'd better go upstairs now before I lose my nerve."

I don't know what she was like with her idiot ex-husband, but if it was anything like she was with me that night in São Roque, I'd have to say his brains must've fallen out with his hair.

At first she was tentative, hesitant to initiate anything, but once she realized that I was in no hurry and was getting pleasure out of making her happy, she began to let go. After that she proceeded to make up for lost time while I seemed to lose track of it altogether. I even forgot that my ribs were supposed to be hurting. I know that we managed to get down to dinner a few hours later for some sort of fish, accompanied by a surprisingly good bottle of Brazilian wine. Then it was back to the room for a reprise of our predinner activities. I don't actually remember falling asleep, so I can only hope that it wasn't at some embarrassingly inopportune time. But I certainly remember waking up in the morning. I was having this incredibly realistic sex dream when it slowly dawned on me that I was awake. I lifted up the covers to find Anne looking up at me from between

my legs and saying in complete girlish innocence,
"Look at Willie. He wants to do it again." So he did.

After breakfast we checked out and hit the road to
Piedade, the town where the second stage of the rally
had begun and the last place James was seen before
his disappearance.

Anne was in a quiet mood, not unhappy, but pen-
sive, as if she was as unsure as I was about what after-
shocks we might encounter as a result of our newfound intimacy.

We found Piedade, a small town off the main São
Paulo–Curitiba highway, without any difficulty. Our
next objective was another dot on the map called
Ventania, about two hundred miles to the southwest.
Based on the route map, we took the main highway
for about forty miles until we reached São Miguel-
Aracujo; then the fun began as we tried to find the old
rally route on our modern maps. The country was
hilly, with numerous river crossings, some of them
on bridges that really made you wonder. Since we
didn't know exactly where we were going or just what
we were looking for, it became a long, rambling drive
through places with names like Capo Bonito, Itabe-
ria, Sengles, and Jaguariava. We stopped in each town
so Anne could ask some of the older residents if they
remembered the rally and if anyone knew of any
wrecked cars off in the woods, down a ravine, at the
bottom of a river, or wherever. We were in luck when
it came to following the actual rally route because
everyone over the age of twenty-five who lived there
at the time remembered it with great enthusiasm.

OVERSTEER

They invariably told us about it with lots of arm waving, body language, and sound effects. The cars were another matter. As we soon discovered, Brazil may well be the elephant's graveyard for old Fords and Chevies. By the time we had checked out our tenth wreck it was apparent that we could easily spend the next decade doing nothing else.

We were about twenty miles from Ventania when we accidentally got lucky. An old man in Arapoti, a few miles back, had told us of a big car near the bottom of a gully that had been there for many years. It took a while but Anne finally managed to spot it with the binoculars. It was quite a way off the road and almost completely covered by the underbrush. The road was gravel and there was a decreasing radius curve around a large jutting section of rock, which had probably caught the driver out, and off he went. I put the jeep into four-wheel drive and made my way down toward the wreck, stopping every ten or fifteen yards so Anne could take another look through the glasses. I pulled to a halt above a swiftly moving stream, looking for a place to cross, when Anne said, "No need to go any farther, I'm afraid. It's a large sedan but definitely not a Rolls."

"Okay, chalk up another one while I get this thing pointed in the right direction."

Anne marked the location of the derelict car on the map with a red *X* while I attempted to turn the jeep around. The slope leading down the stream wasn't overly steep, but when I was in the last phase of my three-point turn, the two inside wheels went down into a hidden rut, and in pure Peckinpah slow motion, the jeep rolled over onto its side. I killed the engine and looked at Anne, who was hanging by her seat belt up above me, trying not to burst out laughing.

"Your turn not to say anything amusing, dear," I told her.

"Never," was all she could get out through the suppressed giggles.

"Open your door, then unfasten your seat belt and I'll give you a boost."

In a minute we were both out, standing beside the now useless jeep. A car went past up on the road but if they saw us they weren't inclined to stop. Anne immediately started scrambling up the slope. "I'm going up and flag down the next car. If they can't help, perhaps they'll call a tow truck or something."

"Okay. Be careful. I'll try and see if I can figure out something to do here."

What I had in mind was to utilize gravity to try to roll the jeep over until it was back on its wheels. It would probably have worked but it was lying pretty close to the stream and there was no way I was going to chance making things any worse by dumping it into the water.

It was while I was checking the wheels and suspension to see if anything was broken that something caught my eye near the muffler. When I moved in for a closer look, I found a small anodized, black metal box about the size of a cigarette pack stuck to the frame. I don't profess to be an expert on Toyota jeeps, but this thing didn't look like any factory option I'd ever heard of. What it looked like was one of those little homing devices that people in spy movies are always sticking on cars so they can follow them. It was secured by a powerful magnet but I managed to pry it loose with the help of a screwdriver. It had no identifying marks of any kind nor the blinking red light they always seem to have in the movies, but I was convinced, for whatever reason, that we were being followed. That interesting train of thought was brought to a halt by a noisy commotion above me. I looked up to see an old, decrepit school bus backing down the road toward Anne, honking its horn. There were about fifty Brazilian men hanging out of the windows, beating their hands on the sides of the bus, waving and whistling at her. I dropped the device in my pocket and started back up the slope.

Anne, who was also waving, was pointing down the slope toward the jeep. I was about halfway up when the bus disgorged its boisterous occupants. Anne said something to them and in a moment I was engulfed by her newfound friends. I turned back to the jeep but by the time I arrived they had it back on its wheels. At their urging, I climbed in, started the engine, and with one giant push from the multitude, went storming back up the hill. Anne, who was all smiles, stood waiting next to the bus.

"What do you say to that, Mr. Hawthorn?" she said smugly.

"I love it. You are obviously a force to be reckoned with, Miss Alcott. Who are they anyway?"

"Farm workers from one of the local vineyards."

The bus driver began honking and signaling to the men to hurry things up and as they came back we shook their hands and said a lot of heartfelt *obri-gados.* I walked over to the door of the bus, stuck my head inside to say thanks to the driver, and managed to stick the mysterious black box to the side of the old rustbucket. As the bus drove away and the men reluctantly stopped waving good-bye to Anne, I hustled her back into the jeep and began following along at a distance. My mind was working overtime, trying to figure out just what I would do if we were indeed being followed, speculating on the who and why of it all. I wasn't really aware that Anne was talking to me until she leaned over and tapped me on the top of the head.

"Peter. You haven't heard a word I've said. What's going on? Is anything wrong?"

"Sorry. I'll tell you about it as soon as I can find someplace to pull off the road out of sight."

We only had to go another half mile before the perfect spot to put my theory to the test presented itself. Just after a blind right-hand corner I spotted a narrow, overgrown, trail leading back into the forest. I hit the brakes, then quickly reversed far enough into the trail to ensure that the jeep was unlikely to be seen by anyone passing on the road. I shifted into neutral, then tried to explain things to Anne.

"While you were flagging down the bus, I was checking the jeep for damage, and I found what I'm pretty sure was a bug, some sort of electronic homing device, stuck to the frame."

"A homing device? You mean someone's actually gone to that much trouble to follow us? Why?"

"I don't know. But if my plan works, maybe we can ask them personally."

"Go on."

"I stuck the bug onto the bus, and if I'm right, who-ever's tailing us should pass by here any minute." I'd no sooner finished saying that than a white Range Rover whipped past, driven by a bald man wearing dark sunglasses. I turned to Anne, gave a little "what did I tell you" shrug, put the jeep in gear, and went after him, feeling positively James Bondian. Fortunately, the gravel roadway made it easy for me to follow him without having to get close enough to be seen while I figured out my next move.

"What now?"

"We'll overtake him, force him to stop, then see what he has to say."

"Suppose he doesn't want to stop? Or suppose he does, but he has a gun or something?"

She was right, of course. Whatever was going on, the bug proved it was pretty serious, and there was no reason to assume the man wasn't armed.

"A far more sensible course of action might be to try and get his license number and give it to the po-lice."

I was about to concede the point when we rounded a curve to find the bus stopped a hundred yards ahead, letting out some of the men. The Range Rover had pulled over behind it, giving me the perfect op-portunity to go back to plan one. If I could confront him there, in front of a busload of witnesses, it wasn't likely he'd start a shoot-out. I stepped on the gas and as the jeep responded I yelled to Anne, "When we get up there, stay in the car and keep your head down."

The driver of the Range Rover must have spotted us

191

in his mirrors because the minute we picked up speed he put the pedal to the metal and sent the car fishtailing around the bus, the stones kicked up by his spinning tires rattling off our windshield like shotgun pellets. As we blasted past the bus in hot pursuit, the workers, recognizing our jeep, gave us a resounding cheer.

At first I was able to close up until we were only fifteen or twenty feet from his rear bumper, but as soon as we hit a clear bit of road the power of the Range Rover began to tell, allowing him to widen the gap. We were already doing over eighty, and while he had a clear road ahead, I was practically driving blind into the huge cloud of dust he was throwing up. It reminded me of driving at Le Mans in the fog, except we were going about half as fast. I was too busy to talk to Anne but I did hear her scream once as we went broadside through a sharp left-hander at opposite lock. I felt the jeep go light under me as the springs and shocks on the right side loaded up. I was ready for their rebound action when we cleared the corner, but the jeep's high center of gravity nearly caused another rollover. I got off the gas and gathered things up, but by then the Range Rover was hauling ass and any hope I had of catching him was long gone. I pulled to a stop, hitting the steering wheel with my fists in frustration. "Goddamn it, we almost had him," I said, turning to Anne. She was staring at me wide-eyed, white as a sheet and taking in large gulps of air. Definitely not a happy camper. She leaned forward, groping on the floor until she found her purse, opened it, and looked at herself in the small mirror. Apparently satisfied that she was still alive, she closed the purse and spoke to me as if nothing out of the ordinary had happened.

"Now that our quarry has escaped, would you mind stopping for a minute while I check something?"

I pulled as far off the narrow road as I could and stopped. Anne got out, walked to the back of the jeep, turned around, came back, and climbed into her seat. "You may go now," she said, with a satisfied smile.

"Are you planning to tell me what's going on?" I asked as I drove back onto the road.

"Did you manage to get his license number? No? Neither did I. The plates were covered with mud. Deliberately too, I should think. But when we first came up behind him, before the roller-coaster ride, I noticed a small triangular red decal on the bottom of his rear window. I thought I'd seen one like it quite recently and I had, in our own rear window. It's some sort of identification put there by the hire-car people."

"You're quite a detective. And a lot better looking than Miss Marple, if I may say so."

"Thank you, kind sir. Now, I'd suggest you find someplace with a proper loo as quick as possible. My bladder is not quite up to the rest of my body when it comes to detective work, I'm afraid."

CHAPTER

19

We talked it over and decided to drive straight through to Rio, even though it meant getting there well after midnight. The team was due to arrive the next day and I wanted enough free time to ask questions at the car-rental office about the Range Rover and to go with Anne when she checked her father out of the clinic. After that I would have to focus my total attention on the test session and preparing the car for pre-qualifying on the morning of the twenty-fourth.

True to form, Anne fell asleep almost immediately, leaving me alone with my thoughts for nearly the entire journey. I couldn't blame her for being exhausted. It may have been a short trip but it certainly had managed to cover all the bases emotionally. For me, a simple effort to exorcise the ghosts of my past was now a matter of international intrigue and, quite possibly, murder. What if all of the incredible events connected with the Cup Rally were not, as Anne had speculated, coincidences at all? What if it was all part of some master plot? There were too many questions with no corresponding answers, and that made the conspiracy theory all the more plausible. I tried to organize the facts in my mind. James disappeared twenty-one years ago somewhere south of São Paulo. Neither he nor the Rolls was ever seen again. The other man in the car, Alcott, had reappeared, but couldn't remember anything. Livesey, the man Alcott replaced as navigator/co-driver before the rally started, died in an explosion in London just after I'd met with him to find out what he knew. Then there was the crew of the second Rolls: Billy Gibbons, the regular navigator/co-driver, was injured in a pub brawl and couldn't do the rally. He was killed years later by a hit-and-run driver. *His* replacement, Richard Harriman, or Harrison, seems to have vanished, or may just have returned to Canada. Windsor, of course, owned half of the team that employed me and without him I wouldn't have been in Brazil at all. He had also been responsible for James coming to Brazil. He owned half of our team because Vitale's original partner, DeStefano, was killed in a skiing accident, a landslide that may have been caused by someone firing a gun. I was beginning to feel like Charlie Chan, laying everything out at the end of the film before exposing the killer. Only I didn't know who the killer was or even if anyone actually had been murdered.

I took time off from my mind games to navigate our way through São Paulo and experienced another inscrutable mystery by not getting lost once. I thought of waking Anne to look for one of those sushi bars but decided it would be better to press on.

Once we were back on the main highway north, I reverted to boy detective. If I accepted the conspiracy theory, then Windsor would have to be the prime candidate for the role of mastermind. But what was he trying to accomplish? Was he looking for something, like the Rolls, or James? Or was he trying to cover up something by eliminating everyone who knew about whatever it was? Then there was the bald man in the Range Rover. Why would he go to so much trouble to follow us? Maybe he was working for Windsor *or* maybe Windsor was working for him? Then I had a chilling thought. What if James was the man in the Range Rover? From the moment Anne had suggested that he might be alive, I had been unable to put it out of my mind. I tried to picture him hiding out in South America like some Nazi war criminal, but it just didn't seem real. Finally, there was Anne herself. She walked into my life that night at the Cavallino in place of her father and had been acting as a buffer between us ever since. Was she part of the "plot," staying close to me and reporting my every move back to headquarters, like some modern-day Mata Hari? "Make him trust you, dear. Sleep with him if you have to. It's all part of a spy's job." Having reached the point of ridiculousness, I switched the whole mess off and began thinking about getting back into the race car. Compared with all the other crap, pre-qualifying was a pleasure to contemplate. Well, almost.

Due to all the new teams entering Formula One,

some system had to be devised to whittle the huge field of forty-one cars down to thirty-two; that being the number permitted to try to qualify for one of the twenty-six starting spots. How well a team did the previous year determined whether or not they'd be relegated to the eight A.M. pre-qualifying sessions. Since there was no Vitale team in 1988, we'd be setting our alarm clocks a little bit earlier Friday mornings for the first half of the season at least. After that the teams would be reshuffled based on their performance in the first eight races. Got it?

Anne finally woke up about an hour south of Rio. Naturally she wanted to talk about what had happened earlier, so I ran through all of the possibilities I'd just come up with. I did, however, leave out any mention of her possible involvement. On the other hand, by sharing all of my thoughts with her, I knew that I was eliminating her as a suspect in my mind.

"What about that letter you found in your mother's diary? Didn't you say your father alluded to something connected to the rally that was going to make him wealthy?"

"You're right. I don't recall the exact words, but he said he was onto something big, something worth a lot of money. There was also the discrepancy with the dates."

"Do I know about that?"

"No, I probably didn't mention it. David Livesey pointed it out to me. In the letter, James said he'd be in New York on the thirteenth or fourteenth of April, but the rally wasn't due to end until the twenty-seventh. I thought he must've just made a mistake but now I'm not so sure."

"What about Windsor, didn't he stop before the twenty-seventh?"

"Yeah, but he crashed in Colombia and couldn't continue. And remember, he went straight back to Brazil to help with the search. In fact, if he hadn't kept the pressure on the officials, your father might not have been found alive. God, I wish he could remember something, anything, about what happened."

"I'll speak to him about it in the morning, and if he's feeling up to it, I'll suggest the three of us get together and talk it through as soon as possible. That's the most I can promise right now, Pete."

"That's okay, I understand."

When we arrived at the hotel we headed straight for our own rooms and sleep. As she got out of the elevator, Anne gave me a quick kiss and said she'd call me after she spoke to the clinic in the morning. I took a hot shower, crawled between the sheets, and was about to turn off the light when I remembered the letter. I got it out of my suitcase and found the relevant passage. "There are opportunities connected with this event that far exceed the excitement or challenge of the actual race. Opportunities that offer great financial reward."

Poor James, I thought, as the words to that old song ran through my head. He never did make it to easy street.

After what seemed like a five-minute nap, the noisy beat of my travel alarm sounded like a heavy-metal band on speed. My ribs creaked painfully as I climbed out of bed, which was just before I stubbed my big toe on the chair leg. The day could only get better.

Anne called just before I got in the shower to say that her father wouldn't be discharged for at least another day. She was going out there to find out what was going on. I offered to come along, but after talking it over, we decided it was more important for me to check out our friend in the Range Rover. We'd meet later at the hotel.

I wasn't sure if car-rental agreements were confidential in Brazil, so I tried inventing a cover story about why I needed the information. The closer I got to the agency on Avenida Princesa Isabel in Copacabana, the dumber the story seemed. So I decided to get my information the old-fashioned way: I bought it.

As it turned out, there were so few Range Rovers in the fleet that they were a cinch to check out. Knowing the color didn't help because they were all white, but of the five the company owned, I was able to eliminate four with almost total certainty. One had been returned at nine the previous evening, and there was no way baldy could have driven to Rio that quickly, unless of course we were being tailed by Fangio. There was a young German couple on their honeymoon, five American students on vacation, and a party of French missionaries. Then there was the fifth customer, a Mr. B. Dutton, who had made the rental arrangements through his hotel, the Nacional. Interestingly enough, the Hotel Nacional was practically next door to the Inter-Continental. I decided to pay Mr. Dutton a visit, but not before I traded in the jeep for the other Range Rover. Now, if I got into another situation that called for a car chase, I'd have a longer wheelbase, a lower center of gravity, and more power. Next time the fat lady was going to sing my tune.

My luck ran out at the Nacional's front desk. Dutton had checked out and when I pumped the desk clerk for information he acted as if I was inquiring about numbered Swiss bank accounts. Well, if Dutton was in Rio he had to be somewhere, so I decided to go back to the Inter-Continental and phone all the major hotels to see if he was registered. As I was leaving the Nacional, a group of about thirty men came in. I didn't recognize any of them but I knew from their looks, and the pile of logo-covered luggage being wheeled in behind them, that the teams had begun to arrive in town for the test session.

The same arrival scene was being played out in the lobby of the Inter-Continental, but on a larger scale. There must have been more than a hundred team members, journalists, and other Formula One types milling around waiting to check in. I noticed Spikings at the same time he spotted me.

"Peter, hello. You're looking fit. How are the ribs coming along?"

"No problem," I lied. "Everybody here?"

"The ones that have gotten through customs at the airport have gone to the circuit to sort out the equipment. The rest are still stuck at the airport, along with Prost, the Williams team, and God knows who all."

"What happened?"

"I'm not sure. Some of the customs officials are stopping people who checked off the 'tourist' box on the immigration card they give you on the plane. I'm going out to the track to check on things in about half an hour, if you want to come."

"Sure. Just give me a ring when you're ready to leave."

I went up to my room and spent the time trying unsuccessfully to locate Dutton. There were hundreds of hotels in and around Rio and he was probably in one of them, but there was no time to check them all. It looked like I'd just have to wait for him to find me.

When we arrived at the circuit, we went to the area of the paddock set aside by Brazilian customs to check in the cars and equipment. Things there were either out of control or proceeding normally, depending on who you talked to. Considering what it took to move the eighteen teams with their cars, equipment, fuel, and even food to Rio, it was a miracle things were going as smoothly as they were. It had taken two chartered DC-10s to deliver the eighteen teams and their accompanying steel shipping containers, each marked with the appropriate team logos and code numbers identifying their contents. A fully loaded 747 was still due in. The Boeing 707 carrying all the fuel had arrived the day before, and its cargo of fifty-liter drums was already stored in the appropriate garages. We maneuvered our way through the organized confusion to the Vitale area, where things were also far from calm. Our team only had fifty-five containers, while the top teams like McLaren and Williams each had well over a hundred. Chaos reigned as the customs officials tried to verify the thousands of serial numbers on the team manifests.

Windsor and Vitale were talking animatedly with one of the customs men, in a conversation that spanned six different languages. "Bloody hell!" There was no mistaking that voice. Rory was down on his hands and knees next to a container with a jagged hole near the bottom. "Fucking forklift drivers ought to be shot!" he shouted to no one in particular. We went over to see what had happened.

"Look at this," he said, sticking his hand into the hole to demonstrate. "They've gone right into the side of the block, the little fuckers have. G'day, Pete. Barry, we've got to do something about this."

"I'll take care of it. Just wait till everything's un-crated, then give me a detailed list of damages for the insurance."

Barry seemed quite calm considering that some-body had punctured a $100,000 engine. He saw the look on my face and laughed. "Too soon to start going over the top about things I can't control. It's a long season and this is only the first of the cock-ups ahead. At least we're not doing this out on the tarmac at the airport like they used to. Then, you were totally at the mercy of the locals. A few years ago during test week the customs boys decided to take the weekend off, so they just locked up and left things there, including one of the Brabhams. Well, the gearbox on the other car broke, so someone on the team loaded it up, took it to the airport, bribed his way in, and switched it for the new one. I wasn't here but I heard it was something to see when they tried to match the serial numbers with the carnet."

Windsor and Vitale had concluded their "discussion." They were both red in the face and Windsor was sweating heavily, but they were smiling, so I guessed it had gone their way. "*Buona sera,* Peter. How are the ribs doing?"

"Fine, Signor Vitale, just fine. Can't wait to get back in the car."

"That's a relief," said Windsor. "When I think about what happened to you and Miss Alcott . . . It was appalling. I've warned everyone on the team not to go out alone, and to stay off the beaches at night."

"You don't have to worry about me," I replied. "I'm only leaving the hotel to get in the race car, where it's safe."

"Yes, quite," he said, not entirely sure how I meant it. "If there's no further need for us here, Barry, Ludovico, and I should like to go to the hotel."

"No, sir. You two go on ahead. I've checked everything over there and it's in order. Maybe Pete could drive you. I want to stay here until everything's unloaded and organized," Barry said.

"Ready when you are, gentlemen."

During the ride they both wanted to know how Alcott was doing. I told them as much as I knew and said they should talk to Anne that evening. Windsor suggested we all meet for drinks at seven. "What happened to Alberto?" I asked. "He take a later flight?" Peter asked.

They looked at each other and exchanged knowing

leers. "Earlier," said Vitale. "Alberto arrived in Rio yeterday to be with the beautiful Brazilian girl which Denis has described to me fully."

"Esmandina?" I asked, already knowing the answer.

Windsor nodded. "Such a lovely girl," he said, coming on like her favorite uncle. "What we wouldn't give to be young again, eh, Ludovico?"

Good for Alberto, I thought as I pulled up to the hotel. I'd have to say something to him about conserving his strength and saving himself for the race car. The way Moss used to before he found out through applied research that it didn't matter a damn.

I met Anne in the lobby a few minutes before our seven o'clock date with Windsor and Vitale, just in case there was something about her father's condition she didn't want to share with them. Fortunately, though, the news was good. If you can call a sprained back good news.

"He tried to get up out of his wheelchair without locking the brakes; it moved and down he went. They've got him on painkillers and some sort of muscle relaxer."

"How long do they think he'll have to stay now?"

"Probably until the end of the week. He's really quite disappointed about missing the test session."

Alberto and Esmandina spotted us as they came out of the elevator holding hands.

"Buona sera, Signorina Alcott, Peter."

"Alberto, it's Anne, remember?"

"Va bene. Anne, may I present Esmandina Bracha."

204

The two women, who had already checked each other out thoroughly, shook hands warmly. "Are you and Alberto joining the rest of us for drinks?" Anne asked.

"No, not tonight. I promised to take Alberto to my favorite Italian restaurant for an early dinner."

"Yes, it is a big day tomorrow. Everybody is here, I think, except Ferrari. Also," he said, lowering his voice, "Esmandina does not wish to sit with Signor Windsor again if it is not necessary."

"Alberto," she exclaimed, poking him in the ribs with her elbow. "Don't talk like that."

"It's all right," said Anne, laughing. "I'm not very keen on him myself."

"I think we'd better change the subject, gang," I said, nodding toward Windsor, who was almost within earshot and closing in rapidly. He arrived and suddenly everything was all smiles and kissy-kissy. Alberto and Esmandina told Windsor about their dinner plans.

"Let me guess. You're taking him to Streghe?"

"Not tonight, no. Streghe is best when there is no driving in the morning and one can lambada downstairs at Caligola. We are dining at Enotria."

"Ah, *sì*, a wonderful choice. *Ecellente pasta con frutti di mare.*" Vitale had arrived unobserved. "And you must be the beautiful Signorina Bracha I have heard so much about from Alberto? I am Ludovico Vitale. I have had the pleasure of meeting your father on several occasions. Wonderful man, even if he did buy a Modigliani from under my nose six years ago."

"Thank you, Senhor Vitale. I told him I would perhaps be seeing you in Rio and he sends his warmest regards. He also wishes me to express his sadness on the death of Senhor DeStefano."

"*Grazie.* He was a dear man, Paolo. A good friend."

"As I told Senhor Windsor, I was in Gstaad when he was killed. It was very sad. Do you know, there is someone else here who was there at the time?"

"In Gstaad?" Windsor said, obviously surprised. "Who was that?"

"I don't know his name. A big man. I saw him here in the lobby today in a crowd of other men from the racing teams."

"Esmandina. We must go soon or your friends will think we are not coming."

"Signorina, will we have the pleasure to see your father while we are in Rio?" Vitale inquired.

"Not this week, but he does plan to be here for the Grand Prix."

"Esmandina?" Alberto was looking impatient.

She glanced at her watch and made a little show of being shocked at how late it had gotten. After promising to join us for dinner later in the week, they left. Anne and I spent the next hour telling Windsor and Vitale about her father and our trip south on the old rally route, purposely omitting any reference to the mysterious Mr. Dutton and his electronic gadgets. As soon as it was polite to do so, we excused ourselves and went up to my room for a light French meal before going to sleep. That night I had no reason to wonder what Alberto was doing.

CHAPTER

20

The paddock and garages were swarming with cheerful people, and there was an unmistakable sense of optimism in the air. That, along with the absence of Ferrari, Tyrrell, and Ligier was a sure indication that this was a test session rather than a race meeting.

It was also the first day of a new season. A season without turbocharged engines. A season during which the unbeatable McLarens (fifteen wins in sixteen starts last year) might yet be conquered. A season during which new teams and drivers might come to the fore, capturing the attention of fans and media. These, and similar delusions of grandeur, filled the heads of drivers, team managers, owners, and sponsor reps. The mechanics, of course, knew the truth. Having worked on the cars for months, they were already mired in the reality that would envelop all but the fastest few over the next seven days. When those who were bog slow would begin to rethink their priorities, making their goals a little more attainable in order to get through the year with whatever grace and dignity they could muster.

But that was yet to come, and on the morning of the first day of a new season every car sits on the pole and no one finishes out of the points.

The crowd in and around our garage showed the other folks that the Vitale team was here in force. Neither car was within an hour of being ready to run, so Alberto and I strolled through the paddock to get a look at the competition and to pick up on some of the latest news and gossip.

One look at McLaren and you knew they were still the team to beat, just as they had been in '84, '85, '86, and '88. Only Piquet in the Williams had been able to break their successive string of driver's World Championships. Maybe that's one reason they'd renamed the circuit for him last year. The current champion, Ayrton Senna, had to settle for having his picture on a new Brazilian postage stamp. *His* teammate, Prost, who had been detained by Brazilian customs for nearly seven hours the day before, was determined to take the championship back to France this year. Benetton certainly looked strong, with five cars ready to roll. Two each for Nannini and Herbert, and one with "active" suspension for works test driver Johnny Dumfries. At the Arrows garage we watched Eddie Cheever struggle to work his way down into the narrow cockpit of the new Arrows A11. God help him when he tried to bail out in less than five seconds, I thought, and made a mental note to congratulate him on the birth of his daughter the week before. But the biggest crowd by far seemed to be around the Minardi garage, including crewmen from most of the other teams.

"Ah, Minardi," said Alberto. "Let us go to say hello to Pierluigi."

"Wonder what's up? You think they brought their new car?"

"Is not the car, is the coffee." Alberto smiled and I could tell he was happy to tell me something I didn't already know. "They have a sponsor, MoKador coffee, and they always bring a big automatic espresso *macchina. Delizioso.* And everybody like Minardi, so is always a big crowd. We will have some coffee too, yes?"

"Lead me to it."

He was right about the coffee, and the ambience, which felt like the days when Grand Prix racing was more of a sport than a business. Somewhere nearby, an engine roared to life, the sound echoing off the walls, scattering crewmen in all directions toward their own teams. The serious stuff was about to begin.

Back at our garage, Rory and the mechanics were checking everything for the last time under the watchful eyes of Windsor, Vitale, and the rest of the team. If wishing could make it so, we were really looking good. Outwardly, the cars seemed much the same as they had during our last visit here, but I knew the tremendous amount of work that had gone into improving the handling. The cars were still without any sponsor identification and my car didn't even have a number on it. Spikings explained that it was just a precaution, in case Alberto had to drive the car.

Other engines were firing now, joining together in a symphonic dissonance that would have pleased Charles Ives.

By the end of the morning, it was apparent that the aerodynamic changes had made quite a difference. The car had gone from severe understeer to a diabolical combination of understeer/oversteer. The corrections needed to make the car turn in were now minimal, but once I was into the corner and back on the power, the rear end immediately started to break loose. On top of that, it was darting all over the place on the bumps and was unstable in traffic. But the good news was that I'd picked up almost eight seconds a lap over what I'd done back in February, with my best a 1:38.04. Alberto had also improved, turning a 1:39 flat on both of his last two laps.

During one of the breaks, while the mechanics were making adjustments, Spikings filled me in on how the competition was doing. Cheever had already lost a gearbox and was out of commission until a new one could be flown in. Neither of the Onyx cars would be ready to run until Wednesday. Rial was having fuel-feed problems similar to those I'd experienced at Daytona. Zakspeed still hadn't been able to get their nose and rear wing through customs and the new FIRST team didn't show up, having decided not to participate at all.

"That's all very interesting," I said, "but some of those cars whizzing around out there are fucking quick. I tried to follow one of the Brabhams and it was a joke."

"Probably Brundle. He and Modena are sharing the one car, but he went out first."

"What was he turning?"

"He was doing 1:31.6s."

Maurice, who had been listening in, spoke up. "Nowhere near quick enough, I should think. I hear from reliable sources that Mansell was turning 1:26s when Ferrari was here two weeks ago."

"Thanks, Maurice. You made my day. Barry, tell me about the teams that are having problems again. Please?"

"Bugger off," Spikings replied with a smile. "Just get out there and stick yer foot in it."

Alberto pulled in, came to a stop behind me, and Spikings went back to talk to him. So much for the big improvement in our times. Last year a 1:35.7 was enough to make the field, but that might not even be enough to pre-qualify now. Looking in my mirrors, I could see Alberto climbing out of his car and going around to the back of it, where a small crowd was gathering. Something must have broken, because no one seemed to be doing anything other than squatting down to have a look.

In a minute, Todd, Maurice, Rory, Spikings, and the rest of the group moved to the back of my car for a look-see. I knew by the way their heads started nodding in unison that a consensus had been reached about something, and when Spikings came around to signal me out, I knew it was serious.

"The gearbox casing on Alberto's car has cracked. It's losing fluid and it's also affected the stability of the wing. Yours looks all right, but we want to tear it down to make sure. If it's sound, you and Alberto can share this chassis until Rory can get the other casing welded. By the way, Alberto's last lap before he noticed the problem was a 1:36.3." Having given me the bird, he winked and headed for the garage.

1:36.3. Shit. Somewhere out there Alberto had picked up a second that I hadn't located, and as soon as the car was checked out I intended to go out there and find it. I wandered out to the pit rail to watch some of the other cars flash past. I was enough of a fan to get a kick out of seeing the cars and listening to the fabulous sounds made by the different types of engines. Piquet's Lotus went by and I wondered how he was coping with the high g-loads on *his* circuit. Spikings had told me that he was also driving with one or two cracked ribs. Of course, being a world champion, he'd gotten his from a fall on his yacht.

"Pete. Pete," Spikings was calling from the other side of pit lane. I waited as one of the Lola-Lamborghinis came in, then went across to meet him. "Rory's gone to heliarc Alberto's casing. Yours seems to be all right, but Todd's ordered new ones to be flown in on Thursday. Now, I'm sending Alberto out in the car and I don't want to hear any whining from you. We want to do a series of standing starts, and Alberto's better equipped to evaluate that than you are. I want you to sit down with the boffins and work on the new problems."

He started to walk away, then turned back. "Cheer up. It's going to start raining soon and you won't have to get your nice suit all wet."

He was right about the standing starts. I hadn't

212

done one for eight years. But I was now faced with the prospect that Alberto would finish the day a second quicker than me. *Quel* bummer.

I went inside to try to sort out the handling problems with Todd and Maurice, the arrival of the rain soon after proving Spikings right yet again. It did sound a lot better hitting the roof of the motor home than it would have beating on the top of my helmet.

About an hour later, Alberto came in. He was soaked, but it hadn't affected his disposition any. "The rain is stopping now," he announced, "and we are doing the same. Is there any coffee?"

"Maurice just made a fresh pot," I told him. "So, why have we stopped?"

"*Scusa*. The clutch is gone, but is being changed."

One glance at my watch told me we wouldn't be going back out. Alberto changed into dry clothes and joined the brainstorming session, which went on until Spikings arrived with orders to pack it in for the day.

I had just gotten out of the shower when the phone began to ring. I figured it was probably Anne, who'd planned to call as soon as she got back to the hotel. She'd spent the day on the shopping trail, visiting Rio's fancy boutiques as part of her current assignment. Nothing like research. When I picked up the receiver, though, it was Vitale, and he was upset. "Peter, I am sorry to disturb you but there has been a terrible tragedy. May Denis and I come, please, to your room, now?"

"Yes, sure. But what is it? Is it Anne? Did something happen to her?"

"No. No, is not Miss Alcott. Is Miss Bracha. Please, we will be there in five minutes."

He hung up, leaving me standing next to the bed, dripping water onto the rug. Esmandina? God, what could have happened? I finished toweling off and had just pulled on my pants when they knocked on the door.

"Sit down, please. What's happened to Esmandina?"

"She has been badly injured in a road accident. I have only just spoken to her poor father, who is coming from São Paulo by plane. Denis, you explain to him—"

"Miss Bracha has suffered severe head injuries. She's in a coma and can only breathe through a respirator."

"Jesus, that's terrible. How did it happen?"

"The man I spoke to at the hospital said her car skidded off the road in the rain and was totally destroyed. It's a miracle she wasn't killed outright."

"Tell him about the phone call, Denis."

"One of the women who works for Miss Bracha at her shop in Rio phoned Ludovico here at the hotel. She wanted to find out how Alberto was doing and what hospital he was in so she could contact Miss Bracha there."

"What's Alberto got to do with it?"

"My question exactly, dear boy. Well, this woman said that a man phoned the shop this afternoon, an Englishman she thought, asking for Miss Bracha. After talking to the man, Miss Bracha became extremely upset and left the shop to be with Alberto at the hospital, where she thought he'd been taken after a crash at the track."

"Let me get this straight. Someone called with a phony story about Alberto being hurt. Esmandina went rushing off to the hospital, crashed her car, and now she's in a coma?"

They both nodded. Vitale was practically in tears. "What are we going to tell Alberto? He will be crushed. If I find the man who make this terrible joke, I will kill him."

Windsor looked shocked. "What else could it be? Ludovico and I decided it must have been someone, a suitor perhaps, who is jealous of Alberto and thought it would be amusing to scare the poor girl that way."

"I guess that's possible. Where is she now?"

"São Vicente Hospital in Gavea. We're meeting her father there in about an hour. What do you think we should tell Alberto?"

"Tell him about the accident, but I wouldn't say anything about the phone call just yet. Do the police know all this?"

"Obviously they know about the accident, but the phone call, I don't know."

"Do you know where it happened, the accident itself?"

Windsor shook his head and looked at Vitale, who shrugged. The phone rang again and this time it was Anne. I quickly filled her in on what had happened and said I'd meet her in the lobby in half an hour to drive to the hospital. Windsor and Vitale went off to wait for Alberto, who was due back at any minute. They'd bring him to the hospital with them. As I finished dressing, I couldn't get the idea out of my head that this "accident," like all the others, was related to the Cup Rally and James's disappearance.

During the drive to the hospital I told Anne I suspected that someone had deliberately tried to kill Esmandina, and she agreed wholeheartedly. When we arrived, there was nothing to do but wait, as Esmandina was in intensive care, where only immediate family were allowed. Windsor, Vitale, and a very shaky-looking Alberto arrived soon after, as did Esmandina's father. Following a short, hushed conversation, Alberto accompanied Mr. Bracha into the intensive-care unit. By now, some of Esmandina's friends and colleagues had arrived and were talking together quietly in the already overcrowded waiting room. Anne, who had visited Esmandina's shop earlier that day, recognized one of the women and went over to speak to her. They chatted briefly before Anne signaled me to join them. "Pete, this is Nina Arruda. She's the one who took the phone call about Alberto."

Nina didn't speak much English but she did speak excellent Spanish, allowing Anne to act as translator as she explained what had happened. When she answered the call, the man asked if she were Miss Bracha. She said no, but started to explain that Miss Bracha was in the next room. The man interrupted to say he was calling from the race circuit and that it was an emergency. She got Esmandina on the line immediately, then hung up her extension. In about a minute, Esmandina ran out of the back office looking panicked. "Alberto's had a bad crash," Esmandina told her. "They're taking him to the hospital." With that she dashed out.

"Ask her if she remembers what time the call came in." She was sure that it was exactly four o'clock. We thanked her for the information and let her get back to her friends.

Four o'clock. At four o'clock Alberto and I were in the motor home with Todd and Maurice. The rain had just stopped and every car that could motivate went back out onto the track. In fact, I remembered commenting on all the noise. I had Anne go back and ask Nina what, if anything, she'd heard in the background when she talked to the mysterious caller. Nothing special, she said, the sound of traffic, a car horn blowing, the usual things you hear when someone calls from an outside pay phone. So whoever had called hadn't done it from the racetrack.

The door opened and an ashen-faced Alberto came back into the room. He looked around without seeming to see anybody until Vitale went over and guided him to the exit with Windsor tagging along behind.

Vitale insisted that Alberto not do any testing on Wednesday, and when I agreed with the idea, Alberto got pissed. He claimed that I only wanted to keep him out of the car because he was faster than I was. I knew that that lousy second would come back to haunt me.

Afternoon rain was forecast again, so we got down to business as soon as the track opened Wednesday

217

morning. As a result of Alberto's enforced absence I had the luxury of two cars, and I intended to make good use of them by having the mechanics set his car up for the anticipated rainy afternoon. Todd had come up with some new end plates, tabs, and splitters for the wings to help stabilize the car in traffic, and we spent the morning trying them on my car in varying combinations. It was only the second day, but already some of the faces in the pits were beginning to look a little grim. Then the thing everyone dreads most, a major crash, took out Philippe Streiff in one of the AGS cars. I had just come into the pits for another wing adjustment when the red flags came out, closing the track to all but the fire, ambulance, and rescue vehicles, which were already on the move. One by one the others that had been out on the circuit pulled in.

The drivers all knew it was a bad one, and as they climbed out of their cars I could see them explaining what they'd seen to their crews. No one had caught the beginning of the incident but the consensus was that he'd clipped a curb at very high speed, launching the car into the air, where it rolled over, smashing into the guardrail upside down. This ripped off the rollbar and part of the fuel tank, effectively cutting the car in half at the back of the monocoque. At least two course workers had been injured by flying debris. After what seemed ages, word came back that Streiff was alive and conscious. We watched as the medivac chopper lifted off to take him to the hospital. The same hospital, it turned out, where Esmandina lay.

OVERSTEER

* * *

Streiff's accident and the widening gap between the haves and the have-nots made it a week worth forgetting for some of the teams. Alberto returned on Thursday. He apologized for his remarks the previous day and we both went back to the work of finding a tenth of a second here, another mile per hour of speed there, trying to remain competitive with the other teams who were busy improving their times. By the end of the week we had both gotten into the low 1:34s, and were looking forward to the last two parts of our test program: a run on Saturday at full Grand Prix distance, and some hot laps on qualifying rubber.

Medical progress reports from the hospital and clinic had become an integral part of each day. Alcott was due to be discharged over the weekend, but that was the only good news. Streiff had broken his collarbone and left shoulder and, more seriously, suffered two dislocated and one crushed vertebra. The doctors were already worried that he might develop partial or even total paralysis. By Saturday, Esmandina's condition was listed as "guarded." Although still in a coma, she continued to show signs of improvement.

Saturday was also the day Todd thought he'd figured out what was causing our handling problems. We had gotten our times into the low 1:33s that morning, but there didn't seem to be any more to come, and even at that speed I was scaring myself once or twice every lap. Todd's discovery involved the car's underbody. Formula One cars are now "flat-bottomed," without the elaborate air tunnels underneath that suck the cars onto the track the way the American Indy cars do. But air does flow in, around and under the cars, and at high speed. Todd said the tremendous g-loads were causing the underbody to flex or deform in some way that screwed up the handling. As a result, we would skip the full-race-length runs in order to work on the problem. Then, if nothing worked, immediately ship the cars back to Italy for modifications. With less than a week before pre-qualifications, it was probably our only hope.

On Sunday, Senna went out on qualifiers and set the fastest time of the week in his McLaren at 1:26.34, just beating Boutsen's 1:26.36 in the Williams. Of the thirty-six drivers, we finished twenty-sixth and twenty-eighth fastest, with Alberto a few-thousandths quicker than me. Not quick enough, but we hadn't been able to use our qualifiers, which should knock off another two seconds.

Sunday was also the day that Streiff was airlifted back to Paris, Esmandina taken off the respirator, and Alcott discharged from the clinic. In fact, Anne brought him to the track in time to catch the end of Alberto's run and have a reunion with the crew before they headed back to Italy. All in all it had been a hell of a week.

CHAPTER

21

I was roused from a deep sleep the next morning by a laser-thin shaft of sunlight that had managed to find a crack in the drapes and hit me right in the eyes. I rolled out of its way, shot a quick glance at the clock, and was surprised to discover that I'd slept for twelve hours. Anne was gone but she'd left a note stuck to the bathroom mirror reminding me that we were having lunch with her father at one; as if I'd forget that. While I was in the shower, I made a mental note to invite Alberto to join us for dinner. Esmandina's accident had depressed him, and before they left for Italy, both Windsor and Vitale had asked that I do what I could to keep him from dwelling on it.

I went down to the outdoor Veranda restaurant just before one and got a table overlooking one of the pools. The table's large white umbrella did a good job of keeping out the sun but couldn't do much about the heat, which was nearing pizza-oven intensity. So, when the waiter arrived, I decided to try the local thirst quencher I'd heard so much about. Caipirinha turned out to taste like a cross between a margarita and Gatorade. Perfect for the climate but undoubtedly worthy of Barry's earlier warning. After a couple of sips I decided I'd have another—after the race on Sunday. By one-thirty, the caipirinha was almost gone and so was my patience. I was sure I'd been stood up again and was already rehearsing sarcastic things to say about it when Anne and her father arrived.

"Hi. Sorry we're late," she said, kissing me on the cheek. "There was some mix-up about father's room that I had to straighten out."

We all sat down, ordered lunch, and spent a while making small talk about the weather and the results of the test session. Then, since nobody else was going to, I brought up Esmandina's condition and Alberto's guilt pangs once he'd heard about the unexplained phone call. I watched Alcott as I talked and I could tell from his lack of surprise that Anne had filled him in on the events surrounding the accident as she'd promised. Then I found out she'd done a lot more than that.

"My daughter's just told me what happened when you two went on your trip south." He paused for a moment as if searching for the right words. "The fact that you were being followed like that seems very . . . organized. I guess what I'm tryin' to say is, if all those accidents that've happened weren't accidents, then I don't want my little girl involved anymore."

"Oh, no. Wait just a minute . . ." Anne broke in.

222

Alcott shook his head and kept on talking. "If you're intendin' to keep lookin' for the Rolls, I insist you take me in her place."

"I don't know . . . I sure would appreciate your coming. I mean, who knows, you might see something that'll seem familiar or—"

"Stop it right now," Anne said angrily. "There is no possible way the two of you are going without me. If there's anybody who shouldn't be going, Father, it's you. You've just come out of hospital—"

"I'm perfectly well and you know it."

"Hey, will you two knock it off? Now, listen. I'm heading south again tomorrow morning. I'm giving myself two more days to see what I can find out about James and the Rolls, and that's it. There's plenty of room in the Range Rover for all of us, okay?"

Neither of them spoke for a moment. They were consciously avoiding looking at one another until Alcott leaned over and put his hand on her arm. "Come on, girl. Pete's right. Let's stop bickering and have a go at it. Maybe I will remember something. Twenty-one years is a long time to be missing a piece of your life."

She looked into his eyes, smiled, and nodded.

"Agreed then. Any questions?" I asked.

"You said you wanted to leave in the morning. How early might that be?" Anne wanted to know.

"We'll meet in the lobby at five."

"Five o'clock? Worse than the bloody army, you are. Would you mind letting me have a look at that rally map you mentioned? Don't know if it'll do any good but I'd like a chance to study it for a bit before morning."

"Great. I'll get it as soon as we're finished. In fact, I'll give you the new maps as well. A lot's changed since 1970."

"Hasn't it just," he said.

While Anne was typing up the notes for her piece on Rio and her father was trying to find a road that led to his past, I was at São Vicente hospital having my ribs checked out. Once the doctor was satisfied that everything was all right, he started asking questions about the test session and the upcoming race until he was practically dragged away to tend to his other patients.

I went upstairs to see how Esmandina was doing and found Alberto seated in the lounge talking quietly with a beautiful and somewhat familiar-looking woman. When he stood to greet me, I could see in his eyes the toll this was taking on him.

"Ah, Peter. It is good of you to come. May I introduce Signorina Constanza Ribeiro, Peter Hawthorn."

As she shook my hand she smiled and nodded. "You are the man from the pool, yes?"

"Yes. I guess I am." So that's who she was. The girl in the dental-floss *kanga.* I could feel myself blushing as I pictured her wearing it. She must have known exactly what I was thinking because she burst out laughing. Poor Alberto was totally at a loss.

"I'll explain later," I told him. "How is Esmandina? Anything new?"

"She is no better, no worse than yesterday. The doctor, he say it could be weeks before she wakes up."

He looked so miserable I didn't know what to say that would cheer him up. "I'm really sorry, Alberto. I wish there was something I could do. . . . I'm having dinner with Anne Alcott and her father tonight and we'd really like you to join us. You too, Miss Ribeiro, if you can."

"Thank you," Alberto replied. "But we must decline. In fact, I was about to ask you to join with us tonight to pray for Esmandina."

"All right. I'll bring Anne. We could meet you at the church. Just tell me where it is and what time to be there."

Instead of answering, he turned to Constanza. "You explain to him, please."

"It is not a church we are going to, Senhor Hawthorn. It is a *quimbanda* house."

"I don't get it. What's that?"

"*Quimbanda* is one of our local Brazilian religions. A spirit cult with roots in Africa and the Amazon."

"A spirit cult? You mean like voodoo?"

"In some ways, yes."

"Hey, Alberto, come on. I know you're upset about Esmandina, but you don't think going to some place where they kill chickens is going to do her any good, do you?" He looked at me with an intensity I'd only seen once before, when he was strapped into the new car for the first time.

"Yes, Peter, I do think it may help her. I am also going to do something bad for the person who make the phone call that almost killed her."

"Jesus. Where is this place, anyway?" I asked Constanza.

"About forty minutes north of here by car. Senhor Hawthorn, I would not expect you to believe in the power of spirits, but do not be too quick to make judgments about things of which you know nothing."

"Peter," Alberto said, taking hold of my arm. "You are my friend and I ask you to come with me, please, at least to drive the car. I do not feel so much like driving today."

It was obvious that with or without me, Alberto was going off to this *quimbanda* place and I thought it would be better for him if I went along. I'll also admit that given a different set of circumstances, I'd have jumped at the chance to see something like that. They were both staring at me now and I was beginning to feel uncomfortable about it.

"Senhor Hawthorn, have you not seen the candles burning at night along the beach, or the bowls of food and bottles of rum placed on the sidewalks or at crossroads out in the countryside?"

Anne and I had noticed things like that during our trip and she'd said they were probably offerings of some sort. "Yes," I answered. "But, if you'll pardon my saying so, I didn't think they were put there by intelligent, educated people."

She smiled. "I do not wish to shock you, but here, in Rio, there are more than a million people who believe in one spirit cult or another, and many of them are far from the illiterate savages you seem to be imagining. Esmandina's father, for instance, is both a Catholic and a believer in *umbanda*. But even if it is,

226

as you probably think, a silly superstition, how can it possibly hurt Esmandina? On the other hand, if it is as I believe, perhaps it will help. Would you deny her this?"

"No. Of course not. The idea just takes some getting used to, is all. I'll certainly be glad to drive the two of you there anyway. When do you want to go?"

"Eight o'clock here?" Constanza answered, looking to Alberto for confirmation.

"*Sì*, eight. When visiting is over. *Grazie*, Peter," Alberto said, shaking my hand, then embracing me. I left them there and went back to the hotel to tell Anne about the change in plans.

After talking it over with Anne, who thought the whole thing preposterous, we decided it would be better if she stayed at the hotel with her father while I went off to visit the spirit world.

I picked up Alberto and Constanza, then followed her directions, driving north along the edge of the Tijuca Forest, past the giant Maracana Soccer Stadium and on to the outskirts of the Mangueira *favela*. Alberto was uncharacteristically silent during the trip, staring out of the windows and methodically biting his fingernails.

After parking along the side of a dirt road, we followed Constanza through the darkness to a large, two-story wooden house that was desperately in need of a coat of paint. As we went up onto the long front porch I looked through the windows into darkened rooms that were barely illuminated by the light of flickering candles. It was only as we neared the open front door that I became aware that there were people inside. Standing alone or in small groups, some held burning candles and spoke in whispered tones, others stared silently into space. Once I was inside, my eyes quickly adjusted to the near darkness, but my nose was another matter. The place stank. Not just a bad odor, like rotten eggs, or spoiled food, or sweaty unwashed bodies; it was all that and more, reeking of putrefaction and death. If it had been up to my nose, I'd have done an immediate one-eighty and headed back to the twentieth century, but not without Alberto, and he was there on a mission. Constanza told us to stay put while she went to find the priest, or shaman, or whatever, who was going to be our spirit guide. Looking at the others in the room, I was struck by the diversity of their appearance. The majority were shabbily dressed and probably lived in the nearby *favela*, but there were also a few well-heeled types, including a middle-aged, European-looking couple who were kneeling on the floor under one of the windows. In front of them was a small towel or blanket that was nearly covered with burning candles, bottles of liquor, and an open box of cigars. The woman was sobbing and I could see tears sparkling in the candlelight as they rolled down her cheeks before dropping onto the objects below.

Constanza reappeared with a tall, gaunt, black man wearing a pair of dirty white shorts and nothing else. He gave me the once-over, then bent down, whispered into her ear, turned, and left the room.

"I'm sorry, Senhor Hawthorn, but it will not be possible for you to accompany us to the sanctuary of the *exu.* You may wait here if you wish, or outside in the car. We will rejoin you in about one hour."

I didn't particularly like the idea of Alberto going off without me but I knew it was too late to start questioning the protocol of the place. "All right, I'll probably be in the car. Tell me something," I said, pointing to the couple with the bizarre little picnic spread. "What are they doing?"

"Everyone here is communicating in their own way with the spirits. The offerings you see, like the ones we discussed earlier, are given to please the *exus,* who are fond of earthly pleasures like alcohol and cigars."

"Who, or what, is an *exu?*"

"*Exu,* Senhor Hawthorn, is our word for the devil." She smiled, took Alberto by the hand, and led him toward the back of the house, where they disappeared into the darkness.

I was about to get the hell out of there when something happened to me. I began to perspire heavily, and in a matter of seconds was dripping with adrenaline-induced sweat. It was as if something didn't want me to leave. I saw a batch of unused candles on a shelf by the door and, without hesitation, picked one up, leaving a handful of coins in the collection bowl next to them. Then I found an unoccupied corner, lit the candle, and allowed the hot wax to drip onto a small dish I'd found sitting on the floor. After securing the candle to the dish, I took an Upmann out of my cigar case and placed it next to the candle. I knew I should have felt foolish, but I didn't. As suddenly as it had started, I'd stopped sweating. I was totally exhausted, my limbs feeling like lead weights hanging off my torso. I left the house as quickly as I could without running, made my way back to the car, got inside, locked the doors, and went immediately to sleep.

I awoke with a start to the sound of Constanza pounding on the window. It had begun to rain while I was asleep and both she and Alberto were getting soaked. As soon as they were inside, Alberto curled up on the backseat and was asleep before I could start the car.

"Is he all right?" I asked.

"Yes. He will need to sleep for many hours, but nothing more. I know you are wanting to ask questions about what has happened but it is best not to talk of it. Thank you for coming and sharing your strength with Alberto. It meant much to him, and to Esmandina. I know something of your own reasons for being in Brazil and I'm sure the *exu* will consider your offering and be of help to you. My car is parked at the hospital, so if you will drop me there, please, I will say good night."

"Sure. But tell me, how did you know I'd made an offering?"

I waited for a response but she didn't answer, and when I turned to ask again she, too, was sound asleep.

CHAPTER

22

After a thorough inspection to make sure our Range Rover wasn't harboring any extra electronic doodads, we set off for São Paulo. Although Alcott had stayed up half the night studying the maps, they didn't succeed in jogging his memory. I'd planned to use the drive south to talk about whatever he *could* remember, but all he and Anne were interested in was my visit to the *quimbanda* house. I recounted the events in detail, omitting only my own unusual behavior with the candle and cigar. I still didn't know why I'd done it, but I was sort of glad that I had. On the other hand, I didn't want them to think I was some sort of nut case. As soon as my tale was told, Anne promptly fell asleep, allowing her father and me to have our first real conversation together.

"Windsor told me that you don't remember running the rally at all, not even the European stages?"

"I'm afraid he's right. I used to give myself headaches trying to remember what happened, but it didn't do any good."

"I don't want to suggest you give yourself a migraine or anything, but could you tell me what you *do* remember? For instance, do you know why you got the ride instead of David Livesey?"

He thought for a minute before answering. "Not really, but I think it might have been James that wanted another co-driver. One that could drive as well as navigate. Not that he'd have asked for me. Although I had driven with Mr. Windsor, you know."

"When was that?"

"The year before, in Wales and up in Scotland."

"But you'd never navigated for James?"

"No, never. He hadn't done much rallying, your father. I knew him from the shop, of course, but that was all."

"What do you mean, 'the shop'?"

"Mr. Windsor's garage. I used to be a pretty decent engine builder in them days."

"Did you do the engine work on the Silver Clouds for the rally?"

"It was me who designed the special exhaust system to keep the pipes out of the water."

"Right. I saw pictures of it. Pretty ingenious stuff."

"Ta. We put a lot of hours into those cars, and a lot of money. I think by the time we were done, Mr. W wished he was runnin' Austins."

"I can imagine. Nothing comes cheap when it's for a Rolls."

"Is that ever so. There was a while there before the

insurance money come when I thought he was gonna pack it in."

"I don't understand. What insurance?"

"Sorry. I thought you must've heard the story."

"No, go on."

"Well, Mr. W, he's a collector, you know. Paintings mostly, I guess. A couple of months before the rally he was robbed. They done him good too. Took everything. Quite a year for it, as I recall. Couldn't pick up a paper without readin' about some manor house bein' tossed."

"What's that got to do with the rally?"

"It was the insurance, you see. On the paintings. Over 200,000 quid. Mr. W's business wasn't doin' so hot and the bills for work on the Rollses wasn't gettin' paid. Somebody even tried to put a lien on 'em as I recall. Anyway, the insurance money took care of everything, thank God."

"I'm not so sure I'd be thankful for it. If the money hadn't come through, my father might still be alive and your life wouldn't have a big hole in it."

"True. True. But I was just readin' the other day that if people don't stop usin' hairspray, they'll be wearin' bikinis at the North Pole, or some such foolishness. What I mean to say is, if you go around worrying about one thing, something else'll come along that's just as bad."

For someone who'd avoided talking to me for weeks, and who rarely said ten words when he did talk, Alcott was suddenly acting like a guest on the Johnny Carson show. I decided to take advantage of his newfound chattiness to see if he could confirm my suspicion that something else had gone on down here nineteen years ago besides the World Cup Rally. I told him about James's letter and the hint of some big money deal connected with the rally, and of the "mistake" he'd made in the dates. It took so long for him to answer that I thought I'd blown it.

"I'm pretty sure . . . more than pretty sure, that you're right," he said. "When Mr. Windsor talked to me about co-driving with your father, he said there'd be a bonus of some sort. I can't recall exactly, you understand. . . . A bonus for me when we finished. I asked him, sorta jokin' like, what would happen if we didn't make it to the finish and he just laughed and said we'd finish, all right."

"How much money are we talking about? It couldn't have been enough for James to start a new life with, could it?"

"I don't know. When I tried to find out, he said not to talk about it anymore. Said he'd explain everything later. 'Course, if he did, I can't remember it."

"Did you get it, though, the bonus?"

"No, and I'm sure I'd remember something like that. In a way, though, I guess I did. Mr. W's been helpin' me out all these years. Not just with doctors and such either. Helped me get my job. Always sent me fifty quid at Christmas. He's real good about things like that. I remember runnin' into Billy Gibbons a few months before he died and he told me Windsor was helpin' him out as well. Hafta give the man credit."

"He said you called him up and asked for a job on the racing team. Is that true?"

"I asked him, all right, but it was him that rang me. Said he'd seen somethin' in a magazine by Anne and just wanted to say how good it was. Then we started talkin' about racin', and one thing just led to another, I guess."

"Did he used to call you a lot then?"

"No, he never. Once a year 'round the holidays. To make sure I'd gotten his check."

After that our conversation drifted back to the team and the upcoming race. I could tell he was really getting tired and when I suggested he get some shut-eye he dozed off almost before I'd finished saying it. I glanced at Anne in the rearview mirror. She was still sleeping soundly. A regular chip off the old block. Alcott's revelation about the bonus certainly was interesting. I added it to the list of things I intended to discuss with Windsor when we returned to Rio.

We arrived at the Hotel Alpino with plenty of time to unpack before lunch. I explained to them that I planned to spend the afternoon in the area between Piedade and Ventania, then all the next day retracing the rally route from Ventania to Bateias. The team would be returning soon for pre-qualifying, so if we didn't find anything in those two days we'd have to quit looking and head back to Rio. Even as I was speaking, the thought of driving the rally route with James's navigator in the other seat had me in a state of excitement so intense I was amazed my cigar didn't just ignite when I put it in my mouth. When we set off, I could feel that we were going to find something out there.

By the time it got too dark to see anything I'd decided that maybe whatever was out there didn't want to be found after all. We had driven over anything that remotely resembled a road and found nothing. Alcott, who had started the search in high spirits, was exhausted, irritable, and had a headache that seemed impervious to medication.

We returned to the hotel for a moodily silent dinner before heading upstairs and collapsing into bed. Once again Anne and I had adjoining rooms, but they were the only things connected that night.

Because we'd had such a long day, I decided to delay our departure the next morning until eight. It would take us a couple of hours to get back to Ventania anyway and I figured the Alcotts, *père et fille,* could continue to catch their ZZZs during that part of the drive. Myself, I was too keyed up to sleep past first light, so I went down to the pool for a swim and a strategy session with myself. If anything was going to happen, it had to happen that day, and if things could be helped along at all by me, I was prepared to do whatever it took. As I swam lazily through the cool water I began to evolve a plan. It was based on dimestore psychology but for someone who'd recently tried to bribe the devil with a cigar it was downright scientific.

True to form, the Alcott family slept for most of the drive to Ventania. Alcott's headache hadn't improved much from the day before and, not surprisingly, neither had his disposition. I didn't think he'd be able to take another long day, so if I was going to try to shake any information out of the dead-letter box in his brain, it would have to be sooner rather than later. Once we were off the main road, and within a few miles of what had been the starting point of the first rally prime, I floored it. In less than a minute we were rocketing along, bouncing through ruts and potholes, looking to all the world like an accident searching for a place to happen. The first jolt had awakened my companions, who found themselves trying to process this unexpected turn of events with minds that weren't yet up to speed. Anne, whose eyes looked like two satellite dishes staring at me in the mirror, found her voice first.

"Peter, have you gone mad?" she yelled over the din. "Slow down before you kill us all."

"Can't do that. We're more likely to get killed if I do slow down. Somebody's been tailing us for the past fifteen minutes or so, and I intend to lose them if I can."

Anne and her father both twisted around as far as they could to look out the back. All they could see was the dust thrown up by our tires, which was just as well since there was nobody back there.

"Can you see 'em?" I asked.

"I can't see a thing," Anne replied. "What color car is it?"

"White. I'm not sure, but it could be that other Range Rover. Keep watch and let me know if it's gaining on us. Trevor, turn around. I'm gonna need another pair of eyes on the road up ahead."

As he shifted around I got a quick look at his face and he looked terrified. I like to think it wasn't my driving that was scaring him but the imagined threat from behind. Then again, either reason would do. "There it is," I yelled as we came sliding out of a corner on opposite lock. "Dead ahead. The start of the first prime. Anne, are they still back there?"

"I think I saw something just before that last corner but I'm not sure."

"Keep looking. Trevor, see if you can judge which way the road up ahead goes. At this speed I don't want to make any mistakes."

We had left a relatively fast, flat section of road for a climb into the hills. The roadway, which was covered with loose gravel, stones, and dirt, wouldn't have been bad at forty but at seventy it was pretty hairy. I was even beginning to scare myself a little. The vegetation, which had been pretty sparse and scrubby, was suddenly much thicker, coming right to the edge of the road in many spots, concealing totally whatever lay beyond, including which way the road went. I hoped to hell this wasn't a truck route. As we crested a sharp rise, the wheels left the ground and we soared for a good thirty feet before banging down with a spine-jolting thud. The second the car was stabilized I pumped the brakes furiously to get us slowed for a sharp right-hander that almost had me fooled. "Trevor," I shouted. "Come on. Get with it."

"Sorry, James. The turnoff's about a half mile ahead on the right. As soon as you get over the bridge and start up the hill you'll see it." I knew it was Trevor Alcott speaking to me, and yet it wasn't. His voice was stronger, more confident. It was the voice of a younger man. Twenty-one years younger. The dam had finally broken, releasing a flood of memories. He started calling out directions. "Left over brow, one hundred . . . Twenty easy right, then long easy descending left to bridge."

I felt Anne moving up between the front seats, leaning forward to see what was going on. "Peter, what's happening? Daddy? Are you all right?"

I took my right hand off the wheel and pushed her back, shaking my head and putting my finger to my lips to signal her to be quiet. Our eyes met in the mirror and I knew I was going to have a lot of explaining to do, no matter what happened. The bridge appeared on cue and with a roar of clattering, rusted metal we were across.

"James, slow down. You'll miss the turnoff." Alcott was hunched over, his hands gripping the dash, peering out the windshield. "There it is," he shouted, pointing to a nearly invisible road leading off into the undergrowth. I stomped on the brakes and made the turn. "Absolute right, thirty," he said. "Then two hundred, flat right. Let's go, we only have fifty-five minutes."

It was practically dark where we were, interspersed with sudden bright pools of illumination as the sunlight pierced the canopy of vegetation. Where the hell was he taking us? I wondered. A look at the compass mounted on the dash confirmed what I already suspected. We were headed northeast, away from the rally route. *Fifty-five minutes*, he had said. *We only have fifty-five minutes*. Alcott was silent now, and when I looked over at him, it scared me. His face was bright red, the veins in his temples bulging as if they were going to burst. He was also awash in perspiration, hyperventilating rapidly, and there was an odor coming off his body that reminded me of the stench in the *quimbanda* house. Whatever I'd started, I felt certain it was about to end, and I was more than a little afraid. The road fell away, down to a small creek, which we splashed through without incident, then back up again around the side of a steep hill. I'd just picked up speed, anticipating another long descent, when Alcott screamed, "It's a slide. Stop. You can't make it." He made a grab for the wheel and came so close to putting us off the edge that my heart all but stopped. I locked up the brakes and skidded to a halt with the right front wheel hanging over a fifty-foot drop. Anne was sobbing hysterically, trying frantically to unfasten her belts while her father hung loosely in his, not moving at all.

I popped open my seat belt, checked Alcott, who was breathing shallowly, then reached into the back and released Anne, who immediately hit me with a couple of stinging blows to the face. "You bastard," she shrieked, scrambling over into the front to look after her father. I got out and ran back up the road to the approximate spot where he'd started yelling. *A slide*, he'd said. *It's a slide.* I looked up at the hillside and tried to imagine a small, or large, landslide coming down to block the road. He'd also said, *You can't make it*, and tried to wrestle the wheel out of my hands. That probably meant that James must have thought he could drive over, or through, the obstruction. There was only one place the car could have gone and that was over the side.

Without a moment's hesitation I plunged into the

thick undergrowth and began climbing, slipping and stumbling my way down the hillside. I turned to look back up and get my bearings, but the road had disappeared completely. I don't know how long it took. I know my clothes were torn and my skin scratched bloody in spots, but there was no concept of time spent searching. It was as if I knew exactly where I was going, yet when I got there, the surprise took my breath away. The journey that had taken more than half a lifetime was finally over.

The Rolls was pointed downhill, the left front collapsed against a giant boulder, but otherwise practically undamaged. Although there were vines going in and out of the windows, the aluminum body was intact, impervious to the ravages of nature and time. My heart was beating so loudly I expected small men wearing loincloths to appear at any moment in answer to its call. I made my way around to the front of the car, looked inside, and nearly blacked out, grabbing onto a tree branch for support. As soon as the dizziness passed, I moved in for a closer look. James, or what remained of him, was seated behind the wheel, held partially erect by the rotting belts, his fleshless skull lolling to one side under the weight of his crash helmet. For twenty-one years he'd been sitting there, waiting for his only son to come and take him home. I got dizzy again and had to drop down to the ground and sit for a minute. I became aware of someone calling my name and as I dragged my brain back out of the fog I realized that it was Anne and she sounded panicked. I tried to shout back to her that I was okay, but could only manage a parched little croak. I tried again and pretty soon was able to make enough noise for her to hear me. I gave the Rolls a brief inspection, but enough to convince me that it had indeed been untouched for all those years. After a silent promise to James that I would return, I began to climb back up to the road. Back to the present.

CHAPTER

23

By the time I'd clawed my way up the steep incline to the road, Anne had stopped calling my name. In fact, she wasn't making any noise at all, which I hoped was a good sign. The car was about fifty yards from the point where I emerged from the ravine. The passenger door was open and I could see her kneeling behind it. Alcott was visible, seated inside, but from my vantage point it was impossible to determine his condition. Anne, who heard me as I sprinted toward them, stood and glared angrily at me through red-rimmed, swollen eyes.

"Where were you? Didn't you hear me calling? Look what you've done." She pointed at her father, who was slumped over in his seat, unconscious. "Did you do all this on purpose, you bastard?" she said, waving her arms to take in the immediate landscape. I knew she was about ready to take another poke at me.

"Calm down. I'll explain in a minute." I gave Alcott a quick check, and aside from his being asleep, he seemed okay. No fever. No cold sweats. Pulse and heartbeat normal. A much better bet to finish the race than his co-driver, who slept the big sleep not two hundred yards away.

"As far as I can tell, all his vital signs are okay, but I think we should get him to a hospital in São Paulo as soon as possible. . . . Stop looking at me like that," I told her as I walked away from the car, indicating that she should follow me. As soon as I was sure Alcott couldn't overhear us if he came out of it, I told her about my discovery of the Rolls and its grim contents. When I'd finished, she simply stared at me, shaking her head in disbelief as tears began rolling down her cheeks.

"Oh, Peter, I'm so sorry." With that she let loose and began sobbing uncontrollably. I took her in my arms and stood there holding her tightly until she stopped shaking. Then we heard the sound of an approaching car and she pulled back, snapping her head from side to side, trying to locate the direction of the sound.

"My God. What if it's them?" she said, her voice on the verge of panic. It was definitely not the right time to tell her that no one had been following us. Actually, considering the way things had turned out, there might never be a right time.

"No. I'm sure we lost them. If not, they'd have been here long before this."

I didn't know if she actually believed me but she obviously wanted to, and that would do for now. "What we should do, and quick, is move the car.

Come on." We ran back, jumped in, and just as I tried to start the engine an old beat-up Cadillac came slewing around the corner, barely missing us with its giant tail fins, then spraying us with stones as it fishtailed away. The engine caught, and after gingerly maneuvering all four wheels onto solid ground, we resumed our interrupted journey to the northeast.

"Don't you think it would be safer to go back the way we came? You don't know where this road goes, or even if it goes anywhere at all."

She had a point, but I was convinced we were going in the right direction. "According to the compass, we're headed toward São Paulo. Plus, that Cadillac had to come from somewhere."

"What happened?" It was Alcott. I slowed immediately and glanced over at him. He looked groggy. "Where are we?" he wanted to know.

Anne leaned forward to comfort him but when she touched his arm he jerked away in surprise.

"Daddy? Are you all right?"

"I think so. . . . Feel a bit confused, actually. Did we have an accident or something?"

"Almost. Some local in an old Caddy nearly ran us off the road. Gave us all quite a scare. You blacked out, I guess." The moment I said it I shot a quick look at Anne in the mirror. Her nod told me that nothing would be said about finding the Rolls—for now anyway.

"Just relax, Daddy. We're going to find a hospital in São Paulo and have you properly looked after."

"No. Take me back to Rio. If anyone's going to look at me, I want Dr. Salazar."

"But that'll take hours," she said, looking to me for help.

"Anne's right. We're a good five or six hours from Rio, and I think—"

"No! I'll be fine. I don't want someone I don't know asking a lot of stupid questions. Just let me be. I'll probably sleep until we get there anyway, tired as I feel. I don't want to hear any more about it." He turned, smiled at Anne, and patted her hand. "It's all right, girl. Just you let yer old dad sleep for a bit and he'll be as fit as a fiddle. You'll see."

"Peter, will you talk to him please?"

"Maybe he's right. The people at the clinic know his history and everything, so maybe we should just get him there as quick as we can." I smiled as reassuringly as I could. She nodded but, in truth, I think she was simply too exhausted to fight about it. I decided the smart thing was just to shut up and drive. After about ten miles we came to a crossroad with a sign pointing toward Itapeva and I knew that my guess about the road we were on had been correct. I started to say something about it but when I checked my passengers they were both sleeping peacefully.

During the long drive, I had plenty of time to think the situation through, making and rejecting plans until I'd convinced myself I had something. Once again, I would need Anne's cooperation, but I knew that this time there was no certainty she'd be prepared to give it.

It was dark when we arrived at the clinic. Alcott was admitted immediately and taken off for a complete work-up while Anne took care of the formalities. I put in a call to the hotel and found that the team had been checked in by Spikings an hour before. Anne and I would have to agree on what information to give, or withhold, before we got back to the Inter-Continental. And if my plan was to work, she'd have to agree to tell more than a lie or two. I went outside for a smoke and to practice the arguments I'd undoubtedly need to convince her.

Getting Anne's cooperation turned out to be much easier than anticipated, particularly when I explained that acting overtly hostile toward me was of vital importance to the plan's success. Her agreement not to reveal the discovery of the Rolls was given, I'm sure, solely to spare her father's feelings. She'd also decided to stay at the clinic for the next twenty-four hours, or until the doctors were sure he was in no immediate danger. At the end of our discussion in the parking lot she pointedly snubbed my attempt at a farewell kiss by turning abruptly to go back inside.

As I climbed into the car for the drive to the hotel I glanced at my watch. Eight P.M. In exactly twelve hours the light at the end of pit lane would turn green to signify the beginning of pre-qualifications. By the time I got to the hotel everyone had already left for the circuit to prepare the cars for the next morning's battle. After calling the hospital to find that Esmandina's condition was unchanged, I took a quick shower and went off to join the rest of the team.

The garage area at the track was as brightly lit and busy as the Las Vegas strip on a Saturday night. It wasn't just the ten teams that had drivers in the morning session, the entire field was hard at work in the bug-infested paddock. As one of the new kids on the block, the Vitale team was off in the boondocks working under large, generator-driven lights. I had to stop from laughing out loud when I got there and saw Alberto seated in a folding canvas chair watching Rory and the mechanics at work on "his" car. Rory caught my eye, smiled, then disappeared back behind one of the sidepods.

"Ciao, Alberto. Everything under control?"

When he turned I could see that he was still in the grip of forces that had nothing to do with Formula One. "Hello, Peter. Yes. Barry says the flexing is solved, so is fine for tomorrow. He has been asking for you. I think he is over there with Todd and Maurice."

"Thanks. Listen, I called the hospital a few minutes ago but they wouldn't say much. Is there any real news?"

"There is not much. But she has begun to, uh, respond to people's voices and she has no difficulties with breathing."

"That's great. Anything new on how it happened?"

"Nothing. The *polizia* still say it was an accident, but I know was somebody trying to kill her."

Although I agreed with him totally, I thought it would be better to try to defuse some of his anger. At that moment he didn't strike me as someone who should be driving a two-hundred-mph racing car.

"Maybe they're right. You know how people drive here. They're crazy. Anything could have happened."

"Is possible. But what about the phone call? That was no accident."

"I know. It was a shitty thing to do, but it doesn't mean whoever did it wanted her to get hurt."

"Peter, where the devil have you been?"

It was Spikings. He, Todd, and Maurice were walking toward us and I wanted to head them off so I could talk privately. "Be right there . . . Alberto, I think you should go back to the hotel and get some sleep. Now! We've really got to be on top of things in the morning. I know that's what I intend to do as soon as I check in with Barry. Okay?"

"Okay, boss." He smiled, and for a moment looked like the Alberto of old. "I will go back to the hotel with you and you may tuck me into bed yourself."

"Deal. But no bedtime stories. Wait here, I'll be back in a few minutes." He was still smiling as I went to join Spikings and the others.

After they briefed me on the modifications they'd made to the cars, I gave them an edited version of what had gone on over the last few days. I also expressed my concerns regarding Alberto's mental state. Spikings said he'd have a talk with Vitale about the situation later that night. Then he told me confidentially that Vitale and Windsor had gone to the airport to pick up a top representative of the team's new sponsor. Naturally, I wanted to know who the sponsor was and that's when I found out about the little "hitch" in the arrangements. It seemed the contract wouldn't be finalized until after the pre-qualifying session.

"Signor Vitale was going to tell you and Alberto tonight, but after what you've told us, I don't think Alberto should know anything about it."

We decided the best thing was for me to get him back to the hotel as soon as possible because the sponsor rep was coming directly to the track from the airport. As I went back to get Alberto I thought about what they'd just said. The sponsor was here to watch pre-qualifying. The deal would be signed after that. Ergo, if we didn't at least pre-qualify, there probably wouldn't be any deal. Pressure? Nah. Now it was doubly important to make sure Alberto got a good night's sleep. But after the bedtime story Spikings had just told, who the hell was going to tuck me in?

I don't know about Alberto but I had a hell of a time getting to sleep. I finally succeeded by resorting to the racer's version of counting sheep: driving imaginary laps in my head. I've always used this technique of visualization the night before a race, but this was the first time I'd had to run a full Grand Prix. It was also the first time I consciously tried to change my driving to pick up some speed. I imagined carrying more revs on the straights, moving my braking points, going deeper into the corners, changing my lines now that I didn't have to fight the car to make it turn in. By the time I finally fell asleep I was sure I'd picked up a few seconds.

After the alarm went off at six, I stayed in bed long enough to do a few more practice laps. Then I decided to go for a quick one running against the clock. In theory, and in practice for that matter, if you time one of your visualized mental laps, you should be within half a second of your actual on track time. I got up, pulled a stopwatch out of my racing kit, closed my eyes, hit the start button, and went for it. Past the pits and through the right-hander, down the short chute to Pace Corner, up into fifth, flat out through Suspiro then deal with the off-camber left. I could tell it was going to be a quick one. Down to second for the Norte Hairpin, then up through the gears for the long straight, the engine screaming at 10,300 rpm. Two hundred mph into Sul Corner. (Two hundred?) Touch the brakes and sweep through using all the track, the curbing, and another of my nine lives. Quick right, left sequence followed by another, tighter-banked left-hander leading onto the stretch to the 90 Graus Corner. Through it in fourth then accelerate to the Vitoria Hairpin, a long 180-degree corner that ejects the car back onto the pit straight. Back up through the gears, third, fourth, fifth. There's the start/finish line. Bingo. I hit the stop button on the watch, opened my eyes, and smiled: 1:31 flat. Seven seconds quicker than I'd gone during the test session and about five seconds quicker than Alberto. I wondered if they'd let me phone my time in. . . . Suddenly, I had this vision of qualifications being run that way. Forty drivers, all suited and helmeted, sitting in chairs, eyes closed, stopwatches in hand, and visualizing like gangbusters. They'd be bobbing over the bumps, leaning into the corners, making engine noises as they shifted gears. Invariably someone would overcook it and turn over his chair. Then Senna and Mansell's chairs would get tangled up. . . . By that time I was laughing out loud and all my anxieties about getting through pre-qualifying had vanished. I was in. Going to the track was just a formality.

The atmosphere in the paddock that Friday morning was pretty grim for most of the fifteen drivers who had to go quick enough during that one-hour session to make the cut. By nine A.M., eight of them would become instant spectators for the first Grand Prix of the season. Based on times recorded during test week, only the Brabhams of Brundle and Modena seemed a sure thing. And me, of course, based on my times back at the hotel.

Before being allowed on the track, all drivers had to prove to the officials that they could climb out of their cars in the requisite five seconds. Everyone managed to squeeze through, even Eddie Cheever, although the Arrows mechanics had to install a special, butterfly-shaped steering wheel to help their tall driver make good his escape. Once I was out on the track, the hour went by so quickly that I was sure they'd thrown the checker by mistake. As the ten cars that were still running pulled back into the pits for the good or bad news, the electricity in the air was enough to light up a small city. The Brabhams were in. No surprise there, with both drivers below 1:30. Foitek's EuroBrun and Larini's Osella also got below the 1:30 mark. That left three openings, and when the numbers on everyone's Longines-Olivetti video monitors became official, both Alberto and I had made it. We were both slower than Schneider's Zakspeed but we were in, with Alberto beating me by four-hundredths of a second. That was something I hadn't visualized.

And the losers? Well, those with garages had to pack up and vacate them immediately so they could be used by pre-qualified teams getting ready for the first official practice session, which began at ten. While Rory and the mechanics swarmed over the cars, Alberto and I had a joint debriefing session with Barry, Todd, and Maurice. Then he and I had to go and get weighed. Before the start of the season the weight of every driver, dressed in full gear, is recorded. This is done so officials can spot-check cars to make sure they conform to the minimum weight limit. Each season the drivers seem to get smaller and smaller as designers look for ways to improve aerodynamics and shave off weight. I'm sure a lot of them would be happy if drivers could be done away with entirely, replaced by a nice, uncomplaining, ten-pound black box. Luckily my 175 pounds wasn't the heaviest, that honor going to Gugelmin, who topped off the list at 176. Okay, it's only a pound. I can count. Alberto's weight of 160 probably accounted for his outqualifying me. At least that's what I told him.

When we got back to our newly acquired garage, Windsor and Vitale were there with a well-heeled-looking man whom they introduced simply as Mr. Parker Smith. Although no mention was made of it, I knew that he was about to become one of the most important men connected with the Vitale team: the sponsor's rep. When Windsor took me aside to inquire about Alcott, I told him that he had suffered a relapse of some sort, but one that was serious enough to preclude his having any visitors. I suggested he call Anne at the clinic for details. I was about to question him concerning the bonus Alcott had spoken of when the ten-minute warning was announced for the beginning of the ninety-minute untimed practice session. Time to go out and play with the big boys like Prost, Senna, Mansell, and the rest of the front runners. There would be thirty-one other drivers out there and some of them were going to be pretty damn quick. I went off to get strapped into the car so I'd have a few minutes to sit quietly and focus my thoughts on the job at hand before going out. There'd be time enough to talk to Windsor later.

That first practice session was a revelation. About half the cars were running under 1:30, and some, like Senna, Patrese, and Berger were in the 1:26s. Alberto had a terrible time with some sort of misfire caused by the electrics that defied all attempts at solving. As for me, I spent so much time looking in my mirrors to keep from blocking anyone that I actually lost time, ending the session three seconds slower than I'd driven in pre-qualifying. There was a ninety-minute break before the first qualifying session and I was going to have a serious talk with myself about how to drive it. I told the crew that the car was set up as well as I could get it and that the only problem was with the driver. I knew that with qualifying tires I'd pick up at least two seconds without doing anything different, but then so would everyone else. Alberto was so jumpy that Vitale finally had to take him off somewhere before he drove the mechanics crazy. They were working frantically in the hundred-degree heat installing a new wiring loom on his engine in hopes of curing the misfire, and didn't need any more distractions than already existed in the overcrowded paddock. After they left and Windsor took the money man off to lunch, I stripped down to my shorts and sat quietly inside the garage until it was time to do it again.

The word that comes to mind when I think of the first qualifying session is *disaster.* On my first flying lap the left-rear half shaft broke as I accelerated out of Norte. I guess if it had to happen, that was as good a place as any, since I was only going about a hundred mph. The car snapped around like a spinning top and came to rest well off the track. I ran halfway back to the pits before I remembered that we had no spare car here. It wasn't due in until late tomorrow and would only be available for the race itself. I knew better than to think I'd get any time in Alberto's car, as he'd already missed the morning session and needed all the stick time he could get. The one surprise of the session was Patrese in the Williams-Renault. He got in one demon lap on his qualifiers for a 1:26.172. Just thirty-three-hundredths quicker than Senna but good enough for bragging rights for the next twenty-four hours. At least Alberto wasn't the slowest. He wasn't quick enough to qualify, but tomorrow, as they say, would be another day. Damn good thing too.

By that time the temperature was well over the hundred mark and Vitale told everyone to knock off for a few hours until it got a little more bearable. Then he, Windsor, and Mr. Smith left, presumably to finalize their deal, saying they'd be back after dinner to see how things were getting on. Alberto went to the hospital to visit Esmandina and I headed to the hotel for a swim and a massage. As soon as I got there I called Anne to find out if everything was okay and to see if there might have been any change in her attitude toward me. No luck on that score but her father was feeling better and planned to come to the track for the race on Sunday. Both Windsor and Vitale had called to see how he was doing and she'd stalled them as we'd arranged, telling them she'd be at the track on Saturday to explain in person exactly what had happened to cause his relapse.

After an early dinner at the hotel, I went back to my room, ordered a pot of coffee from room service, and spent a relaxing hour with a cigar and an issue of *Blade* magazine that I'd been carrying around for a couple of weeks. By ten o'clock, without the aid of barnyard animals or imaginary hot laps, I was sound asleep.

The untimed session Saturday morning was mechanically uneventful, allowing me to concentrate on driving the car in traffic. Unlike the previous day when my main concern had been staying out of everyone's way, I began to pay some attention to the track in front of me. The fast cars were still fast but I was able to run with the cars I'd be dicing with during the race itself. If I made the race. I have to admit that my confidence was somewhat eroded by my performance on Friday. The final sixty-minute qualifying session would begin at one P.M., and based on Friday's times, I was going to have to get below 1:31 to make the race. When I pulled in at the end of the session, I saw Anne talking animatedly with Windsor. I hoped she was telling him all about our "unsuccessful attempt" to find the Rolls and my despicable behavior toward her father. I caught their attention and waved. Only Windsor returned my greeting. Way to go, Anne. I didn't see Vitale anywhere but I assumed he was still taking Mr. Smith around, showing him what he was getting for his money. I gathered from what Spikings had said that the deal was done and the announcement would be made as soon as Smith's boss arrived at the track later that day.

After Alberto and I completed our standard debriefing for the Vitale brain trusters we looked for a relatively quiet spot where we could talk privately. I say relatively quiet because there were probably fifty thousand Brazilian fans at the track, and when it comes to motor racing, the Cariocas rank second only to the *tifosi* in their enthusiasm. By the end of the weekend I would develop an extraordinary empathy for caged birds, monkeys, and other creatures who are constantly being stared at by millions of eyes. At least we do it by choice. We finally ended up in a hospitality motor home belonging to one of the local sponsors, where, in exchange for autographs and Polaroids with the guests, we got one of the tiny rooms for as long as needed. After some discussion of the practice session I got to the point.

"Alberto, you were quicker than me yesterday and now you're four seconds off your own pace. Something's gotta be screwing up your concentration.

Right?" He started to reply but I cut him off. "I'm not trying to pry into your business. I know you'd normally confide in Signor Vitale, but he's got his hands full on the sponsorship deal. So if you want to talk about it, try me. Okay?"

He didn't seem offended by my questions. In fact, he looked relieved. *"Sì.* Is from when I go to the hospital this morning."

"Is Esmandina worse?"

"No, not worse. Better. She is awake today. I was only permitted five minutes but she spoke to me. Peter, she tell me what happened."

"Jesus. What'd she say?"

"She say a man try to kill her. He come up behind her car and, bang, he hit her bumper once, twice, and that's all she remembers until today."

"You said 'he.' Did she recognize him?"

"It was the man from Gstaad."

For a second I drew a blank, then I remembered. She'd talked about seeing someone she recognized from Gstaad in the lobby of the Inter-Continental. "Did she say what he looked like?" He shook his head. "But she was sure it was the same man?" He nodded. "Did she say what kind of car he was driving?"

"I ask her that but she did not know. Was white, she say. A white car. Peter, this man, if he tried to kill her, I think maybe he had something to do with Signor DeStefano's death."

"Have you told anyone else about this?"

"Only her father. He tell me to say nothing to anybody. Not even Signor Vitale. He say if the man knows she remembers, he may try again to kill her."

"I hate to say it, but he's probably right. What about the police?"

"He say he will take care of it. I think he will also move her to another hospital if the doctors permit. Tell me, Peter, you think what we do is the right thing?"

"Yes. Esmandina's father is a very powerful man. I think he'll do whatever's necessary to protect her *and* to catch the man responsible. I know you're worried, but right now there's nothing more you can do for her. What you can do, for your own sake, is concentrate on putting your car into the race. We've got about half an hour before the session starts. I think you should stay here where it's quiet and get your head together. All right?"

"Yes, is all right. Thank you, Peter. You are a good friend."

"No need to thank me. I intend to outqualify you today and I don't want you to have an excuse for getting beat. *Ciao.*" I gave him a big smile and left. That should be a little extra incentive to get him out of his funk.

After working my way through the crowds jamming the paddock, I arrived at our garage to find it deserted and locked. I was about to head for the pit lane when Windsor, Vitale, Anne, and Mr. Smith came walking up. Three warm handshakes and a cold shoulder later, Windsor suggested the others go on ahead while he and I had a little talk. Anne must have done some job.

"Peter. What on earth transpired between you and Miss Alcott? I thought you two were something of an item and suddenly the mere mention of your name has her dripping with venom."

"Probably pretty much what she told you. I was trying to jog her father's memory about what happened during the cup rally and I guess it was too much for him. Believe me, if I'd had any idea he was going to react like that, I would never have done it."

"Of course you wouldn't have. That's the trouble with women. They're always overreacting to things. Something to do with hormones, no doubt. But tell me, dear boy, what did he do? She said he started yelling gibberish at you, then he passed out."

"It wasn't gibberish. It was his pace notes from the rally."

"Good God. You don't mean to say he remembered them after all these years?"

"No. That's just the point. He didn't. He tried to direct me completely off the first stage back toward São Paulo and when I wouldn't go that way he went nuts and tried to grab the wheel. We wrestled for it and almost crashed; that's when he blacked out." I could see the wheels turning in Windsor's brain, trying to determine how much I might know and how much he could say about whatever he knew. I decided to push things a bit. "Before it happened, he started telling me about some sort of bonus he was going to get when the rally was over. Something you'd promised him, I gather, and quite a large amount too."

"Why, yes, I had promised him a bonus, your father as well. Five hundred pounds, as I recall. Nothing extraordinary. Strange he should remember that of all things."

For the second day in a row our conversation was cut short by the blare of the loudspeakers announcing the imminent start of a session. I felt caught between two worlds, each vying for my attention. Windsor wanted to talk some more but I told him it would have to wait until qualifying was over, the urgencies of the present having again pushed 1970 aside. He didn't argue and I left him behind as I trotted off to the pits. I was already in my car when Alberto arrived. He gave me a big grin, then shot me the finger. I responded in kind. It looked like he'd rejoined the human race. I only hoped it would help him to qualify for the Brazilian one.

About forty minutes into the session the crew signaled me that I'd gotten down to my target time of 1:31, so I pulled in for my second, and last, set of qualifying rubber. The crew changed the tires, gave the car a quick check, and sent me back out. Just so I don't forget, let me state here and now that Formula One qualifying is flat scary. Aside from the opening lap of the race itself, the next three minutes would be the most dangerous I'd face during the entire race meeting. The sticky qualifying tires might increase your speed by two or three seconds a lap, but since they were only effective for two laps, it was necessary to take chances you'd never take under normal conditions. And while some drivers were letting it all hang out, others were out there tooling along like they were off to Grandmother's house for Sunday dinner.

Villenuve died during qualifying at Zolder, and if it could get him, no one was immune.

I was lucky on my first hot lap, with a clear line through almost every corner. The car felt perfect and I knew the second lap would be even quicker. Wrong. I was following one of the Brabhams—Brundle, I think. He was obviously going for a quick one when something went wrong as he came up on one of the Ligiers. The next thing I knew, the Brabham was spinning and the moment I hit the brakes any chance of improving my time went up in the wisps of blue smoke coming off my Pirellis. I headed straight to the pits to await my fate. From the looks on everyone's face when I pulled in, my first lap must have been okay. The second I came to a stop, Spikings placed the timing video monitor on the cockpit cowling so I could see for myself: 1:30.911. A quick count of those that were slower showed seven drivers, including Alberto, who had just gone out on his last set of qualifiers. The other drivers didn't just want to beat Alberto, they wanted to knock *me* out of the race. For years I'd watched the TV coverage of the last day of qualifying for the Indy 500. It was called the "Man on the Bubble." The driver with the slowest speed in the field had cameras and television sportscasters all over him as, one after another, cars went out to try to knock him out of the race by beating his qualifying time. Now I was less than half a second from becoming the bubble man, and I didn't like it one bit. As the session drew to a close, the final lap times flashed onto the tiny screen and I began to sweat the kind of sweat that has nothing to do with temperature.

If Alberto could top Alliot's 1:31.009 he was in. A look at the monitor showed just how high a mountain we had to climb. Senna had done it again, the World Champion picking up where he'd left off last year; on the pole with a 1:25.302. It didn't seem to matter if he had turbo power or wound up rubber bands, he somehow managed to end up on the front row of the grid. Alberto's first flier was a 1:31.501. Close, but no cigar. It seemed to take forever for him to come around again. Finally, he blew past the start/finish line just as the session ended, his time popping up on the tiny screen: 1:31.125. He hadn't made the field, but he was first alternate. Me? I was in. My first Grand Prix in nine years and I was in. Anyone standing in front of the car at that moment without sunglasses would have been blinded by my smile. For Alberto, it meant he would be left twisting in the wind until the light turned green on race day, hoping that some other poor soul would have a problem and be forced to withdraw. I really felt sorry for him but I was sure glad it wasn't me.

The official introduction of our new team sponsor was to take place that night in the main ballroom of the Inter-Continental. Spikings told Alberto and me to go back to the hotel and study all the information in the press kits that had been placed in our rooms. We were required to appear thirty minutes prior to the eight P.M. start of activities, in order to have official team photos taken. New drivers suits, bearing the appropriate logos, were already hanging in our closets. "I guess that about covers it," he said. "Any questions?"

"I don't mean to pry or anything, but do you think we might be told who the sponsor is? I know we only drive the cars but . . ."

"Bugger off. I thought you already knew. As of now, we're all officially toiling for Allied International Services, Ltd."

I started to ask the next obvious question, but Spikings cut me off. "Don't ask me what they do. I tried to get a straight answer from the boss, but it all sounded like something out of the *Financial Times*. Let's just say Allied moves piles of money around from one country to another and while they're being moved they get bigger or smaller. Lately, I gather, they've gotten huge. It's all in the press kit."

"Maybe is not important now," Alberto said almost sheepishly. "You say we have new driving suits with this Allied company name, but you don't say who pays us for the names on the suits?"

Way to go, Alberto. After all, our deal did give each of us the right to sell sponsorship space on our driving gear. Spikings produced one of his patented enigmatic smiles. "You'll find the paperwork covering helmet and suit signage with the rest of the stuff at the hotel. If I were a betting man, I'd wager you'll both be happy with what it says." He glanced at his watch. "Must run. Have to talk to the lads about the new paintwork. See you at seven-thirty."

After he left, Alberto and I looked at each other and shrugged. "I think we must go to the hotel," he said.

I agreed, and we did.

OVERSTEER

* * *

My new suit and helmet with the large A.I.S. logos looked almost as good as the personal sponsorship contract I found lying on the desk. One hundred thousand dollars was what it said. A hundred thousand big ones for extolling the virtues of Allied International Services whenever the occasion arose. Did I read the material about the company? You bet. Did I understand exactly what it was that they did after I had? Not really. Did it matter? Nope. On to the party.

If I had expected colored lights, samba bands, half-naked ladies, and gallons of champagne (which I had), I would have been disappointed (which I was). The champagne was there, as was the spare car, now neatly done up in A.I.S. livery, but other than that it was a pretty businesslike affair. There were short speeches by Windsor, Vitale, and Parker Smith, followed by a question-and-answer period for all of us. The absence of Allied's CEO, Howard Orloff, was commented on by a couple of the reporters present. According to Smith, pressing business in Switzerland had made Orloff's trip to Brazil impossible, but that he would certainly be at the next race in Imola.

By nine-thirty it was all over. In twelve hours we'd be taking the cars out onto the circuit for the first time in A.I.S. colors. I sure hoped the new paint was fast.

CHAPTER

24

When I arrived at the track early Sunday morning I was surprised to see the stands jammed with people. Eight hours in an open grandstand in Rio with forecasters predicting 106-degree heat? I was impressed. I was also impressed to see that all three of the race cars now sported the A.I.S. livery. Someone hadn't gotten much sleep after the press conference. On the other hand, they hadn't been rousted out of their rooms to go stand in the parking lot like the rest of us. Somebody, it seemed, had phoned and said there was a bomb planted in the hotel, so we were all evacuated while the police searched the place. I heard they'd found something, but no one would confirm it officially. Alberto, who was already there when I arrived, still wore the mournful expression he'd had the previous night; failing to qualify had further dampened his already flagging spirits. He was distracting himself by showing Esmandina's father some of the car's features.

"Alberto, Senhor Bracha, good morning. I heard the good news about Esmandina. Is there anything new this morning?"

Bracha looked around before answering quietly. "Yes, thank you. The doctors say she will have a full recovery, in time. We have not yet told anyone but yourself the truth of her condition. I think you know the reason for this?"

"Yes, Alberto told me she'd recognized the driver. You have any idea who it is?"

He shrugged and held up a Polaroid camera that was hanging from a strap around his neck. "We have moved her to a private hospital. I will take pictures of some people here today and bring them to her for identification."

"I don't suppose you'd care to say if you suspect someone?"

"I am afraid I cannot at this time."

"He won't even tell me," Alberto said, sounding exasperated.

"No, my young friend. You are too quick to anger, and until we are sure, it is better to remain calm. Senhor Hawthorn, Alberto has told how you accompanied him to pray for my daughter. Thank you. I am forever in your debt."

I started to protest that I hadn't really done much, but before I could open my mouth his attention shifted and he called out, "Ludovico, *bom dia.*"

Vitale and Smith had just entered, followed by Spikings, Todd, and Maurice. Bracha went over to greet them. "Your two drivers were kind enough to show me these magnificent machines."

As Vitale introduced Bracha to everyone, I took Alberto aside to discuss the 8:30 warm-up. That thirty-minute session would be our first real indication of how the cars would behave in the race itself. Up to that point, every minute we'd spent testing had been focused on getting enough speed out of the cars to make the starting field. Well, we'd done that, albeit with only one car, and that on the last row of the grid. Now I had to get out there and (I hoped) run flat out for nearly two hours in what was an almost totally different car. Different because we'd never had the time to do any serious testing with a full load of fuel, or run a full Grand Prix distance. The addition of over three hundred pounds of gasoline meant the car's behavior would be considerably different from what I'd experienced in qualifying. Also, the handling would be changing constantly as the fuel burned away and the abrasive surface of the track scrubbed the rubber off the tires. The Goodyear Tire people thought that it would be a two-stop race, but like some of the other Pirelli runners, I was planning only one. I'd start with a harder rubber compound, exchanging better grip for longer wear, then switch to softer, stickier tires about halfway through the race when the car had gotten lighter.

As first alternate, Alberto would also be driving in the warm-up. He'd be using the softer compound and half-full tanks for at least part of the session in order to gather more data for me. While he and I were talking I noticed that Bracha was taking pictures of everyone in front of the cars. I wondered what they'd think if they knew they were posing for mug shots.

At eight o'clock, Rory and his gang arrived from the pits, where they'd been setting things up in preparation for the session. As they moved the cars out of the garage, Bracha managed to get their pictures as well. In about an hour everyone would know if the quickest cars in qualifying would still be on top in race trim, and with luck, Bracha would have captured a killer's likeness on celluloid.

The car on full tanks was not as different as I'd feared. In fact, the extra weight had nearly eliminated the last vestiges of our understeer problem. My best time in the session was a 1:38.011, while Alberto clocked in with a 1:35 flat, which was good enough for sixteenth fastest. Even allowing for half tanks, it was a good showing and would, I hoped, restore some of his self-confidence. Prost was quickest at 1:32.274, with Senna next, then Patrese. The real surprise was Brundle. All the way up to fourth quickest, and like our cars, the Brabhams were on Pirellis. Some of the other favorites were not so lucky: Piquet had a fuel pump drive fail and never completed a lap, while both Ferraris had problems with their new electronic gearboxes, consigning Nigel Mansell to a lowly 2:10.117.

As we were changing out of our driver's suits after debriefing, Alberto told me that Senhor Bracha had left by helicopter for the hospital. If her doctors said it was all right, he planned to show his collection of snapshots to Esmandina, then fly back in time for the race. Talking about Esmandina made me think of Anne and I realized I hadn't seen her all morning. According to our plan, she was to bring her father to the track in time for the warm-up, after which the three of us would have a "discussion" with Windsor about the Cup Rally. By then, she already would have told her father about the discovery of the Rolls, making its revelation a shock only to Windsor. A shock strong enough, I hoped, to make him reveal something about the car's disappearance. A quick check with the team determined that no one had seen them arrive. Even more strange was that Windsor hadn't shown up at the track either. Vitale had told Spikings that Windsor would be late, but he hadn't elaborated any further. Hearing that made my stomach take a dive. Something was really wrong. I needed to find Vitale immediately. Spikings said he was playing host at the hospitality tent. Before he'd finished the sentence, I was off and running.

Vitale had just finished his introduction of Alberto when I burst into the tent. As the fifty or so guests of the sponsor applauded, I waved my hand, trying to get Vitale's attention. I got it all right, but he completely misunderstood my signal.

"Ladies and gentlemen. It gives me the greatest pleasure to introduce our American driver, Peter Hawthorn, who as you already know is making his return to Formula One with the Vitale team. Peter, come, please."

There was nothing I could do but smile, accept the handshakes and applause, and try to extricate myself as soon as I could without appearing rude. I stepped up onto the small wooden platform, and after clasping Vitale's hand, I embraced him in an enthusiastic, Italian-style bear hug. He seemed delighted by this, and as we pounded each other on the back, I whispered in his ear, "I need to speak to you privately. Now. It's urgent."

He pulled back, looked me in the eye, nodded, and grabbed the microphone. "My friends, you must excuse us for a moment while we discuss a technical matter. Alberto will be happy to answer whatever questions you may have concerning the team and the race."

He and I both smiled and nodded our way to the exit and stepped outside as Alberto began explaining the qualifying procedure to the guests. Vitale's smile immediately disappeared. "Peter, what has happened? Is something wrong with the car?"

"No. No. The car's fine. Maybe everything's fine. I don't know. That's why I had to talk to you." He seemed understandably confused. "Do you know where Windsor is?" I asked.

His expression changed and he looked as if he now knew exactly what I was talking about, which was more than I could say for myself.

"I'm sorry. Denis and I thought it best not to bring it up until after the race. A mistake perhaps, but the timing was not right. . . ."

"Wait a minute. Hold it. What're you talking about?"

"Signor Alcott." The way he said the name I knew what was coming. "Signor Alcott has died."

"When?" I asked, my mind racing. Christ. Another death. Poor Anne.

"Sometime last night, I think. Denis called before breakfast to say he was taking the car to drive Miss Alcott to the clinic. He said we should not say anything to you because you might not be able to concentrate for the race. Like Alberto in pre-qualifying? I am sure he will be back before the start if you wish to ask him about it."

Alcott was dead. Anne was at the clinic, probably with Windsor, whom I didn't really trust, and I was virtually helpless to do anything until after the race. Four more hours. A lot could happen in four hours, I thought, and I didn't like any of the possibilities that presented themselves. I just stood there, numb, staring at Vitale.

"Peter, please. Tell me what is wrong. I'm sorry we don't tell you but I thought it was best, really."

"No. You were right. It's quite a shock. I think I need to go back to the garage and get my head together . . . get focused on the race. Will you make my apologies to Mr. Smith and everyone inside?"

"Yes, of course. You do whatever you must to be ready for the race."

"Thanks." As soon as he was back inside the tent, I went looking for a telephone. After seeing the long lines at the few available pay phones, I went over to the press center. Naturally the macho guard wouldn't let me in. No press credentials. Telling him I was one of the drivers didn't cut it either. He'd heard that one before. He and I were just about to get into it when Innes Ireland arrived. He was covering the race for

Road & Track, and after the usual remarks about my resemblance to James, he whisked me inside. There were phones, all right, but they didn't do me much good since all the phone circuits out of the track were hopelessly overloaded. After thanking Innes, and promising him an exclusive interview if I ever became newsworthy, I headed back to our garage to get changed before the driver's meeting. Then I really would have to get my act together for the race, which was less than two hours away. I wished there was someone I could talk to about everything that was happening, but after what Esmandina had said, I didn't know who to trust other than Alberto, and he already had enough to think about. This was definitely not the way I'd planned to renew my Formula One career. Here it was, my first race, and I was allowing the real world to intrude on my concentration. Before long I'd be worrying about famine, or the greenhouse effect. Shit. It wasn't funny.

At noon, thirty minutes before the cars had to leave the pits to drive around the track and form up in their proper grid positions, I made my decision. I would withdraw from the race and get my ass out to the clinic as quickly as possible. The fact that Alberto was first alternate, thus allowing the team to remain in the race, helped me to rationalize my decision. I hoped Vitale would understand and not fire me on the spot, but I knew I could never live with myself if something happened to Anne just because I wanted to drive in a Grand Prix. After all, I was Mary's son too.

Once I'd made up my mind, I had to find Vitale

immediately so he could officially withdraw my entry and get Alberto onto the grid in my place. It was only when I began to look for him that I realized how crowded the pit area had become. It looked like an open casting call for *Life-styles of the Rich and Famous*. I finally pushed my way through the beautiful people to the back of the grid where I found the mechanics busily polishing the car to a mirror finish. Vitale, however, was nowhere in sight.

"Maurice, is Signor Vitale around?"

"Afraid not. He and Mr. Smith are off trying to sort out some problem with the pit credentials. Seems they won't let one of Smith's people in, if you can imagine such a thing with this mob larking about."

"Thanks. I'll be back in a minute." Or never, I thought.

I moved off to look for Vitale, trying not to let myself be slowed down by well-wishers wanting to shake my hand, get my autograph, or discuss the meaning of life. The loudspeakers had just begun sounding the second warning to clear the pits when someone called my name, then grabbed at my arm. I jerked away and kept moving. "Peter, stop." I turned to see Senhor Bracha standing there and, next to him, Anne. All at once I felt relief that she was safe, anger that I'd almost thrown my career away, and anxiety about the race I was no longer mentally prepared for.

"Anne, are you all right? I tried to call you but I couldn't get through."

She nodded, but her attempt at a smile said she wasn't.

"Was it another stroke?"

"The doctor said he died in his sleep, but I think he was murdered."

I knew she was right. I'd felt it from the moment Vitale told me.

I also knew from the tone of her voice who she held responsible. The loudspeakers began bleating again, but this time they were talking to me. It was time to get in the car.

"Senhor Bracha, did Esmandina look at the pictures?"

"Unfortunately, no. The move to the clinic last night was very tiring for her and the doctors would not permit anything stressful at this time. Tonight, perhaps, after she has had more time to rest."

"You said 'the clinic.' You don't mean the same one that Anne's father . . ."

"That's right," Anne said. "I couldn't believe it when we ran into each other out there. That's how I got here, in Senhor Bracha's helicopter."

"Peter, for God's sake, are you trying to give me a heart attack?" It was Spikings and he looked distinctly perturbed. "It's five minutes to start engines, if that's of any interest. I'm sure your friends will excuse you. Yes?"

"Sure. Sorry. Anne, Senhor Bracha, don't go away. I need to talk to both of you after the race. Did Mr. Windsor fly back with you as well?"

"Windsor?" she replied. "He said he was coming over here hours ago. Eight, eight-thirty this morning."

Now it was Spikings who grabbed hold of my arm, and hard. "Peter, let's get to the grid. Now."

The run back to the car took less than a minute

now that the walls of tanned flesh had disappeared. I'd just about gotten belted in when the signal was given, and with an incredible roar from the engines and the crowd, the field came to life.

At least I hadn't had time to become nervous about the start of the race. As the cars ahead of me began to move out, I selected first gear and set off on the two-pace laps that precede the start of every Grand Prix. Before I'd gotten halfway through lap one, I knew I was in trouble. The clutch had begun to slip and I had less than sixty seconds to decide what to do about it. Suddenly I found the time to be nervous. I knew I could race competitively without a clutch—any professional could do that. The problem would come when I stopped for tires. If the clutch was working at all, I could probably baby it enough to get out of the pits, but if it was completely shot, I'd have to do the entire race on the tires that were already on the car. Considering the forces that would be placed on the clutch at the start, when the car would be accelerating from a standstill to well over a hundred in less than four seconds, I decided it wasn't worth the risk. I'd have to pull into the pits immediately and switch to the backup car. It meant I'd be forced to start the race from the pit exit after all the other cars had gotten away, but since I was on the last row of the grid anyway, I figured it wouldn't matter much. (Ha!)

As soon as I could I got on the radio and told Spikings what had happened, and by the time I got there the spare was ready to go. The transfer accomplished, I drove to the pit exit and came to a stop beside Alberto, who was still hoping for some miracle that would allow him to start. I was using hand gestures to try to explain what had happened when I heard a gigantic shock wave of sound as the light turned green. Twenty-five accelerators jammed to the floor, unleashing eighteen thousand raging horses, all stampeding toward the right-hander at the end of the pit straight. I brought the revs up, put it in first, and waited for the official standing by the front of the car to wave me off. The car began to creep forward and I started screaming at the guy to turn me loose. I knew he couldn't hear a thing over the howling of the engines, but it made me feel better. Then, just as I was sure I'd lose the clutch out of that car, he waved me out.

After one of my better standing starts, I rocketed out onto the track, where I could just see the tail end of the pack heading into turn one. There was already a yellow flag out and I could see bits of bodywork scattered around, but no immediate sign of the cars involved. A few seconds later I saw one of the Minardis off at the side of the track and, a little farther on, Berger's Ferrari, which was also stationary. At least I knew I wouldn't finish last. Two down, twenty-three to go.

For the first couple of laps I was really driving badly, trying too hard to catch up with the field and falling farther behind as a result. In fact, I scared myself pretty good a couple of times, nearly losing control after bouncing over the curbing. That forced me to have a talk with myself and within two more laps I had begun to settle down and get into a rhythm, my lap times becoming more consistent as my concentration improved.

As I passed the pits on lap twelve I saw two bits of good news hung out on my signaling board. I'd just turned a 1:39 flat and I was up to nineteenth position. Mind you, I hadn't passed anybody. Hell, I hadn't even seen anybody. But everyone knew the attrition rate was going to be high, given the heat and the fact that it was the first race of the season. The car was handling all right and obviously I wasn't having any problems with traffic. In truth, it seemed more like a practice session than a race. Over the next five laps I managed to shave another half second off my time and, finally, began to move up on the other tailenders.

I got my first view of the McLarens in my mirrors as one came up behind me. It was Senna, and he went by so effortlessly I might as well have been in reverse. But even Senna couldn't have come around to lap me that quickly. He must have been in the pits with some sort of problem. God, I might actually have been ahead of him. Something to tell the grandchildren.

From lap twenty to my scheduled stop on lap twenty-nine I picked up a couple more spots. I finally discovered who was leading when Mansell, Prost, and Gugelmin all lapped me, the Ferrari showering me with sparks as the skid plate bottomed on the rough track. Mansell was certainly a surprise. Up to then he'd never managed more than eight laps in the car before having some sort of problem, and there he was, in the lead.

By lap twenty-nine, my tires, particularly the right

front, had just about lost all their grip and that last lap before I pitted was like driving on glare ice. I knew the crew was ready. We'd practiced the routine a hundred times. I just hoped no one, especially me, would do something stupid to screw it up. I know it doesn't seem like much, driving in and stopping for a few seconds while some guys change your tires. But when you've been running at 180 mph for a while your perspective changes. The cars may be whizzing past the grandstands in a blur, but on the track there is no real sensation of speed because everyone around you is going just as fast as you are. Then, all of a sudden, you have to drive down a narrow road, absolutely jammed with people, come to a stop with your tires on two small bits of tape stuck to the ground, keep the engine running and the rear wheels from spinning while sixteen men go crazy yanking the car up off the ground, changing tires, dropping it back onto the pavement, and trying not to get run over as you light up the tires in your hurry to get back into the race. We did it in eleven seconds. I didn't plan to stop again until the checker dropped.

The race had just reached the halfway mark. Mansell's Ferrari was still in front and I, in my own unobtrusive way, had moved up to seventeenth. On a track as large as Rio with only seventeen cars running, it's possible to go for long stretches of time without doing any real racing at all. So it was a happy surprise when I discovered I'd rejoined the action sandwiched between Schneider's Zakspeed and Alliot's Lola.

I managed to get a good run on Alliot entering the long back straight, sticking my nose right up under his rear wing, waiting for just the right moment to flick the car out of his slipstream and motor past before we hit the braking zone for Sul. The plan was sound but it didn't take into account the speed he was getting out of the twelve-cylinder Lamborghini engine. I could stay with him but I couldn't make the pass. While this was going on, Schneider moved up on my tail, and when I had to back off as Alliot braked earlier than I expected going into Pace, the Zakspeed got us both. I managed to make my move between Suspiro and Nonato, but by then Schneider had begun to pull away. During the next two laps I began to close the gap, keeping an eye on my mirrors for the Lola, which was trying to move back up on me. On lap thirty-seven, Cheever's Arrows passed me going into Norte and I followed him down the back straight as he moved up behind the Zakspeed.

Cheever made his move as they entered the braking zone for Sul when something happened to Schneider's front suspension, causing the car to slew sideways. Cheever, with nowhere to go, clouted him and sent both cars spinning off into the sand trap. As suddenly as that I was fifteenth. At that point my luck began to run out along with the oil in the gearbox. I wasn't sure exactly what was wrong but I knew it was serious when, a few laps later, I lost third, then fourth gear. Alliot was by in a flash as I tried to baby the transmission in the hope that it would last the remaining fifteen laps. On lap fifty-one, second gear went south. Patrese's engine let go on the same lap, ending a great debut for the Williams-Renault. Rio was his 177th Grand Prix, breaking Graham Hill's long-standing record. All that and he's only a year older than I am. Oh well, now I was fourteenth. I went past one of the Ligiers, which was smoking badly. Then Mansell came by again, still in the lead. I kept watch in my mirrors and pretty soon Prost came through with Gugelmin right up his exhaust. I could actually hear the Brazilians in the stands going bonkers as they urged Gugelmin to pass the Frenchman.

Now I was four laps down with less than ten to go, and I was just about out of gears. I don't think I drew another breath until it was over. By then I was barely crawling around, driving well off the racing line with one hand in the air to warn the other drivers. The gearbox gave up the ghost as I came into the last corner, so I turned off and coasted into the pit lane, waving my arms until somebody started pushing the car to get me out of the way. Rory and the mechanics came running toward me and in a minute I was gliding along toward the Vitale pit at a pretty fair clip. I could see the mechanics in the mirrors as they pushed the car along. They looked like they'd just won the lottery. The Brazilian Grand Prix was history and the DV-1 had hung in there. I was sure we hadn't completed enough laps to be officially classified, but we'd ended up ahead of a lot of other cars *and* almost cracked the top 50 percent of the field. Even though we hadn't done a lot of actual racing, we were around at the finish and I knew from the smiles in our pit that the results had given the team a real lift.

I popped the belts, removed the steering wheel, took off my helmet and balaclava, and tried to get out of the car. I couldn't do it. I had just enough energy left to crack an enormous smile as Rory and Alberto lifted me out of the cockpit and sat me down in a folding chair under an umbrella held by Signor Vitale. I knew everyone was talking to me, but even after taking out my earplugs, I couldn't hear anything but the high-pitched scream of the engine. I drank some water while Spikings poured another bottle over my head and down my back. Then he helped me to peel off the top half of my soggy suit and long-sleeved turtleneck Nomex undershirt. Rory held up the digital tire temperature gauge in front of me, then knelt down and touched the probe to the concrete: 142 degrees. He looked at my face and burst out laughing. Mechanics are very humorous people.

After I'd sat there for ten or fifteen minutes I began to feel human again. I heard "God Save the Queen" playing over the loudspeakers, which meant that Mansell had hung on to take the victory. It also meant that my ears were beginning to function as something other than a place to hang sunglasses.

"Was it Prost and Gugelmin after Mansell?" I asked Alberto.

"*Sì*, with Herbert just behind, then Warwick and Nannini. Was a good race. And you, Peter, you finish fourteen. Is very good. Everyone is very happy."

The moment the rest of the team realized I was functioning again they crowded around, offering congratulations, shaking my hand, slapping me on the back. Anyone would have thought I'd won the race. And it was a victory of sorts. We'd survived pre-qualifying, qualifying, and fifty-six laps of a Grand Prix with a brand-new car and a slightly used driver. Not too shabby. Vitale, who had been watching over me like a mother hen, leaned down and whispered into my ear. "Peter. You think you are okay now to walk into the garage? There is something we must discuss."

The way he said it brought back all the thoughts I'd stopped thinking once the race had started. "Is it about Windsor?"

He shook his head. "Is about the other car. Your car. When Rory push it back into the garage, the wing was loose and when he check it he find out is sabotaged. If you did not change cars, you would certainly have had a big accident."

I stood slowly, my legs still rubbery, my ribs yelling unprintable things at me, and followed Vitale toward the garage. The whole pit and paddock area was fast becoming a madhouse, with crazed Cariocas swarming over everything, grabbing anything that wasn't tied down and lots of stuff that was. I even saw a kid in the crowd carrying a nose cone from one of the Lotus cars. Another fan, who looked totally spaced, was running along, wearing an open-faced crash helmet and holding a steering wheel out in front of him, going "Vroom, vroom, vroom." I pointed him out to Vitale, and as we laughed, I caught a glimpse of a face that seemed familiar. It disappeared for a moment behind a waving Brazilian flag, then there he was again. Bald. Dark sunglasses. The man in the white Range Rover.

CHAPTER

25

Mr. B. Dutton, if that was indeed his name, was only about fifty feet away, but before I'd covered even ten of them, he spotted me and took off, dodging into the enormous crowd. I knew I was too exhausted to run him down, so I yelled the first thing that came to mind as I stumbled after him. "Stop, thief. Help. Stop that man." People did turn to look at one or both of us but no one made any effort to stop him. I guess most of them didn't even understand what I was saying.

Then I heard Alberto call out from behind me. "Peter, what's wrong?" He ran up beside me, scanning the crowd. "Who are you after?"

"Bald guy, wearing a blue shirt and dark glasses. There he goes, over there. I think he's the guy that tried to kill Esmandina."

That did it. Alberto took off like a top-fuel dragster, screaming at the top of his lungs, the crowd parting in front of him like the Red Sea for Charlton Heston. By that point I could barely walk, the pain in my ribs making it difficult even to catch my breath. Then Vitale caught up with me and I leaned on him for support as I gasped out an explanation of what was going on. We continued on until we saw a big group of people jammed together, their backs to us, cheering and waving their fists in the air. I knew that Alberto had gotten his man. Once Vitale and I had elbowed our way through, we saw Alberto and Dutton rolling around on the ground, hitting each other. Dutton, who seemed to be giving a good account of himself considering his younger, highly motivated opponent, was hollering for the police. Odd, I thought, for a crook to want the police. Then, when he saw me, he called out in perfect English, "Hawthorn, for God's sake, call off your friend before someone gets hurt."

Things definitely weren't adding up the way I'd figured. "Alberto, okay, stop. We've got him." I don't know if he heard me or not but he obviously had no intention of stopping. Vitale stepped in where Alberto could see him. He yelled something in Italian that did the trick. Alberto got up warily, never taking his eyes off Dutton for a moment. Vitale gave Dutton a hand up and there we stood, surrounded by curious Cariocas, staring at each other until Dutton broke the silence.

"Before things get any further out of hand, I wonder if we might go somewhere a bit more private," he said, indicating the onlookers.

"Well," I replied. "You were just calling for the police, why don't we go see them? Their office is over there somewhere."

"If you insist, but I'd just as soon we didn't get them involved just yet."

Alberto, who had been taking this in without quite comprehending why we all were acting so civil, suddenly lashed out and gave Dutton a shove that nearly knocked him over. "Come, we will go to the police and you will tell them why you try to kill Esmandina."

After Dutton regained his balance, he reached into his pants pocket, pulled out a small folding wallet, and opened it. "Sorry to disappoint you chaps, but as you can see, I *am* the police."

I reached out to take the wallet but Alberto angrily ripped it out of his hand. After staring at it for a moment I watched his expression change from total rage to confusion. He looked bewildered as he put it into my hand. "Peter, you say he was the one who attack Esmandina?"

I nodded as I checked out the picture ID and badge. It seems I'd just had Alberto beat up on CID Inspector Bernard Thomas Dutton of New Scotland Yard. Terrific. I handed the ID to Vitale.

"It's quite legitimate, I can assure you," Dutton said. "If you still have any doubts after our talk, I'll be glad to accompany you to the local police or, better yet, the British embassy. Fair enough?"

Vitale seemed satisfied that his credentials were genuine. *"Scusi.* My young friend here really did think you were someone else."

"That was my fault," I said without explanation.

"Look, Inspector, you're right about us not talking here. We don't know who's standing around listening to everything we say."

"I'll say." He looked intently at the dwindling group of onlookers still standing around us. "Ever heard of Ronnie Biggs? No? Remember the great train robbery back in the sixties? They made a movie about it? Right. Well, Biggs was one of the gang. He escaped from prison and now he lives here in Rio. Married some local girl and had a kid, so he can't be extradited. I'm sure I just saw him, brazen as life, strutting around like he owned the place. Forgot all about you lot for a minute, or you'd never've spotted me." Dutton, it seemed, was as worked up about this Biggs character as Alberto was about him.

Vitale looked at his watch, then made a suggestion. "In fifteen minutes everyone on the team must be at the hospitality tent. We can go to our garage and talk there."

"Perhaps," Dutton said. "But, uh, this is a bit awkward, I'm afraid. Will Mr. Windsor be there?"

Vitale responded angrily. "No. Denis is not here at all. The first Grand Prix for the Vitale team, and he is not here."

Dutton seemed quite surprised by the news. "You mean he never came to the track today at all?"

"*Sì.* He and I shall have strong words about this, I can assure you."

Dutton really looked agitated. "All right, in that case, to your garage, and quickly, please. We may have more to talk about than I'd thought."

When we got to the garage we found Anne and

Senhor Bracha waiting for us along with the rest of the team. The three race cars were inside, with my primary car back against the far wall, covered with a tarp. Rory was seated on one of the rear wheels, guzzling a huge can of Foster's, apparently guarding whatever evidence there was of the sabotage to the rear wing. Vitale took Spikings aside, and after a few words, they began shepherding people out. Rory got up to leave but I signaled him to stay put, figuring the attempt to make me crash would have some bearing on what we'd be discussing. As soon as the seven of us were alone, I pulled down the security gates, locking us away from the throngs of people still milling around the paddock, and quickly introduced Dutton to Anne, Bracha, and Rory.

"Before I go into any details of my purpose here," he said, "I should like to know if any of you has any idea of the whereabouts of Denis Windsor?" Receiving no response, he continued. "At approximately eight-thirty this morning, I observed Mr. Windsor leaving the Santo Antonio Clinic, driving a yellow Fiesta. Unfortunately, due to the traffic congestion caused by the race, I lost sight of him shortly after that. My assumption, which I now realize was erroneous, was that he was on his way here."

"That's where he told me he was going," Anne said. "He'd driven me out to the clinic to help with the arrangements concerning my father—" She stopped there, her composure beginning to slip.

"That's all right, Miss Alcott. Mr. Hawthorn told me about your father and—"

"Did he tell you that he was murdered?" she demanded, in control again.

"That's a very serious charge," Dutton replied. "Do you have any proof?"

Before she could answer, Bracha spoke up. "I have notified the authorities on Miss Alcott's behalf, and the circumstances surrounding the death of her father are being investigated. Perhaps you are aware that an attempt was recently made on my daughter's life?"

"Yes, and we'll return to that in a moment. But first, Mr. Hawthorn, I'm going to ask you a question, and if the answer is what I expect it to be, it may explain much of what has been going on here."

"Ask away."

"Have you recently discovered the whereabouts of the Rolls-Royce driven by your father, James, in the 1970 World Cup Rally?"

"Yes. I found the car on Thursday afternoon." That certainly got everyone's attention. Dutton seemed to be thinking over very carefully what to say next.

"Have you told anyone?"

"Only Anne Alcott. She and her father were with me at the time. It's complicated, but Mr. Alcott was only semiconscious and I'm pretty sure he didn't know I'd actually found the car. Isn't that right, Anne?"

"I think he may have suspected it, but that was all. And before you ask, no, I haven't mentioned it to anyone else."

"Could anyone have found out in any other way?

Was anything on paper? Is it indicated on a map? Anything like that?"

"There is a map, yes. It's back at the hotel. It doesn't have the exact location, but it'll get you pretty close."

"Could Windsor have gotten hold of it, or seen it, even for a moment?"

"I don't see how, unless he broke into my room, and quite honestly, I can't picture him doing that sort of thing."

"A man will do a great many things for forty million pounds, Mr. Hawthorn." If he was looking for a reaction, he got one. We all stood there, looking collectively stupid, until Rory spoke up.

"Maybe he's right, Pete. Windsor was out here last night. I'd just sent the lads off to bed, in fact. He said he had some things to do an' that he'd lock up when he was done, so I left."

"Just what are you getting at, Mr. Hite?" Dutton wanted to know.

"I'm not sure, but somebody sabotaged Pete's car here, an' it was only dumb luck kept him from having a helluva shunt."

Vitale, who had been quietly taking this all in, spoke up. "Moment. Wait. Denis Windsor is my partner, not some Mafia gangster. And what is this forty million pounds you are talking about?"

"Sehnor Vitale is entirely correct, Inspector. Before we give any more information, I, too, would like an explanation of these things." Bracha looked around and we all nodded our support.

"Yeah, and I'd like to know why you bugged our

jeep. What the hell does my looking for my father have to do with Scotland Yard?"

Dutton thought about it for a moment before replying. "All right. But I must warn you that whatever information I pass on is not to be divulged to anyone without my permission. Is that understood?" Assured that he had our agreement, he continued. "I have reason to believe that certain contraband valued at somewhere between thirty and forty million pounds is hidden in the Rolls-Royce Mr. Hawthorn discovered last Thursday. Furthermore, I believe it was hidden there by Denis Windsor with the full knowledge of the driver, James Hawthorn, and co-driver, Trevor Alcott. I ask you now, do any of you have any knowledge of this?"

As we looked at one another, things began to come together in my brain, like one of those connect-the-dot picture puzzles. Rory took the last swig of his beer, tossed the can into an empty oil drum with a clang that made everyone jump, and said, "What is it then, drugs in the rocker panels like that car in the *French Connection* movie?"

Before Dutton could answer, Anne exploded, her anger giving her a fierceness I hadn't seen before. "Stop it. All of you. That's my father you're talking about. He died last night because of all this and I won't have you accusing him of being a drug dealer." Her face was bright red and her hands were balled into tight fists. When I made a move to comfort her, she stopped me in my tracks with a withering look.

"Please calm yourself, Miss Alcott. No one is accusing your father, or anyone else, of dealing in narcotics. Now, Mr. Hite, in answer to your question, it's not drugs I'm looking for, it's Degas."

"You mean the painter?" said Bracha, sounding as surprised as I felt.

"That's correct. A number of Impressionist paintings were stolen from Mr. Windsor's estate in early 1970. It was one of a series of burglaries I was investigating for the Fine Art, Antique, and Philatelic Squad, as it was called then. In fact it was my first big case. It took us five years but we managed to recover most of the stolen works and even put some of the gang away for a bit. Thing is, they all claimed to a man that they had nothing to do with Windsor's collection, and I believed them. I think he saw an easy way to pick up some tax-free money and he took it. He'd steal his own paintings, collect the insurance, then smuggle them out of the country and sell them to some rich collectors who could be counted on not to ask any embarrassing questions."

"And you think he was bringing them here?" I asked. Dutton nodded. "But why Brazil? Why not one of the other countries the rally passed through?"

"I'm afraid I don't know the answer to that yet. But I do know that one of the stolen paintings surfaced last year in Cali, Colombia."

As soon as he said it, I knew he was right. "That's where the Rolls Windsor was driving broke down," I said. Everything fit. The wrong dates in the letter weren't wrong and neither was the strange route they'd taken away from the rally. They were on their way to deliver the paintings to someone when they crashed.

"Correct, Mr. Hawthorn. When I heard about it I was reminded of the theft of seven Renaissance masters from the Budapest Museum of Fine Arts in 1983. The criminals placed the paintings in a hidden compartment in a Fiat, drove to Athens, and sold them to a well-known Greek industrialist. Then, when I saw in the paper that Windsor and James Hawthorn's son were coming to Brazil, together, it seemed more than a coincidence. My apologies, but that's the reason I felt it necessary to track your movements electronically."

"But what good does it do to buy a famous painting if everyone knows it's been stolen?" Anne asked him. "You can't resell it. You can't even show it to anybody."

It was not Dutton but Bracha who answered. "Miss Alcott, imagine having the *Mona Lisa* to look upon whenever you chose to. The possession of such beauty would make an exquisite secret."

"I'm afraid he's right, miss. There are a lot of collectors, very wealthy and highly respected I might add, who have two collections. One that's known to the world and another known only to themselves. That's one of the reasons why art theft is the second-biggest criminal activity in the world, after narcotics."

"*Scusi, l'ispettóre.* If what you say is true, how could Denis hope to gain from these stolen paintings? You say, thirty, forty million pounds. It does not seem possible."

"Signor Vitale has a point," I said. "The paintings are worth that much only on the open market. How could he expect to sell them for that if everyone knows they're stolen?"

Dutton smiled. "Because they're his paintings. If they're recovered, he can do whatever he likes with them. Van Gogh's *Irises* fetched 53.9 million four years ago, if that makes all this easier to understand."

"What about the insurance company?" Anne said. "Weren't they defrauded when they paid the claim?"

"Certainly, but that was in 1970. The statute of limitations ran out long ago. As a matter of fact, the statute of limitations has run out on the burglary as well."

"If that is so, then how do you expect to stop Senhor Windsor from doing just as he wishes?"

Bracha had a point, but there was another aspect to the case that he wasn't aware of. "Because there is no statute of limitations on murder."

I could tell that Vitale was shocked by my suggestion that his partner might somehow be implicated in a murder, but before he could say anything, Spikings called out to him from outside the locked gates. "Signor Vitale? Can I see you for a minute?" Vitale excused himself, with some relief, I'm sure.

"Well," Anne said. "Is it true, what Peter said? Is Windsor a murderer?"

Dutton answered without hesitation. "All I can say at this moment is that Mr. Windsor has not been charged with any crime. Mr. Hawthorn, how long would it take to drive to the spot where the Rolls is located?"

"About six and a half hours, I guess. But not today, if that's what you're thinking. Traffic around here will be totally screwed up for hours. You think that's where Windsor went, don't you?" Dutton nodded.

"Where is the location of the car?" Bracha asked.

"It's between São Paulo and Ventania. I'd have to show you on a map."

"If we leave now, my helicopter can have us at Santos Dumont Airport in ten minutes. From there it is only a forty-five-minute flight to São Paulo."

"I don't know," I said. "But I'd be willing to bet that all the flights to São Paulo are jammed with people going home from the race."

"That is undoubtedly correct," Bracha said with a smile. "But they will not be flying in my plane."

When Dutton heard that, he actually smiled for the first time since I'd laid eyes on him. I glanced over at the gate and saw that Spikings was now talking animatedly with Alberto while Vitale had gone over to talk with Rory.

"Senhor Bracha?" Anne said. "How many people will fit in this airplane of yours?"

"The helicopter will carry seven, including the pilot, and the Lear will hold ten."

"I don't know about anybody else," she said. "But I certainly intend to come along."

I could see that Dutton didn't much care for the idea, while Bracha simply looked amused. Vitale, who had also been listening to the exchange, spoke up. "Regretfully, neither Alberto nor myself will be able to join with you. This is a very, uh, embarrassing situation for the team. If what you say about Denis is true, I must go and prepare the people from Allied International for the bad news. Inspector, you have my word that neither Alberto nor I will say anything of this to anyone." He stepped over, put his arm around my shoulder, and turned me away from the others. "Peter. I know you must do this thing. All I ask is that you do whatever is possible to protect the team. Yes?"

"Of course, and thanks for understanding."

"Is no problem. I will tell everyone that you have damaged again your ribs and is too painful for you to join us. *Ciao,* and good luck . . . Come, Alberto, we have work to do."

Well, he seemed to have it covered. He could even pass a lie detector test with that story about the way my ribs felt. I'd assumed Rory would be going with them but he was still sitting there, working his way through another Foster's.

"Rory. You don't have to stick around anymore if you don't want to."

" 'S all right, Pete. I'd better come along. If you lot have to dismantle a Rolls-Royce by yourselves, you'll be out in the jungle for a week."

"Senhor Hite is correct. We may well have need of his skills. I think if we are going we should be on our way. There are already less than four hours of daylight remaining."

"Right then, Mr. Bracha," Dutton said. "We'll follow you."

CHAPTER

26

The trip from the circuit to São Paulo was as quick and effortless as a few million dollars could make it. The Bell LongRanger helicopter was only a short walk from our garage, and by the time we were all buckled in, the pilot was ready to go.

As soon as we lifted off we began to see the thousands upon thousands of cars that were clogging every road leading away from the circuit, their angry horns audible even over the roar of the aircraft's Allison turbine. The pilot had radioed ahead, and by the time we touched down next to it, Bracha's gleaming new Lear 55 was cleared for takeoff and ready to roll. Once again we seemed to be airborne the second our bottoms touched the seats.

The first ten minutes of the flight were spent going almost straight up, the plane climbing at five thousand feet a minute until we reached our cruising altitude of forty-one thousand. Reminded me of the banking at Daytona. I don't think Dutton enjoyed it much. By the time we'd leveled off, he looked greener than the rain forest. I knew Anne wasn't crazy about flying either and wondered how she was taking it, but since she'd deliberately seated herself all the way in the tail I figured it was best to leave her alone.

The interior was small, somewhat cramped but elegant, with coffee, soda, and a fully stocked bar available. Bracha was the perfect host, making sure we all had whatever we wanted before going up to talk to his pilot. A beer can popped as Rory picked up where he'd left off back at the garage. I took a sip of coffee and leaned over to Dutton. "Inspector, can you tell me if the deaths of Paolo DeStefano and David Livesey are a part of your investigation?"

"Yes, we're making inquiries into both of those cases. But that's all I can say right now."

"Okay. Good. But to the best of my knowledge, Windsor has airtight alibis for both of those incidents." I waited, but he didn't offer any comment. "Well, if that was true, and he was involved, then it stands to reason he must have had at least one accomplice. Right?"

While I was talking, Bracha returned and sat down opposite us. "Are you by any chance discussing the attempt to kill Esmandina?"

I shook my head, but before I could explain anything, Dutton wanted to know more about her accident. "I know the basic facts, Mr. Bracha, but is there any, more recent information?"

"You know of course that we have moved her to the Santo Antonio Clinic?" Dutton nodded. Bracha went on to explain that Esmandina had recognized the man who hit her car as the one she'd seen in Gstaad and at the Inter-Continental. He described the Polaroids he'd taken at the track, and how he'd left the pictures at the clinic for her to identify as soon as her doctors would permit it.

"Let's talk about what we're going to do once we get to São Paulo," I said.

"My pilot, Gustavo, is arranging to have two cars waiting for us at the airport. I had planned to charter another helicopter but unfortunately, as you will soon see, the weather at São Paulo is not so good, with rain and high winds. Still we should be able to get to the Rolls before dark."

He was right about the weather. The trip back down was really bumpy, with the kind of sudden drops that try to relocate your stomach somewhere up between your ears. Bracha had gone forward again, leaving the rest of us sitting there trying to act unconcerned. The pilot made a perfect landing and I applauded silently as we taxied to a stop near one of the hangars, then waited in the plane while Rory and the pilot went to check on the cars. I was dying for a cigar but since I'd had no time to get changed out of my driving gear I didn't have any with me. I asked Bracha if there were any on board. He smiled, opened a small cabinet next to the bar, and produced a box of Monte Cristo coronas. He scooped out a handful and dumped them into a large Haliburton attaché case. The pilot reappeared to announce that the cars were waiting on the opposite side of the hangar.

* * *

The rain was coming down pretty hard as we began to go over the maps that had come with the cars. They weren't very detailed, but were good enough to get us to the spot where the prime had started. We decided that Rory and I would do the driving and that Anne and I would go in different cars, in case we all got separated along the way. Dutton decided to go with them in order to avoid being asphyxiated by the cigars Bracha and I had already lit up.

About forty minutes outside São Paulo we hit fog. It was patchy ground fog but pretty thick in spots. That, coupled with the fact that there was quite a bit of Easter Sunday traffic, made it a little hairy to maintain a decent speed. We left the highway at Itapeva and for the next fifteen or twenty miles were stuck in a convoy of slow-moving locals who apparently were going to, or coming from, some sort of festival, given the costumes they were wearing.

During the drive I filled Bracha in on everything I knew about my father, Windsor, and the Cup Rally, in the hope that it might somehow help to identify Esmandina's assailant.

"Well, is difficult, you see, because of the concussion and the medication. Her account of what she remembers seems sometimes confused."

"What exactly did she say?"

"Exactly? It's hard to be sure. It sounded like, 'man with beard gone at hotel.' It was impossible to say more because the doctors want her to sleep. I think she meant that the man checked out of the hotel."

"Wait a minute. Nobody ever mentioned anything about his having a beard."

"No. I thought it best to keep some information to myself."

I thought back to when he'd been taking the Polaroids, remembering how he'd taken a couple of pictures of Maurice. "Is that how you decided who to take pictures of?"

"Yes. There was only so much time available, so I went through the pits, shooting everyone with a beard whose team was staying at the Inter-Continental."

"I sure hope it works. When are you supposed to check with the clinic to see if she's seen the pictures?"

"I told them I will call around six."

"Six? Christ, I hope we can find a phone."

That seemed to amuse him. He turned around, got his case out of the back, opened it, and produced— what else?—a telephone. I started to laugh, but Bracha's expression suddenly changed, cutting it short. He turned around again and said, "The other car is gone."

I slowed to a crawl and looked for a place to pull off and stop. "They were there when we got mixed in with the bunch of cars that turned off about a mile back," I said, trying to remember just what I'd seen in my mirror. "If they made a mistake and went that way, they'll probably turn around and look for us."

Bracha was looking intently at the map. "Perhaps you are right, but if they did turn off there, it is possible for them to continue on and rejoin this road

301

about ten miles ahead. It is my opinion that we stick to the plan and continue on as quickly as possible."

"Yeah, you're probably right." I got on the gas and in a moment we were back up to speed. If they'd spotted the same thing on the map that Bracha had, we might still be able to hook up with them a little later. But we were only an hour away from the Rolls, and since that was about all the daylight that was left, we couldn't afford to lose any more time.

When we came to the intersection where we'd hoped to meet the others, they were nowhere in sight. We continued on and soon began to encounter more local traffic, this time going in the opposite direction. Cars that were also full of people done up in their holiday finest. As we climbed higher above sea level and left the fog behind we were able to pick up the pace. I had just asked Bracha to check the map again when the engine coughed, sputtered, and then died as we coasted down a slight incline.

"What's wrong?" he asked.

"Beats me. It just quit. If I didn't know better, I'd say we were out of gas." I pointed at the gas gauge, which was still registering full, as it had when we started. "Can't go by that. It's obviously broken." I turned off the ignition, pumped the accelerator a couple of times, then tried to start it again. Nothing. I dashed out into the rain, opened the hood, and quickly determined that everything visible was in order. The more I thought about it, the more apparent it became that we had simply run out of gas. Shit. I was about to get back in to tell Bracha the news when I saw a car bouncing down the road toward us. I thought that if the driver had a siphon of some sort, maybe he'd sell us some gas, or at least go for help, so I stepped into the middle of the road and began waving my arms. For a moment I thought he was going to run me down, until I realized that he was trying to stop the car, but wasn't having a lot of luck. It began lurching from side to side, the brakes squealing like some deranged banshee. I jumped out of the way as it slid on by. The car, an impossibly dilapidated Hudson Hornet (remember those?), shuddered to a halt about thirty feet past where I'd been standing. As I started toward it the door opened and a small man with a patch over one eye and an enormous black beard got out and began yelling at me in rapid-fire Portuguese.

"Boa noite, senhor," Bracha called out from behind me, following that up with what I hoped was an appeal for gas. Soon Bracha and the bearded man were deep in conversation while I stood anxiously, getting drenched, awaiting the outcome. "Peter. I must introduce you to Senhor Antonito Arigo, who cannot believe he has almost run over a famous Formula One driver."

As I shook hands with Senhor Arigo, he took in every aspect of my driver's uniform with a sort of religious awe. I was checking him out as well. I didn't know about the eye patch but the beard was certainly false. I wondered what his story was. Bracha must have realized what was on my mind. "Senhor Arigo and his family are on their way home from an Easter costume party for the local children. He says he listened to the race on the radio and is honored beyond belief that you should wish his help."

"Great," I said, grinning at Arigo like a fool as he kept pumping my hand. "Does that mean he's going to give us some gas?"

"No. But he *is* going to give us his car," Bracha said, before launching into more Portuguese. Arigo finally let go of my hand and ran back toward his car, yelling and waving his arms in the air.

"What the hell is going on?" I asked Bracha, who was laughing and shaking his head.

"I promised him you would send him the autographs of Piquet, Senna, and Gugelmin."

"Okay, but what's so funny about that?"

"He has named his two sons Nelson and Ayrton. Look, there they are."

Arigo was coming back with two little boys, about three and five, and a very pregnant woman. The moment we saw her we looked at each other and said, "Mauricio."

As soon as I'd met the rest of the family, Bracha took them back to our car so they could get in out of the rain, which was still falling lightly. I went to the Hudson, got it going and backed up next to our car. Bracha had opened his case and taken out a couple of the Monte Cristos. Arigo put one in his mouth and was about to light it with an old Zippo when his wife yelled something to him. He laughed, reached up, and pulled off his beard, handing it to her through the window. As he lit up he spoke to Bracha, who translated for me. "He says she reminded him that the beard belongs to his brother and if he burns it he will have to pay for it."

Bracha continued to talk about the arrangements

he'd made with the man to switch cars, but I wasn't listening to him anymore. I was listening to a girl lying in a hospital bed five hundred miles away as she told us who was responsible for the deaths of at least three people. I grabbed hold of Bracha's arm so tightly that he jumped. "Peter. What is it? What's wrong?"

"The man didn't check out of the hotel," I said, going over to our car. I put my hand through the window and pulled out the false beard. "She wasn't telling us the man was gone. She was telling us his beard was gone. He'd had it in Gstaad, but when she saw him at the Inter-Continental it was gone. He'd shaved it off. And he didn't get lost back there, he turned off deliberately. Now he's out there somewhere with Dutton and Anne. Jesus."

"You mean it's Rory, the mechanic? Rory tried to kill Esmandina?"

"That's right," I said, trying to plan the next move. "Tried to kill me too. He was the one that sabotaged my car, not Windsor, even though I'll bet they're in it together. Jesus, I can't fucking believe it. Look, get on that phone of yours and get hold of the police. Try Itapeva, or maybe Arigo here knows some that are closer. Anyway, have them meet you here, then bring them to the Rolls as quick as you can."

"No. I will call, but I am going with you."

"You can't. Look, you know pretty much where the Rolls is, but it could take them hours to find it." He started to protest again but he knew I was right. By the time he'd started to question Arigo about the local police, I was in the Hudson and gone.

I spent the next hour mentally kicking myself in the ass for not having suspected Rory, while trying to keep Arigo's Hudson from killing me before Rory got his chance to do it. Figuring that Anne wouldn't have been able to guide them to the site without taking the old rally route, I went in from the north. The rain finally had stopped and the sun had come out for the last half hour of daylight, throwing long shadows across the landscape. Leaving the car about two hundred yards from where the Rolls had gone off the road, I walked as quietly as I could, listening for any sound that might signal the presence of Rory and the others. I heard something, all right, but it wasn't at all what I'd expected and it scared the hell out of me. At first I couldn't make out the words, just a man's voice screaming obscenities. As I got closer I could tell it was Rory doing the yelling with Windsor on the receiving end, though I still couldn't see them down there—"stupid fool," "double-crosser," and "fucking idiot" being the most repeated epithets. The car Rory had been driving was parked on the same little outcropping of roadway that I'd ended up on four days earlier. Four days. Seemed like another lifetime. I looked in the car windows and my heart nearly stopped.

Anne's body was on the floor, facedown, wedged between the front and rear seats. Opening the door, I folded the front seat forward and touched her to see if she was alive. She reacted as if I'd jabbed her with a cattle prod, sending my heart rate supersonic. When she saw it was me she started to cry. I told her not to make a sound as I peeled the racer tape off her mouth and then tore through the strips of it that bound her wrists and ankles. "Where's Dutton?" I whispered.

"I don't know," she replied. "Rory made him tie me up, then he took him out of the car. I think he killed him." She began crying again.

"What makes you say that?"

"He has a gun. After they left he put something in the trunk and a little later I heard shots. Peter, why is he screaming like that? I'm scared. Let's get out of here."

"Anne. I want you to do exactly as I say. There's an old green car parked a couple hundred yards up the road. I want you to walk back to it, then hide in the bushes where you can see it clearly. Don't come out until either the police or I get there. Got it?"

"But I don't—"

"I don't have time to argue. Just do it, please?"

"You'll be careful, won't you?"

"You can bet on it. Now get going." She reached up, kissed me on the cheek, turned, and walked away. I watched until I was sure she'd get there safely, then shifted my attention back to the problem of what to do about Rory and Windsor. I hadn't figured on the gun. Playing the hero is only valid up to a point, and looking down the barrel of a gun was not on my agenda. Since I knew exactly where the Rolls was located, I figured I could get pretty close to it without being seen. The wet conditions would certainly help keep the noise down too. Then again, as long as Rory kept yelling that way, they wouldn't hear me if I came in with a marching band.

I worked my way down the slope, trying not to lose

my footing in the wet grass and mud, until I was within fifty feet of the Rolls. At that point I got down on my stomach and wriggled forward until I could almost reach out and touch the car. Suddenly Rory stopped yelling at Windsor and I froze in place, hardly daring to breathe. As I watched, Rory came into view in front of me. He had a gun, all right, some sort of pistol that was clutched in his right hand. But it was his face that held me spellbound. He looked totally demented, like some horror-film doctor who'd injected himself with the wrong formula. Without warning, he lashed out with his foot, kicking the fender of the Rolls again and again, until the aluminum was twisted beyond recognition. That act must have exorcised whatever demons were possessing him, because by the time he stopped, he looked like the Rory of old instead of a raving maniac. Great, I thought, now he's just your average killer with a gun in his hand.

There was still no sign of Windsor or Dutton, and as long as he had that gun, I didn't dare make a move. My hope was that the arrival of the police would occupy his attention enough to allow me to jump him, or hit him on the head with a rock, or something. If the police arrived in time, that is. While I was busily hatching plans, he started talking to Windsor again, this time in a normal tone of voice.

"So, Denis, you old fart. Time for me to be movin' on. Think I'll try Canada again. Somewhere out west this time. I wish I'd had the pleasure of killing you myself, but life is full of little disappointments. See ya in hell." Just as he said that, Anne screamed. "Bloody hell," he exclaimed, and went crashing off through the undergrowth, back toward the car. As soon as he disappeared from view, I jumped up and stepped out into the tiny clearing surrounding the Rolls. The light was pretty dim by then, but not enough to hide a truly grotesque sight. Windsor, who was obviously dead, was seated with his back against the side of the Rolls, his body covered with something that looked like confetti and surrounded by sheets of clear plastic wrapping. A quick search showed no sign of Dutton, so I took off up the hill after Rory. Whatever had caused Anne to scream, I hoped it hadn't driven her out of her hiding place to where Rory could get his hands on her.

As I climbed the slippery slope toward the road, I heard a car start, then saw lights come on. Too close to be the Hudson—it had to be Rory in the other car. I heard it accelerate rapidly, its tires spinning on the wet roadway as Rory slammed his way up through the gears. He was no more than fifty feet away when I heaved myself up onto the road and stood in the bright glare of the car's headlights. The second he saw me, he jerked the wheel to the right, slamming the car into the side of the cliff, then bouncing back onto the gravel, nearly hitting me as it whipped past. I can still see the fear on Rory's face as he looked at me, twisting his head as he passed to keep me in sight. It was that, as much as anything, that sealed his fate. By the time he'd turned back to the road he was only a few feet from a sharp right-hand corner. He hit the brakes, throwing the car into a slide as he tried desperately to negotiate the curve. I watched the rear end start to come around, stopping momentarily as he tried to correct the oversteer, then snapping violently in the opposite direction as the rebound skid sent the car into the rock, then spinning off the road down the embankment.

I arrived at the spot where he'd gone off, and followed the trail of broken trees and flattened foliage down the steep grade. The car was sitting on level ground at the bottom of the ravine where it had smashed headfirst into a large tree. As I came up behind it I could see Rory, still seated behind the wheel. He seemed to be struggling to get out of his seat belt. Then, as I got closer, the struggling stopped and everything got unnaturally quiet. I knew he still had the gun, but something told me I didn't have to worry about it anymore. I moved up to the driver's-side window and looked inside. Rory had been struggling, all right, but not to get out of his seat belt. One of the branches of the tree he'd hit had come in through the windshield and run right through his chest. When I opened the door to see if there was anything that could be done, he turned his head toward me, whispered, "Hello, James," and died.

With Rory beyond help, I immediately began yet another climb out of the now dark ravine. As I reached the road, I could hear the welcome wailing of police sirens approaching, and by the time I'd gotten within sight of the Hudson, I could see their flashing red lights dancing through the trees.

Anne, who had been sitting on the hood of the car, saw me approaching. She jumped down, ran over, threw her arms around me, and began talking a blue streak. "Peter, thank God you're all right. What about Rory, and Windsor? I heard the car. Did they get away? What about the paintings, did they—"

"Whoa. Slow down. First things first. Are you okay? I heard that scream. What happened?"

"Oh, God. I was hiding, just as you said, when I heard this sort of bumping and scraping sound coming from the road. I put my head up to see what it was and saw this body rolling down the road toward me. That's when I screamed, I'm afraid. I hope it didn't spoil anything?"

"What? What body? What are you talking about?"

"Inspector Dutton. You didn't see him then?" I shook my head and she continued. "Well, Rory had hit him on the head and dumped him into the boot of the car, but he didn't get it shut properly, and when Dutton came to, he kicked it until it opened. Then he crawled out and hopped along the road until he fell down in front of me and I screamed." She took a quick breath and forged ahead. "Then, as soon as I helped him get out of all that tape, he ran off to look for you at the Rolls. Now it's your turn."

It was about then that Bracha, the Arigo family, and the local police arrived. Over the next hour they were joined by every city, state, national, international, and for all I know, interplanetary, cop within a thousand miles. They all claimed to have jurisdiction and none of them had a clue to what was going on. If Bracha and his portable phone hadn't been around, we'd probably still be there. But by midnight, he, Dutton, Anne, and I were on our way, by government helicopter, to São Paulo. After a bath and a few

hours of sleep, we made our statements to the authorities and held a press conference for the media. Soon
the story, complete with grisly pictures of James,
Rory, and Windsor, was appearing in newspapers,
magazines, and on television shows throughout the
world. A few of them even got it right.

Windsor had robbed his own art collection with the
help of Richard Harriman, aka Rory Hite. The paintings, sealed in airtight plastic wrapping, were hidden,
with the full knowledge of their crews, in the rollbars
of the two Rolls-Royces. After splitting the proceeds
from the sale of the art that made it to Colombia,
Rory and Windsor went their separate ways. Windsor
returned to England where he prospered, Rory to
Australia where he didn't. As worldwide art prices
skyrocketed, one, or both of them, must have decided
to find the missing paintings no matter what it took.
Even murder.

Rory was in Gstaad when DeStefano was killed,
near London when Livesey died, and minutes away
from the clinic where Alcott breathed his last. And
Billy Gibbons? He probably had nothing to do with
any of it. Rory was doubtless responsible for the beating that had kept him out of the rally, but his death
was probably nothing more than an unfortunate accident. As for Windsor, I don't think that he would have
willingly been involved in murder, but Rory was a
dangerous man to have as a partner, particularly
when the stakes were so high.

There's something else we'll never know, but I'd be
willing to bet that it was the sight of James, sitting
behind the wheel, that caused Windsor's fatal heart

312

attack. Just as it was the sight of me, driver's suit covered with dirt, climbing up onto the road in front of
Rory, that caused him to lose control and crash.

Like a pendulum that had swung as far as it could
go, the forces set in motion twenty-one years before
came hurtling back with enormous force, destroying
everyone in its path.

I went back to the Rolls later that afternoon to su-
pervise the removal of James's remains. The Brazilian police were still going over the area, which had
now been cleared of foliage, exposing the car to the
roadway above. Inspector Dutton was there, sifting
through the tiny bits of canvas that I'd thought were
confetti. Forty million pounds' worth of paintings reduced to rubbish. Poor Dutton. He looked devastated.
"Peter, come over here and take a look at this, if you
will," he said, holding up one of the rollbar cross
members. "The paintings were inside this, sealed in
plastic, and would have been fine if some idiot hadn't
done that."

I looked closely where he was pointing and saw
that a small hole had been neatly drilled through the
metal. "Do you have any idea why someone would
drill a hole like that? Whoever did it punctured the
plastic sheeting, the insects got inside, and now everything is destroyed. God, what a waste."

"I can tell you exactly what that is," I said. "It used
to be standard practice before the start of any championship rally to drill holes at random in the rollcage.
They did it to check them for the proper thickness, so

people couldn't cheat with some lighter, narrow-gauge tubing to save on overall weight."

He shook his head sadly as particles of Renoir, Degas, and Matisse dropped out of his hand and fell slowly to the ground. "By the way, after the police towed your car in last night, they found a hole in the gas tank. Must have been a stone."

Right, I thought. A stone named Rory. He'd only been alone with the cars for five minutes at the airport but it had been enough.

"What's going to happen to the team now with all this mess?" Dutton asked.

"I'm not sure. Vitale and the others have gone back to Italy to get things sorted out. I think we'll be all right as long as A.I.S. sticks with us. But losing Windsor's money will certainly hurt. I have a feeling those bits and pieces of canvas were meant to pay for our new wind tunnel."

"Oh, I found this under the car," he said, handing me the rally map I'd gotten from Livesey in London. "I figure Windsor must've dropped it there since I found a vial of his heart medicine on the ground next to it."

"I wonder how he got hold of it?"

"Probably during the bomb scare at the hotel. I was keeping pretty close to him at the time and I noticed that he was about the last guest to come out that night. . . . Well, must get back to work. Best of luck. I'll be watching for you on the telly. Might even come out to Silverstone for the Grand Prix, if I can get away."

OVERSTEER

"Write and let me know," I said, shaking his hand. "I'll see you get a pass."

"Thanks. Sorry about your dad. Good-bye."

As he walked away I saw an ambulance come to a stop on the road above. James's final journey, to a cemetery near Miami, was about to begin. I walked over to the edge of the clearing, opened the bag I was carrying, took out a bottle of Remy Martin, a hotel ashtray, and a couple of Bracha's Monte Cristos. I lit one, placed the other in the ashtray, and sat it, along with the cognac, back out of sight in the tall grass. As Fats Waller once said, "One never knows, do one?"

EPILOGUE

In the five months since we were in Brazil, the team's fortunes had been about as volatile as the stock market. Without Windsor, the flow of cash that had been so abundant at the beginning of the year was reduced to a trickle, curtailing our development and testing programs drastically. Luckily, A.I.S. decided to hang in with us, despite all the negative publicity. As it turned out, we were not the only team to suffer the adverse effects of sensational offtrack events. The owner of another team was arrested for murdering his wife, the chairman of a second was forced to resign after being implicated in the DeLorean affair, and one of the sport's top designers died by his own hand. Before long, we were old news.

With Esmandina on her way to a full recovery, Alberto regained his touch and outqualified me at both Imola and Mexico City, although neither of us finished either race. I didn't mention Monaco because we might as well have stayed home, the principality offering little glamour to those who didn't pre-qualify.

The U.S., Canadian, and French Grands Prix saw us make the field but fail to finish in the points. As a result, the race at Silverstone was an all-or-nothing affair, our last opportunity to drag ourselves out of the pre-qualifying rut. In my case it was certainly "nothing," as my crash ended our chances in spectacular fashion.

I'd hoped to see Anne when we returned to England for the race, but she begged off, saying it was best we go our separate ways. My involvement in the death of her father, however innocent, was something she might forgive but, obviously, could never forget.

Silverstone wasn't all bad news, though. Inspector Dutton and I were able to spend some time together, and he brought me up to date on the Windsor case. The Yard had satisfied itself that Rory was indeed responsible for the deaths of Alcott and Livesey and the attempted murder of Esmandina. They confirmed that he was present in Gstaad when DeStefano was killed, but since they lacked hard evidence to the contrary, the cause of death would remain accidental. Another revelation came from Interpol. They discovered that Rory's fingerprints matched those of a man named Henderson, who had escaped from the psychiatric ward of a prison in Perth, Australia, in 1985. But the most fascinating bit of news, as far as I was concerned, was the recent discovery of two missing Cézannes that had been left in a church confessional in Rio, paintings that Dutton was sure had been in

Bracha's possession for many years. Just between the two of us, he said, he always suspected that Bracha was the man James and Alcott were on their way to meet when they crashed. If that was so, then the attack on Esmandina was yet another example of the high price paid by everyone involved in the affair.

They just threw the checker at Spa and I have to say the conditions looked so miserable I'm almost glad I wasn't there. (I said *almost.)* Senna won again, for the fifth time, and looks like a good bet to repeat as World Champion. Alberto finished tenth, our best result of the year. That, coming on the heels of a fourteenth in Germany and an eleventh in Hungary, may mean that things finally have turned around for the team. Five races to go. Unfortunately, I'll miss Italy and Portugal, but that still leaves me three chances to score some points before the season ends.

Well, I think it's time to uncork the Chappellet Chardonnay, light one of the Monte Cristos Bracha sent me, and hobble out onto the terrace to see how the coals are coming along in the grill. Gail should be here any minute with the shrimp, and given the way things are in the world today, we might even attempt something meaningful when we finish eating them.